Dear Readers,

It's even more [...] [...]u'll want to own all four of [...] [...] [...] So stack 'em up, curl up in a comfortable chair, and indulge!

Kate Holmes, multipublished as Anne Avery, used to work for the state department in South America—hence the romantic Rio de Janiero setting for her first Bouquet romance, **Amethyst and Gold.** A shy young teacher and writer, Melisande visits Rio to do research, never dreaming that she will be swept into the sensual rhythms of Carnavale . . . and into the arms of a handsome tycoon!

Veteran author Ann Josephson (you may know her as Sara Jarrod) has created one of the most appealing romantic heroes we've ever encountered in Brand Carendon—lawyer, athlete, and father of an eleven-year-old son he never knew he had . . . until first love Dani Murdock finds her way back into his life. Brand vows to make up for lost time . . . and to find **Enduring Love.**

Newcomer Debra Dawn Thomas takes her readers into the exotic, breathtakingly exciting world of Spanish bull-fighting in her debut novel, **Wrap Me In Scarlet.** Sensible Stephanie Madison, a journalist looking for a story, finds much more in the arms of "El Peligro"—"The Dangerous One"—in a world of intoxicating adventure . . . and passion!

Suzanne Barrett, herself a facility engineer, gives her exciting profession to feisty heroine Karin Williams. She's sent to England to prove her skill alongside Rowan Marsden—a man who'd vowed never to work with a woman again. But Karin's talent, wits, and beauty combine to provide success in a business partnership and, ultimately, in **Taming Rowan.**

Decorate your life with a Bouquet on every table . . . four fresh new ones every month!

The Editors

HE ART OF SEDUCTION,
MEDITERRANEAN STYLE . . .

"Buenos tardes, señorita," the man said, showing perfect white teeth.

Whatever she had expected from meeting Miguel Rafael, it certainly wasn't supposed to be a physical response—a definite roll of her normally steady heart rate. She found herself unable to move under his hypnotic gaze. His eyes were like green olives—the sun glinting off their ripe skins, glowing almost, and absolutely beautiful. His gaze moved down the swell of her breast to just short of being rude, and then he finally released her hand, as if he'd forgotten he held it and only now remembered.

"Stephanie . . ."

He'd said her name like a sigh and it reverberated up her spine as if he were a broadcasting station and she an antennae.

They called him *El Peligro*—The Dangerous One—and Stephanie already felt herself falling under the spell of this irresistibly charismatic, too-handsome man. As a journalist, falling in love with the subject of her writing assignment was definitely *not* on her agenda, and she had to keep their relationship strictly professional. . . .

WRAP ME IN SCARLET

DEBRA DAWN THOMAS

Zebra Books
Kensington Publishing Corp.
http://www.zebrabooks.com

ZEBRA BOOKS are published by

Kensington Publishing Corp.
850 Third Avenue
New York, NY 10022

Zebra and the Z logo Reg. U.S. Pat. & TM Off.

First Printing: August, 1999
10 9 8 7 6 5 4 3 2 1

Printed in the United States of America

Kelly, my beautiful daughter, your life now stretches out before you. Dreams do come true—make yours happen.

ONE

Stephanie Madison wanted her editor's opinion of the story about the homeless she'd E-mailed him for Sunday's edition.

"Good stuff," Bob said when she had him on the phone. "I want you to interview John Stevens, the television actor who started a food bank for the homeless up in Santa Monica. He said you could meet with him tonight at his house in Pacific Palisades."

"Can't tonight. I'm going to my brother's for dinner to meet a new client of his—some bullfighter from Spain. I'll call Stevens and set up another time."

She stretched out on the bed, suddenly exhausted, and wary about the crazy notion of meeting a bullfighter—especially when she suspected her sister-in-law, Adria, was up to her matchmaking tricks again.

"Is the *matador's* name Miguel Rafael?" he asked.

"Yeah, that's right. How'd you know?"

"Find out what he's doing in California."

Bob's request sounded like an order. She sat up, something warning her. "I already know what he's doing here. He's making some business investments with my brother's firm. Why?"

"There's a lot of publicity about this guy right now. Not just because he's one of Spain's greatest bullfighters, but because he's been seen hanging around the Hollywood crowd, including Jenna Starr. He's some kind of Latin lover boy to the rich and famous."

Jenna Starr, the hot-tempered punk rock singer turned actress, turned socialite? Interesting, Stephanie thought, and wondered why her sister-in-law, Adria, had left out this detail.

"Get a story for our Spanish edition."

Now that was an order.

"I'll try to set up an interview, Bob, but you'll have to find someone on staff who knows something about the *Fiesta Brava*. Why not Ray? He speaks fluent Spanish. He's been to Spain, and photographed bullfights." *Or why not Suzie Muller, who writes 'Hollywood Tidbits?' "*

"Miguel would never agree to a planned interview, or I'd turn this over to the editor of the *Variedades* to assign. I'm asking you because you have access to Miguel."

Stephanie almost snorted. "Richard isn't going to appreciate me pestering one of his investors at a dinner party. And just because I have access to Miguel doesn't mean I know anything about bullfighting. And I can't speak Spanish."

"You can wing it."

"What's my angle on this story, anyway?"

"You're a reporter, and a professional. You'll think of something. Consider it an assignment."

She twisted the phone cord and wanted to use it as a noose—on herself—for making the call to Bob in the first place, and for mentioning the bullfighter.

"Get me something, Stephanie. Turn on some sexy charm. I hear he can't resist women."

"Bob! One of these days you're going to say that to the wrong woman employee and end up in court."

"Yeah, yeah, but not Stephanie Madison. She's one of the boys. Oh—Miguel's in *People Magazine* this week. Read it for back story."

Stephanie let the phone drop into the cradle and hurried over to the pile of unread mail. *One of the boys!* she fumed. She'd picked up the title after covering the local sports scene for a few years, including a couple of locker room interviews.

Finding the current *People Magazine,* she dropped down on the sofa and flipped through the pages looking for a *matador.* Then she moaned, *loudly.* Both her cats looked up from their comfy spots in front of the fireplace, curious, or bothered by her noise.

Miguel Rafael was beautiful, if a man could claim the adjective. His skin was paler than she had expected, an engaging contrast to his thick, raisin-brown hair. The only visible flaw marred his right cheekbone—a thin white scar shaped like a question mark. She read:

> *Miguel Rafael, known as* El Peligro, *meaning* the Danger, *is ranked number one, and he's enjoyed the title for nearly ten years, astonishing crowds at every performance. One of the greatest bullfighters of his time, he is a man richly rewarded for facing some of Spain's most savage bulls.*
>
> *He recently accepted a challenge from a younger* matador, *and the scheduled contest in Madrid is two weeks away. Tickets sold out hours after going on sale, and are now fetching astronomical prices in*

the plazas around Las Ventas. *It's being publicized as Miguel's last bullfight. Wagers guarantee that the younger* matador, *Francosis Gaona, will be the victor, and Miguel will die a hero.*

Miguel seems unconcerned with his possible demise, and was seen at the Hollywood opening of Jenna Starr's new movie, "Vamp."

Die a hero? Stephanie thought it sounded too dramatic. Why shouldn't Miguel be in California working a few deals, soaking up the sun with a starlet or two? All he had to do in a couple of weeks was put on a performance. The only death would be that of a defenseless animal. She'd rather write a story about the rights of bulls!

Miguel and Jenna Starr made a superb looking Hollywood-buzz couple. Jenna wore a Versace black velvet gown, the top and bottom separated by two thin, gold chains that exposed her flawless, flat stomach. Miguel looked like a Perry Ellis ad in *GQ*. Gray suit over black turtleneck. Timeless. Classic. Modern.

Sexy.

Stephanie glanced up at her closet. Forget jeans. She still had time to make it to the mall in the name of good journalistic reporting.

At eight sharp Stephanie stood on the spacious balcony off her brother's living room in a gorgeous new Donna Karan dress. The purchase had sent her Nordstrom's bill over the limit—red, silk, clinging, and dangerously low off the shoulders, just enough to draw eyes to her cleavage.

Something warned her that for physchological leverage she'd better look down on this guy tonight, and to help facilitate the notion she wore a new pair of black velvet heels which added another three inches to her five foot six inches. She banked on Miguel Rafael being short if he had to maneuver around bullhorns.

A desperate phone call to her hairdresser had smartened up her shoulder-length blond hair and added honey highlights. She felt confident about the way she looked, but doubted she could, or would, compete with Jenna Starr. Did Miguel only date bimbos, rich and famous ones? The idea nagged at her—gave her reason to dislike him a little.

Richard's Balboa Island home faced the bay and had an extended view of the peninsula. The cool, spring ocean breeze caressed Stephanie's face as she watched a ferry toil across the water. It docked at the island and released cars, bicycles, strollers, and lovers. She felt no more relaxed now than she had all day. Even the wine wasn't helping.

Since Bob's call, Stephanie'd focused on how to slyly get her story now that, with the help of the dress, she might at least have the interest of the *matador's* libido. If the *matador* hated reporters, she didn't wish to jeopardize her brother's business venture with the man.

In spite of her difficult assignment, thoughts of her humble beginnings intruded.

Richard had done well for himself, she mused. It was still hard to believe they'd started from such modest beginnings. Their mother, abandoned by her husband, left with two small children, was unprepared to join the workforce with so few skills, and she struggled those early years for the simplest necessities.

Stephanie focused on the distant lights of The Pavilion and The Newport Harbor Yacht Club. Her spiteful ex-husband now took his place in her thoughts. She'd married Steven Fisher right there, and could almost still see the flower garlands woven around the rails, the candles twinkling under the canopy, and the three-tiered layer cake gracing the patio table. Steven had loved the view, loved Balboa, envied what her brother had, but he'd never wanted to work as hard.

What started out for him as a brilliant career in marketing had turned into one job after another. He couldn't hold down a position and finally found another woman, Kimberly Harris—sadly, one of Stephanie's acquaintances—to support him in an extravagant lifestyle. Their affair had devastated Stephanie more than any single factor in her unhappy marriage, verifying her fears that he'd really wanted a woman with money and had only married her to get to her successful brother.

"More wine?" Richard called, bringing her out of her troubled thoughts.

"Sure." She stepped back into the house and extended her empty glass toward her brother—her only relative. They were just eighteen months apart, and both had worked hard to get out of San Diego's poor neighborhoods. He'd put himself through college on a soccer scholarship, and Stephanie had taken out financial aid—just paid off this year, thanks to Richard's generous gift.

After he filled her second glass to the brim, he set the carafe back on the table. The dining room walls were paneled in mirrors and gave the room a lavish appearance. All looked elegant and romantic under the light of the many candles lit and placed around the room.

"You rescued me from bad memories," she said, never one to hide problems from Richard. "I always remember Steven out on that balcony."

"Look how much better you are without him." Richard smiled at her, showing the same kind of right dimple she had. "By the way, you look breathtaking in that dress. Are you trying to stop our clocks, or the heart of a *matador?*"

"Thanks." She spun around for him, like a little girl showing off a Sunday dress. What he'd said about her life was true, but a lingering bitterness remained. She didn't think she could ever trust another man with her heart. The Madison women were destined to be alone.

"It'll take me a year to pay this off, but your client is used to seeing women in *Versace*, not jeans. You look pretty dapper yourself, Richard."

His blue suit contrasted nicely with his dark blond hair and blue eyes. He'd always been popular with the girls, including Adria, but Richard hadn't even *noticed* Stephanie's best friend until after she'd graduated from San Diego State and landed a job at his brokerage firm. Adria wouldn't be working much longer. A baby was due at the end of the month.

Richard moved the centerpiece over by a half inch and took a step back as if to consider the new location. "Is Adria matchmaking again? Is that why you accepted her invitation?"

"She never gives up, but I'm not romantically interested in your client." Stephanie tucked a curl behind one ear and took a long drink of her wine. "How's business?"

Richard stopped fussing with the table arrangement and glanced up sharply at his sister. "Good—great, really."

"Thanks in part to Miguel Rafael." She picked up a cloth napkin, shook it out, and flourished it back and forth like a cape. "Rich foreigner who wants to gobble up American property and American women. Where's your star client? He's late."

Richard snatched the napkin away, refolded it, and placed it back next to a Noritake china plate. "He'll be here, and you're right, he's an important client. I could retire on what he's bringing into my company and never have to worry again, so I'm going to ask you *very* nicely to behave."

Stephanie thrust out her lower lip and pretended to pout. "Me? I always behave."

"Not if you're after a story."

"I didn't tell you I was after a story!" Stephanie should have known her brother would guess her motive.

"That's an on-assignment dress. But Miguel won't talk. He *hates* reporters, and I'd rather not have him hating you, since we're related." Richard stepped down into the living room.

"Gee, another famous person who hates reporters. What else is new?"

"Steph—"

"My editor put some pressure on me to get something." Stephanie ran her hand across the silk tablecloth, the one she'd given them as a wedding gift. "The *Express* has a Spanish edition, the *Variedades,* which has a huge Hispanic circulation. They want a story."

Richard adjusted the volume on the CD player before he turned back to Stephanie, a strong look of disapproval on his face. "Stephanie, no."

"Miguel isn't going to hate me if I just *ask.*"

"You can *ask,* but if he says no, it's no. End of story. Promise?"

She pushed her lips out in a pout, then said, "Promise. Where's Adria?"

"Still getting ready. She thinks she looks fat in everything she tries on."

"One of the disadvantages of being eight months pregnant." Stephanie held up a crystal wineglass and admired it. "Miguel's occupation seems barbaric to me. It's hard to believe the sport is still popular going into the millennium." She drank the rest of her wine before her astonished brother's eyes. "I suppose I should be interested, or at least sympathetic to, something that's part of one's heritage. Then again, what do we know about our own? What do we remember about our father, other than he was a bastard for leaving mom with two kids?"

Richard stepped back up into the dining room and took her glass. Looking up at him, she saw concern etched on his handsome face. Stephanie thought he looked a lot like their truant father, and understood why their mother had loved him so much. Where was the senior Madison today? Did he ever wonder about them?

"Stephanie, don't harbor so much resentment. It isn't healthy."

She forced a smile and accepted a hug from him. "Doesn't it bother you that he just left?"

"It used to," he said, solemnly. "But we have to move on with our lives."

Spoken like her always positive brother, she

mused. "Just get over it—move on and entertain the . . . *matador?*"

Richard released her, but kept his hands on her shoulders. "I didn't exactly mean that—but try, you know—to have some fun tonight."

"With a Spanish jock?"

"Bullfighting isn't a sport. It's a tradition that's alive and well. I hope you don't plan to show your disapproval. Miguel's investments are making a solid future for my unborn son." He set the wineglass on the table. "Try not to offend him."

"Don't worry. I'll keep quiet."

"Not if you get drunk."

She eyed the empty wineglass guiltily. "I'm just a little nervous dressed like this. A few days ago, I was dressed like a homeless person."

"Miguel's going to see that the next generation of Madisons are not one of them. No one's asking you to agree with what he does. Just hang loose and have a good time."

That was easy for him to say, Stephanie thought as she watched him dart up the stairs in search of Adria.

She turned toward the dining room table, poured herself another glass of wine, and checked herself in the mirror, considering the sexy dress, a really extravagant change for her. She hoped the bull-fighter liked the color. *Red*. She smiled at her own secret joke.

"Jenna Starr, eat your heart out," she said.

The doorbell rang.

She glanced up the stairs. No Richard. No Adria. Time to play hostess. She left the mirror and went to the door and opened it. What registered first were dark green eyes framed in long, black lashes. They looked her up and down, *slowly.*

"Buenos tardes, señorita," the man said, showing perfect white teeth.

Whatever she had expected from meeting Miguel Rafael, it certainly wasn't supposed to be a physical response—a definite roll of her normally steady heart rate.

"¿Perdóneme?" He peered over her shoulder and stretched to a solid height of six feet.

So much for leverage, she thought. *"No hablo español,"* she said.

"Ah, I speak English. We are saved."

"If you're looking for Richard Madison, you've found the right place." Stephanie stepped back and let him pass. A pleasant scent followed him, not too overbearing, but definitely male.

"And you are?" he asked with a thick Castilian accent.

That was the smile she'd seen in *People Magazine.* Guarded. Secret. *Cataclysmic.*

"Oh, sorry. I'm Richard's sister, Stephanie." She couldn't take her gaze from him. "He should be right down." Bullfighting *couldn't* be the only feat that had earned Miguel his reputation as *The Danger.*

"Nice to meet you," he said, and took her hand.

In Stephanie's mind he might as well have pulled out a club and whacked her, since she found herself unable to move under his hypnotic gaze.

His eyes were like green olives—the sun glinting off their ripe skins, glowing almost, and absolutely beautiful. His gaze moved down the swell of her breast to just short of being rude, and then he finally released her hand, as if he'd forgotten he held it and only now remembered.

He stepped down into the living room and strolled over to the window. In the distance several sailboats motored around a ferry. Their lights twinkled in the bay, and he seemed to be following their movement.

In the unobserved moment, she studied him. He wore a dark green turtleneck sweater and a tan linen suit, obviously custom-made, with a hidden Italian label.

Stephanie had expected someone smaller, and thinner, who could easily slip and slide around a bull. Miguel carried himself like a dancer, compact and exact, with a precise pose, even now as he stood at the window.

She could visualize him standing in a bullring just the way he stood now—on the hot sand, the heat shimmering around him, under an implacable Spanish sky, with roses littered at his feet. The mental picture caused her mouth to go dry.

He turned around, the same way he might acknowledge a cheering crowd. *"Stephanie . . ."*

He'd said her name like a sigh, and it reverberated up her spine as if he were a broadcasting station and she an antennae.

"Bonito."

Beautiful! Stephanie knew a few Spanish words. Did he think the view from the balcony was beautiful, or her? She took the step down into the living room to join him, ignoring the tremble in her legs. Miguel affected her, and she didn't quite know what to do with experience, since men in general had been off her list for two years now.

Adria kept telling her that she was too young at twenty-nine to entirely give up the male species, but until just moments ago, Stephanie had been content to do just that. Now, she was reconsidering her wounded heart. Perhaps it was time to make repairs, move on, as Richard might say, get over it and test the waters.

She might drown in this guy.

His thick, dark hair was longer than in the photographs she'd seen. He wore it with a light gel, brushed back to one side, with one of those modern, angled cuts, exposing a straight forehead and dark, arched eyebrows. High cheekbones, the right one slightly marred, and the aquiline nose suggested Spanish nobility somewhere in the bloodline. His mouth looked hungry, full and luscious, the kind a woman could get lost kissing. His eyes—huge green, piercing orbs—once again bore through her.

He taunted more than animals, she thought. *How long has it been since I've been with a man? A year? Longer? Don't get any ideas. What's he doing later?*

Heat flooded her face. "I'm a reporter," she said, very aware of her taut nerves. "The *Variedades* is interested in a story about you."

He turned back toward the ocean view as if dismissing her, as if *any* interest in her was now lost.

"I'm not here tonight as an official reporter," she said, trying to make some verbal repairs. "I know you—"

Miguel spun around on brown leather loafers. "I *donn* like reporters." The Spanish accent was suddenly pronounced.

"Yes. So I understand." She contemplated a polite reply, and remembered that this man, no matter how abrupt, was an important client of Richard's. "I didn't come to do a story. Well, that's not altogether true. I mean . . ." She glanced down at her hands and tried to gather her wits because she'd lost them sometime after he'd walked through the door. "I came tonight because my sister-in-law invited me as a dinner guest, not a reporter. But I had hoped I could ask you some questions. Informal, you know?"

She sat down and tried to pull her skirt down, but it refused to budge. Miguel sat next to her on the black leather sofa, his attention focused on her legs. He brought a faint smell again, unique, arousing.

"No interviews."

Something cruel dominated his expression, something the bull must see before the sword made the final plunge. Did women see this expression before he came deep within them? Stephanie felt perspiration gather under her arms, and her heart rate accelerate.

"Let me get you something to drink. Wine?" She stood up, tried to find balance on her high heels, and glanced in the direction of the stairs. Where were Richard and Adria? Good Lord, she would singlehandedly lose this account for Richard if he didn't appear soon. Yet she felt strangely driven to continue on the current course and pursue an interview.

Her hand shook as she poured the wine from the table that butted the back of the sofa. She handed Miguel a full glass of merlot. He reached for it, and his cuff slipped up to reveal a glittering gold chain laced in a light smattering of dark hair around a tan wrist.

When he accepted the glass their fingertips brushed. Like a conduit, an electric jolt ran up her arm, and color flooded her face. *He's a Spanish bullfighter who dates Jenna Starr!* she told herself. *Get a grip!*

"How much trouble could it be to answer a few

questions?" she asked, incredibly agitated. The man broadcast highly charged pheromones that were aimed and firing in her direction. She had never become aroused—actually wet—from a man she'd just met, and she didn't know what to do with the experience.

"Have you even seen a bullfight?" he asked in a smug tone, one arm hung over the sofa to see her better behind him.

"Of course!"

He scoffed. "¿*Cuándo?*"

"What?"

"Ah, you have *never* been to a bullfight, *señorita.*"

She ventured back around the sofa, thinking about his truthful statement, and sat down, not ready to give up just yet. "Shouldn't you be in Spain getting ready for an important fight in a few weeks?"

"Even if I wanted to answer your questions— which I *don't,* would you be willing to negotiate for it?" He cracked a *proud-of-himself* smile and waited, it seemed, for her to be shocked.

She held his bemused gaze and refused to let him see anything but complete control and calmness, even though his implication was entirely clear. Sex for a story. "Name the price, and let me decide."

Richard and Adria came down the stairs before he could answer.

Over roasted baby artichokes and soft-shell crabs Richard talked about local investments Miguel might look into, which included a house on the island that had just come on the market. Miguel never talked directly to Stephanie, nor did he even glance in her direction across the table.

His cold shoulder perplexed her. Apparently he

didn't want Richard to know anything had happened before he'd arrived on the scene. But Adria had psychically picked up *disaster,* and kept looking at Stephanie with that *well?* look.

After the dishes were cleared, Adria refused Stephanie's help with dessert, a creamy lavender ice cream.

While Richard and Miguel continued to talk stocks over coffee, Stephanie found another moment of solitude on the balcony. She leaned against the rail, took a few deep breaths of ocean air, and wondered about her reaction to Miguel. He'd really stirred her up. She didn't want to say goodnight to him. That would mean good-bye.

When would she ever see him again? Through Richard, but when and how? Not promiscuous by nature, the idea of a one-night stand startled and excited her at the same time. It was never too late to break a few moral codes, she thought, smiling at her steamy thoughts—for a good story, that is, which she apparently wouldn't get tonight. No wonder the Hollywood starlets were all over him. Miguel Rafael was hot—hell, he was molten lava.

The door behind her slid open, and Miguel stepped into the night to heat things up.

"Nice view," he said. He fished out a pack of cigarettes from his pocket. He offered her one.

She couldn't remember the last time a man had done that, or the last time she'd had a cigarette. "No thanks."

He shrugged, tucked the pack away, flicked open a lighter and produced a light.

She looked past him, but saw no sign of Adria or Richard in the dining room. How had fate allowed them so many moments alone? She suspected Adria had something to do with it. Stephanie took a few steps toward the door, instinctual preservation at work now. "I'll go see if I can help Adria."

Miguel blocked her path with one step and she came up short, her hip bumped his. "She has it handled, *Stephanie.*"

She saw a strange light in his green eyes as they stood so loosely joined.

"Do you want the terms of the interview?"

The smoke rose between them, then lifted off with an ocean breeze. "Sure," she whispered, her throat gone dry.

"In Spain it is not uncommon for a *matador* to pay the reporter for a good story."

This she didn't know, and now she felt a little embarrassed for thinking he'd propositioned her. "We are not in Spain." She swallowed hard. "How much would it take?"

He took a long drag off his cigarette. "I already have lots of money."

She'd been right the first time! "Then we have no terms."

"Come back to my hotel room tonight, and you'll get your interview." His free hand reached out, and his fingers touched the bare skin of her shoulder, slid up to her neck and under her chin.

If she were a lightbulb, she would have been lit brightly enough to light the peninsula across the bay. Maybe her body was charged, but her brain had short circuited. *I should be offended. I should slap him. I should do something!* "Let me have a cigarette," she said, instead, and brushed his fingers away.

He smiled, slipped the pack from his pocket, and held one out. Her hand trembled as she put it to her lips and accepted his light.

"In the end the price is too high for you?" he said, seemingly unconcerned. He took a drag from his own cigarette and blew a line of smoke over his shoulder. "But you are dressed like a woman who could come up with the funds."

She stared at his moist, parted lips, thinking she should be insulted and run, but something else—frustration, inner emptiness, plain old *desire*—held her rooted on the balcony. *Get a grip! Get a grip!* She took a drag, almost choked.

He leaned against the rail, enveloped in moonlight and smoke, smiling slightly—no doubt at her consternation!

"I don't understand you," she finally said. "You insulted me, but why? Because I'm a reporter? Do you really hate the press that much? Or do you hate women?"

A dark brow arched. "I hate it when *people* pretend they know bullfighting."

"Okay, so I don't know about it, and I didn't even know about you until this morning. But you could give me a break."

He took a long drag from his cigarette, and his gaze darted up and down her. "I am willing to do more."

She tapped her cigarette nervously. "Oh, please. Spare me." She turned away from him and looked out over the water, her shoulder still sensitive where he'd touched her. An involuntary gasp escaped her mouth when his hands wrapped around her waist, and he literally turned her around to face him.

"You do not wish to be spared," he said, and slipped his hands down her hips, following the lines of the tight dress. They rested on her bottom and pulled her against him. She easily felt his hardness.

When he released her, she stumbled back a few inches just as the door opened and Adria announced that dessert was on the table.

TWO

Bed was a prison. Stephanie tossed and turned for hours, thinking of Miguel. He had lit a disturbing hunger in her. All that Spanish tradition bottled up in one man had played havoc with her vivid writer's imagination. Suggesting sex in exchange for a story was perverse, and he must have thought it a big joke out on that balcony.

Could there be a streak of cruelty in his arrogance? If he murdered innocent animals, what kind of man could he be? At least she'd escaped her brother's no worse for wear—but without a story.

Rain now pattered unseen outside the open window. There hadn't been any clouds earlier, and Stephanie thought about the homeless people that she'd interviewed in the past few days and how hard it was for them to find shelter when the weather turned bad. She shivered and pulled her blankets up tighter around her neck.

The phone rang, jolting her into a sitting position. Her heart slammed into overdrive. Flower print sheets were pulled off the corners and twisted around her like deadly vines, evidence of her fitful night. "Hello?" she said, and squinted in the direction of the clock. 2:30 A.M. *Someone had better be dead,* she thought.

"Stephanie? *¿Puede usted ayudarme?*"

"*Miguel?*"

"*Sí. ¿Quisiera usted salir conmigo esta noche?*"

"Speak English, please." How had he gotten her number?

There was a long pause and some crackling on the line. "Can I come in?"

His request didn't register right away. "What?"

"It is cold out here and raining. Crazy California weather!"

"*Where are you?*"

"I am on your stoop, *señorita.*"

"My—*shit.* Hold on." She threw the phone down, jumped out of bed, remembered that her robe festered on the laundry pile, and had to settle for a pair of sweats. She caught a glimpse of herself as she charged through the hall—makeup wiped off, hair askew. *What was he doing at her house?*

She opened the door and one of her cats bolted out before she could grab his swishing, victorious Siamese tail.

"*Juno!*" she cried, dashing past Miguel after her pet. "I have to get my cat. He's not allowed outside. *Here kitty, kitty.*" She searched under the overgrown, dripping rhododendrons, and then a rosebush.

Miguel leaned against the wall, cell phone still in his hand. "*¡Gato! ¡Gato!*" he called in an apparent attempt to help.

Stephanie scooped up the animal, received a snag from the rosebush for the effort, stormed back up the sidewalk, and stopped in front of Miguel. "How did you find me? Or should I ask, *why* did you find me?"

"Adria gave me your phone number and address." He leaned heavily against the wall and crossed his loafers. "You still need your interview."

Was he drunk, insane, or just on an ego trip, assuming she'd wanted to see him again? *Oh, but she had!*

She couldn't believe Adria had given Miguel her address without some warning. The cat meowed and struggled to get out of her arms. "Come in," she said, exasperated, and turned toward the door. "It's wet out here."

"Let me get something," he said, and bolted back down the sidewalk toward a black BMW parked in her driveway.

While she waited for him, the damp chill and the wet smell of the eucalyptus that grew around her property came into the house. He came up the slick path holding a full bottle of tequila.

"What do you plan to do with that?" she asked suspiciously, moving to let him pass.

"Drink it, of course." He stopped in the middle of her living room and looked around, as if he wondered how he'd come to find himself in a small house on the canyon in Laguna Beach.

It dawned on her that they were completely alone except for her two cats, one that demanded to be let down now that his escape attempt had failed. When she obliged Juno, he twitched his tail and licked his back a few times.

She snapped on a light. "None for me," she said when Miguel held the bottle up for her apparent inspection, or approval.

"You have a story to write, eh? All good *taurin* stories are shared over a few drinks."

Stephanie weighed the situation for a moment,

then made a snap decision. She would get her story, she thought, even if she had to down a shot or two.

On the way to the kitchen she took a detour into her bedroom long enough to change into a comfortable, blue cotton shift, and make a few repairs to her face and hair. When she returned to the living room she found that Miguel had shed his jacket and was now stretched out on the floor. He leaned against the oversized floor pillows that matched the green velour sofa behind him.

He'd made himself comfortable and turned the lights off and the gas fireplace on, casting the room in an amber glow. He looked very comfortable, *too* comfortable. Juno now sat on his lap.

"Where's your other dress?" he asked. He scratched Juno's ears.

"I think that dress got enough mileage for one night," she said, surprised at her calm state, since the scene was so intimate. "Don't you think it's a little dark in here?"

"No." He moved the cat and filled both shot glasses.

"Don't we need lime and salt?"

He shook his head. "That is how the Mexicans drink it."

"How do the Spanish drink it?"

"Any way it will go down!" He laughed at his own joke.

She managed a weak smile. "Just one," she said. She'd drunk three glasses of wine earlier, and the aftereffects were just starting to make themselves known. A small, dull ache radiated between her temples.

She grabbed her purse from the coffee table, took out her tape recorder, and tried to act like she wasn't nervous with this gorgeous Spanish man casually sprawled against her pillows in a fire-lit room, watching her with dark, intense eyes. But she was a wreck, and felt strangely exposed, as if he knew she'd been fantasizing about him since they'd said their goodnights.

But what woman could resist him? Hadn't *People Magazine* reported the same? Women flocked to him in droves. *Well, not me! I refuse to act undignified. Or even the least bit interested in him! I'm not going to do his bidding!*

She turned on a few lights, but he asked her to turn them back off. Scowling, she obeyed, then tried to remember the last time she'd sat on the floor in her living room with a man. This was her sanctuary.

He didn't seem to care much about his surroundings, and downed his shot without wincing and indicated impatiently that she should do the same. She hadn't shot tequila since her sorority days. The liquid burned all the way down, and made her eyes water.

"Ah, now we can relax, *eh?*" He smiled, leaned his head back against the sofa, and closed his eyes as if waiting for the effect. Juno stretched and sauntered off.

"What about the terms of this interview?" she asked, concerned. If he thought she'd go to bed with him for an interview, he was dead wrong. A few shots of tequila, maybe. Sex, never. Still, the idea of this man on her, *in her,* worked on her imagination. "It seems the location is different than the original recommendation."

Now he seemed to notice his surroundings. He looked around her house, which needed a good cleaning—just under nine hundred square feet and furnished with homey, Early American antiques and hooked rugs. She felt momentarily embarrassed that he'd come by without warning, catching her place in disarray. The laundry pile hadn't gone down much since last week. Newspapers, magazines, and unread mail littered the old sea chest she used as a coffee table, and just about every pair of shoes she owned had gathered in the living room for a conference.

His gaze settled back on her. "This is much better than my hotel room."

Tequila has a funny way of sneaking up on you, Stephanie thought, and felt a little too cozy with rain pattering against the window, a fire dancing before them, and soft, huge pillows to lie on.

What are you expecting? What am I willing to give?

The firelight played on his sculpted face, and she found herself admiring his passionate features. Heritage was evident in every inch of his body—thousands of years of Iberian sun—Spain's natural beauty right here in her living room.

He drank down another shot and reached for his pack of cigarettes. He lifted an eyebrow in question. "*¿Puedo?*"

"Let me get you an ashtray." Stephanie jumped up and found him a little ceramic bowl to flick his ashes in.

"*Gracias.* Someday I will quit." Miguel clicked open the silver lighter and a blue flame touched the tip of his cigarette. He blew a line of smoke away from Stephanie.

He poured her another shot and Stephanie boldly picked it up and drank it straight down. She told herself that that was it, no more, even if Bob did think she was one of the boys. "You didn't answer my question."

Will I have to make love to you? Kiss every inch of your Spanish body? Those terms didn't seem so bad at the moment.

A slow smile broke out over his face, as if he continued to read her thoughts. "*Señorita,* it is refreshing for a woman to think that *I* am the one who wants more than good company."

"Is it?" She felt herself growing warm and fuzzy inside. *God, he was so beautiful! Of course women wanted him!*

Good company! Wait a minute. Is that all he wants tonight?

He scratched the top of his nose. "Women seem to think that I am some kind of hot Latin lover, when I am usually just a tired old bullfighter." He gazed into the gas fireplace for a few minutes. "You can relax. I want nothing from you."

Nothing? Stephanie felt a little disappointment, refused to analyze the emotion. "Why did you lead me to believe that you wanted more than good company?"

"At first, I was angry that Richard had let a reporter into his house," he said, thoughtfully. "Beautiful reporters are just as much a nuisance as ugly ones."

He thinks I'm beautiful? "What changed your mind?"

His lips puckered a little, and his eyebrows lifted. "Because you are not impressed that I am the greatest bullfighter who has ever lived, and you look at me as a man and not a legend."

She laughed and put her hand over her mouth to stop herself, cursing the booze. "I'm sorry, it's just that you sound so serious—a little full of your-self."

"I am serious," he said, but smiled again. "You are unlike any reporter I have ever encountered because you have no interest in the subject of bull-fighting—but a little interest in the *matador?*"

"Of course I have an interest in bullfighting." She turned on the tape recorder and set it on the table across from them. "And a *little* for the *matador.*"

He shook his head as if he didn't believe her. "No. Some editor found out I was in town, and then he found out that you had access to me."

"That's just want happened!"

"See? So, now your editor is going to have his wish. But what is your wish—now that you have a *little* interest in the *matador?*"

That you'll make love to me. Stephanie reached over, snatched his cigarette out of his hand, and took a few drags before handing it back, then wondered why she was smoking again. It seemed like an inti-mate thing to share with him, along with the fire and listening to the rain. "I don't have any wishes," she finally said, "other than to complete this inter-view." She fluffed her pillow, leaned back. "But, to be honest I don't like the idea of defenseless animals being baited to their death."

He gave a little shake of his head, flicked an ash into the bowl. "Defenseless? A bull's not defenseless, but he is going to die. There's brutality in the *cor-rida,* but also physical courage and beauty. Every-thing in the ring is symbolic."

His head gave a little jerk to one side, his shoulder a minute tug, as if a chill had gone up his spine. Stephanie saw a subtle transformation in his features while he spoke. A kind of savagery appeared—that same odd cruelty she'd seen at Richard's. This was *El Peligro* who spoke to her from her living room floor, the legend who took his occupation seriously, a proud Spaniard.

"You see, Stephanie, the bulls are raised for fighting. They're not your jersey cows munching grass in the sun, who one day find themselves facing a *matador.*" He butted his cigarette. "The bull that dies in the ring dies proudly, which is more than one can say for the cow who's led to the slaughterhouse. I am forced to point out all those leather shoes over there, and ask how the owners lost their hides. Americans have a lot of double standards."

For a man who'd downed several shots of tequila right before her eyes, and—she suspected—several before he'd arrived, he spoke with articulate passion. She, on the other hand, felt on the border of being drunk, and suspected that if she stood up the line wouldn't be so hard to define.

"You will understand more about bullfighting when you come to Spain. You'll be swept up in the pageant and forget about saving bulls. I'll dedicate the first to you."

Come to Spain? Right, mark that one on the calendar right after going up to Pacific Palisades to interview Stevens. Of course, Miguel was just being nice; he didn't plan to take her anywhere, other than her bedroom. For a moment her thoughts grew wistful, romantic, but what woman could resist such dreams with someone as handsome as Miguel stretched out on the floor on a rainy night?

"Tell me something about your family?" she asked, interested in his heritage.

"My *madre* used to tell me stories that my great-great-great-great grandmother was descended from

the queen of Aragon and Castile. Her legendary
Moorish palace still stands in Granada. I think my
madre told me these things to help me forget about
the hunger. I didn't have a full belly until I was fifteen. Perhaps I will show you the palaces in Spain."

"I'd love—" *Wait a minute. Too much tequila!* "Sure,
whatever. So, why did you become a bullfighter?"

He seemed to be thinking of some private moment and leaned back and tucked his hands behind
his head. "I knew I would fight the bulls the first
time my *padre* took me to the ring. I was just five
years old. It was as if God struck me with lightning.
A spiritual experience—a vision."

"And a way out of poverty?"

"Ah—hunger often drives a boy into the ring. Perhaps you know more about the *corrida* than you pretend."

Through the warm haze of the tequila she studied
the scar on his right cheek. It started just under his
right eye and moved like a question mark down to
his jawline. It wasn't deep, or keloid, but a thin white
ribbon, flush against the rest of his skin.

"How did you get this scar?" On impulse, she
reached over and ran a finger lightly across the im-
print.

He closed his eyes, and her finger trailed up and
across his cheek, over his ear, until the strands of
his hair slipped through all her fingers. His breathing changed, deeper, a little ragged.

He opened his eyes and she jerked her hand back.

"Not a bull, *querida*. Something less predictable
and more dangerous."

One of his hands did the drifting now. His finger
touched her calf and lightly stroked it in little small
circles, round and round. Then the back of his fin-

ger rubbed back and forth, up and down, a little farther, slowly advancing up her leg until the crook caught her dress and moved the fabric higher, exposing the flesh of her thigh. His eyes came up and met hers in a question.

Stephanie wondered if he could hear her heart pounding against her rib cage. His simple stroking unleashed long-forgotten passions. Since her divorce she hadn't found a man worthy of an intimate relationship—hadn't allowed a man this close to her, mentally or physically. Miguel was more than worthy on the physical side, but did she want a one-night stand?

Unable to bear another moment, Stephanie reached over and found the *People Magazine* in the clutter. Her move knocked his hand off her leg.

"What's this about you and Jenna Starr?"

He took the magazine away from her and tossed it into the fire, unaware, or unconcerned, that it wasn't a woodburning unit. He made a chuckling sound deep in his throat, reached over and pushed her down on the pillows, arching over her, easily pinning her down. "Don't believe everything you read."

His hair had fallen over his forehead as he held himself up on his elbows. His dark green eyes seemed smokier than the magazine on fire, and flickered over her face.

She tried to remember what she'd read in the magazine that was now curling up around the edges, but the fire *outside* the grate was tossing around her thoughts. So far she didn't have much to build an interview on, but at that moment she didn't care.

"Can we sit up, please?" she asked, and didn't

know where she'd found the strength to make the request.

He buried his nose between her neck and collarbone and kissed that place, sending little ripples throughout her body, signals of pleasures long forgotten—some never felt. Her hand, as if on its own, ran through his coarse, dark hair.

"What makes this fight so different from all the others?" she whispered with her eyes closed, drifting on the sensual moment but managing to get her interview just the same.

He sat up abruptly. A cold draft replaced his warm body, jarring her back to drunken reality.

"To put it bluntly, these fights are matching a brave old champion—me—and a foolish young challenger." Down went another shot, and out came his cigarettes again.

Stephanie straightened up, pulled her dress back down, and fought the wild excitement his sudden pouncing had created. Was it over? Was he going to behave now? Did she want him to?

"If you're the best, what are you worried about?"

He flipped his lighter open again and lit his cigarette. "I am the best." He rotated his shoulders a few times, ran a hand through his hair, looked around the room. "But I have plenty to worry about. Young Francosis is forcing me to fight him at *Las Ventas*. I have avoided that ring for ten years. My aversion has cost me dearly in the pocket."

Even though she felt the serious haze of the tequila, a sudden deluge of decent interview questions began to formulate in her mind. "Why did you accept the challenge in the first place, and how did he force you? Why is *Las Ventas* such an issue, and what do you mean it cost you dearly in the pocket?"

He shook his head and frowned at her. "Now you're firing questions like a reporter."

"I *am* a reporter."

He moved closer to her, and their shoulders touched. "Why don't you be a woman right now?" He took one of her hands, seemed to be examining her fingers, and then kissed the palm.

Everything around her disappeared except the sensation lingering in the middle of her hand. She retrieved it, checked the time left on her tape recorder. "Why did you agree to this fight in the first place?"

"Many times a *matador* has no say in his scheduled fights, and is forever proving his soul indestructible. Francosis made trouble for me in the press, forced me to accept a fight at *La Plaza de Toros del las Ventas* because he knew it would give him the edge—not just because I'm superstitious about that ring, but because I will not have the favor of the crowd."

He took a long drag from his cigarette, seemed to be staring at the fire now, and looked tired. The smoke floated up, lingering around Stephanie in the same way her incoherent thoughts seemed to be drifting.

"The bull will sense my fear, *señorita*, and so will the audience. But they'll pay a high price to see me sweat—or die."

Back to señorita, *no more* querida?

"Aren't bullfights staged—choreographed? What difference does it make where you fight?"

He flicked his cigarette into the fireplace, a little annoyed. "You are so naive in that thinking. Anything can happen in the ring. How can you communicate to a bull how he must move during a fight?

You have no way to anticipate his moves, only your own."

In the firelight he suddenly turned as pale as one of her struggling yellow roses in the garden beyond the window. "I'll tell you something, but not for your story." He reached over and turned off her recorder. "I've been having a dream—a nightmare— that I am fighting again at *Las Ventas,* and take a horn." He ran his hands through his hair, across his face. "It's a bad omen." He shook his head a little.

He believes in dreams? Okay.

"So, why aren't you at home preparing, either physically or mentally?"

"I'm tired of these questions, because they sound like Domingo's."

"Domingo?"

"My manager." He poured another shot, put the liquid in his mouth, cupped her neck and drew his lips to hers. Mixed with tequila, his tongue swirled with hers, drowning her in more than the gold honey.

He stood up suddenly, pulled her with him, then led her swiftly to the bedroom as if he lived there and knew the layout. She fell straight back onto the bed and pulled him down with her. They both laughed, belly to belly, nose to nose, as if they were longtime lovers and not strangers.

He lay on top of her now, holding some of his weight off. She ran her hands up his back, across the texture of the sweater, enjoying the feel of a man over her. *I thought I wasn't going to do this, but the thought of never seeing him again . . . only tonight can he be mine, then gone—back to his bulls and adulation.*

"You are very beautiful," he whispered. "I have wanted you all night." Warm, hot lips came down on hers, and she opened her mouth to accept his tongue, which gently probed her tender mouth.

He tasted like liquor and cigarettes, not a combination she might normally find appealing, but tonight all the rules were thrown out. Through this taste of vices, his unique scent enveloped her, seeped into her own pores.

"Stephanie," he whispered into her mouth. *"Siénteme . . . ah . . ."* His hands moved down her back, gripped her bottom, and rolled her on top of him.

The playful move flipped her world upside down. Tequila rushed to her brain, whirling everything and *everyone* in it out of control. Blackness replaced all, and she went back to her dream, the one where Miguel came to her house to give an interview, and whisked her into bed to make love to her.

Why is the phone always ringing? she wondered. *Why is my head pounding?* She opened her eyes and a laser beam of sunlight zapped her pupil, sending crushing pain to her head. She moaned and sat up slowly. Her shaking hand reached for the phone.

"Good job, Stephanie," Bob said in a cheerful tone.

Good job? The homeless story? She stared directly into her dresser mirror. She felt as if she had walked through the Mojave Desert—on her tongue. More pain shot through her head. "W—What are you talking about?"

Why am I naked?

"You going to Spain with Miguel. You should hear the buzz running through the *Variedades!*"

Stephanie dropped the phone. It hit the floor and scattered the two cats, who had come into the bedroom to remind her that it was time for breakfast. She fought with the twisted cord, brought it back to her ear, and wondered if she were awake.

"When were you going to call me, Stephanie?"

Why am I naked? What happened last night? Did we? She lifted the sheets and checked for evidence. What kind of evidence, if he'd worn a condom? Did he bring one? I don't have any! *I think I passed out! God, how embarrassing!*

"Steph, you there?"

"Yes, Bob," she managed, rubbing her temples. "I—I was going to call you. But what are you talking about?"

"Rafael agreeing to let you do an exclusive on this upcoming bullfight in Spain. The editor of the *Variedades* is out of his mind with excitement—and jealousy. I was damn surprised when he called. Going to Spain to watch and report on a bullfight— Steph, that's some jump in confidence about a subject you know nothing about, and only last night didn't want to touch."

She suppressed a laugh. Suddenly it seemed so absurd. It was like playing blindman's bluff. How dare Miguel—but that was just it—what had he done? What had *she* done? And how was she going to get out of this now that her boss thought she'd secured a top story?

She felt as if she careened along in the dark, yet it was a very bright morning. There was no sign of the storm that had raged outside, and inside her bed, the night before.

That was no dream. Miguel had been here. She could smell cigarettes and that scent of his, all mixed up in her sheets. Bits and pieces came back to her— laughing, tumbling on top of the feather comforter, kissing, and unabashed exploration of each other's bodies—but she'd been stoned drunk, and the details were a bit fuzzy.

"Ray's going. He can help you with the language."

Ray? Did he say Ray? How did her friend and staff photographer get involved? Another curveball thrown.

"Ray?"

"He wants to do the photo shoot. Marc Garcia, *Variedates* editor, talked to Miguel this morning, not me. I don't know all the details, and since you didn't think it was necessary to tell me, I guess you're writing this for *Variedades* now."

Bob felt betrayed! And she didn't blame him!

After she hung up the phone she charged into the living room. Solid evidence suggested that Miguel had not been an aberration. An empty tequila bottle, cigarette butts, and her tape recorder littered the table. She picked up the recorder and rewound it a little: *"Because you were not impressed that I am the greatest bullfighter who has ever lived, and you look at me as a man instead of a legend."*

She heard herself laugh.

She stumbled to the bathroom and threw up.

THREE

Miguel splashed cold water on his face and then stared transfixed at his reflection under the bright sunlight. He could hear his brother, Galleo, talking on the phone to his manager. Galleo was the best *picador* in bullfighting—his tight muscular body gave him the strength to handle the lance—but he had no talent when it came to dealing with Domingo, who only wanted to talk to the *matador*.

The phone receiver hit the cradle. Galleo's reflection appeared in the mirror. "We have to get back to Madrid," Galleo said in Spanish. "Domingo is going to come and get you himself. He thinks you should be at *La Libra* resting for *Las Ventas.*"

Miguel squinted in the mirror. Bloodshot eyes stared back. He had a pounding headache. "I don't need to be at *La Libra,*" he snapped, and reached for an aspirin bottle. His hands trembled when he shook out two white tablets.

La Libra was his bull ranch in Spain, where he normally spent time away from the plazas. But lately he didn't like being told what to do, or who to do it with—his main reason for the escape to California, a trip that should have waited. Business and starlets could always wait—the *corrida*, never.

The scheduled fight at *Las Ventas* wasn't the only predicament currently guiding his fate. His manager was pressuring him to make a public announcement that he would soon marry Paloma, the daughter of Juan Aguilar, Spain's late, beloved *matador.* Juan had died at *Las Ventas* ten years ago, because of Miguel's foolish challenge. An engagement could turn the crowd in Miguel's favor at a bullring that would remind them of his youthful pride.

Since Juan's goring, it had been speculated that when Paloma grew up Miguel would marry her and make amends for her father's needless death. An engagement now had deeper implications beyond Miguel gaining the favor of the crowd, and his manager continued to remind him of that fact.

His young challenger was in love with Paloma.

Paloma had not told Miguel about her involvement with Francosis, but Madrid had eyes that worked for Miguel—reported her moves in the nightclubs around the plazas.

Francosis could do nothing about the fate of Paloma—which alone belonged to Miguel. This was a powerful edge that could drive the young challenger into an emotional corner.

Miguel was Paloma's benefactor—her guardian, as stipulated in Juan's will. She would do as she was told. Though Miguel had no plans to marry Paloma, he couldn't have Francosis declaring his love for her, either—a fatal public mistake for *El Peligro.*

"It's only been a week since my last *corrida,*" Miguel said over his shoulder. Then he searched his leather travel bag for a razor. "Domingo worries too much, and so do you. We'll be in Madrid in plenty of time before the opening parade."

"Domingo worries because you're fighting at *Las*

Ventas and that ring is bad luck for you. You have decisions that need to be made. Don't pretend you're not also worried, and do not pretend that your leg isn't bothering you."

"It *is* bad luck," Miguel agreed, willing the muscle in his left thigh to stop twitching; today there was a dull pain where the jagged scar twisted down his leg like an angry snake. "My decisions are made, and my leg has bothered me before. It means nothing."

Drastic blood loss and shock had nearly killed him when a bull had crushed him against the *burladeros* one week after Juans death—a goring Miguel deserved for facing a bull drunk.

The doctors first said he was as good as dead. Then they said he would never walk again, let alone fight. Except for an occasional dull ache, Miguel had survived the worst goring of his career, and had proved the doctors wrong. Six months later he was walking, and also fighting better than ever. That was when the rumors started that he'd made a pact with the devil.

"Let me rub some liniment into it," Galleo offered.

"No."

"But, *Matador*—"

"Enough!" he said, knowing Galleo would not take his outburst personally.

Everyone thought Miguel was about to break his rhythm. He'd let Francosis goad him into the upcoming *mano a mano* at *Las Ventas*. Francosis had publicly stated that *El Peligro* fought where his dead mother's soul could watch over him, but since God barred her soul from *Las Ventas*, he would not fight there.

This slander against his mother had been too

much for Miguel, who was used to jabs about his avoiding the Madrid ring.

"And I know, *Matador,*" Galleo said, "that you did not sleep last night."

"You are wrong, brother. I slept like a baby." That was a lie. He had finally fallen asleep at dawn, but not restfully. The nightmare had come again, the terrible dream where an enormous black bull drove a hole in his body and he watched helplessly as his life drained out on the sands of *Las Ventas.*

He woke up in a cold sweat, and had wanted to call Domingo and tell him he was retiring. Instead, he had a vision that Stephanie Madison sat in his box at the ill-fated bullring. Still aching from their aborted joust in bed last night, he'd left her contentedly dozing in a tequila haze, unwilling to bring himself to finish the job, even though it would have been so simple. People could say what they wanted about *El Peligro,* but he was no pig.

Still, he felt driven to follow his intuition on the matter of Stephanie, and maybe his heart. He was too suspicious to do otherwise. He would bring her back to Spain, regardless of the reception.

He'd called the *Varíedades* first thing in the morning and made arrangements for a coveted interview—an exposé, provided he could choose the reporter. His suggestion as to which reporter that might be was not met with enthusiasm, but he held firm and got his way, as he'd known he would.

"Try not to worry, Galleo," he said lightly. "You know I'm the best. Francosis has nothing on me, and we're going home—but not alone."

Annoyance was etched on Galleo's sun-bronzed face. "What do you mean, not alone?"

"I have arranged a little surprise."

"This is not the time for surprises, *Matador.*"

"I had a message—I think from God. I cannot argue with God!" Miguel slammed the bathroom door, then caught his pounding head between the palms of his hands.

Stephanie tipped the valet at the Hyatt Newporter Hotel and asked for directions to the ladies' room. The mirrors told her what she knew, that she looked pretty good considering that she still had a hangover. She couldn't believe she'd behaved so wantonly last night. She attributed it to the booze, which she wouldn't have drunk in the first place had she not been after a story. She'd found no evidence that they'd had sex, other than the bed being in complete disarray.

Miguel had her hunting the racks of Nordstrom's again for something spectacular to wear, but she rationalized that it was safer to dress up than down for The Hyatt Newporter, and her choice of the tan linen suit and matching shoes had nothing to do with the bullfighter.

She went up to the hotel desk surrounded by fountains and live plants in the airy lobby. The petulant little man behind the counter hung up the phone and informed her that Mr. Rafael would meet her in the hotel bar.

A half an hour dissolved before he appeared. Miguel tossed a black linen jacket on an empty chair, and that same unique man's cologne hit her senses, reminding her of their intimacy the night before.

He settled into his chair and gazed at her with his languid green eyes. "I'm sorry that my brother, Galleo, made you wait down here," he finally said, pulling on the cuffs of his white silk shirt. "He wanted to make sure I would call my manager. Galleo knows that Domingo can't be put off."

Miguel waved a waitress over and ordered two glasses of wine. "I'm happy to see you again."

"I don't want wine," she snapped, more than a little irritated that Miguel was making all the decisions right off the bat.

He raised one eyebrow. "What do you want?"

"Ice tea."

He motioned the waitress back over and changed the order.

"*Didn't* you think I'd find out what you've been up to?" She'd managed to say her words in a low, hushed tone, but she was seething. "What kind of games are you playing with my career?"

"*Game?*" His eyes rested on the low neckline of her suit, on the swell of her breasts hidden there. "You mean the all-expense paid trip to Spain for you and a photographer, with luxury accommodations at my villa in Madrid, and ringside seats for a *corrida* sold out weeks ago? You mean an exclusive story about the world's greatest *matador* alive, and possibly his last fight? An interview you may not think very worthy of your time, but will sell for more money than you'd make in a year writing for a local paper. That game?"

"I'm on assignment. I won't make any more money."

"You are wrong, *señorita*. I have personally made certain the *Variedades* doesn't have exclusive rights."

She returned his self-satisfied smile and told herself that she'd been right. He was cruel and arrogant, and maybe a little twisted, too. He had all the answers, and he wanted to see her squirm, wanted her to suffer. Maybe he had no intention of taking her to Spain. Maybe he only meant to humiliate her, as if she were not humiliated enough after last night. But how far would he take this?

"I'm not going," she stated flatly, because she wasn't, not setting one foot anywhere with him. "I don't care what happened between us last night."

He laughed, loudly. "Nothing happened! You passed out—in my arms—or we'd be facing each other as lovers this morning."

His words stunned her into silence for a moment.

The waitress brought their drinks. Miguel held up the contents and examined the dark liquid. A devilish glint came into his eyes. "The editor of the *Variedades* said you wouldn't take the assignment."

Stephanie's jaw dropped a little. "He did?"

"He said you can't speak Spanish, and couldn't possibly handle this kind of story. It was out of the question."

Her fingers clenched the table edge. "He said that?"

"I didn't believe him." He waved his hand in the air in a casual manner. "And I called him a liar."

"You did?" A nervous laugh escaped her lips, and she pointedly looked away. At first she was totally bewildered that Miguel would believe in her, but not an editor. Then indignation replaced confusion. She'd worked hard the past few years, proved time and again that she could handle difficult investigative reporting on a variety of subjects.

The liquid from his glass passed over his lips, and when he drew the glass away his tongue ran over the lower one. He chuckled and one shoulder lifted slightly. "He wants to assign another reporter. I guess I'll have to consider his offer."

"Just because I can't speak Spanish doesn't mean I can't write the story! Maybe I just don't *want* to write about the brutal deaths of innocent animals!"

"I think he might be right. It's too much for you. You can't possibly learn—"

"Listen, I could write a story in Sanskrit if I had to!" After the words flew from her mouth, she wanted to yank them all back. What was she saying? That she'd go?

His hand reached across the table and covered hers. She hadn't expected him to touch her again, hadn't expected violent desires to wash over her in the middle of a hotel bar. She tried to free her hand, but his fingers quickly circled her wrist and held it firm.

"Then write it," he said. "Prove everyone wrong."

She needed fresh air, thought she might swoon from the way Miguel was looking at her—lusting after her. It was disgusting—no, it was wonderful!

She jerked her hand free of his, scraped the chair across the floor, and hurried from the room to curious glances from other patrons. She gulped air when she burst through the hotel doors, intent on getting as far from him as possible. It smelled as if it were going to rain again, and she could see storm clouds coming from the direction of the ocean, not visible from the hotel.

She hurried down a path and followed it through the maze of hotel rooms. It ended at a park-like setting where a man played catch with a dog. She considered which way to go, wondered what she was running from. In twenty-four hours her life had turned into chaos, and confusion was something she didn't like, or need. How would she ever explain this mess to Richard and Adria?

Miguel's warm hand on her shoulder startled her. His touch sent a shudder through her body and weakened her resolve to escape him.

"Stephanie," he whispered in her ear, and pulled her backside close enough to feel his warmth. "Stop resisting and come to Spain." The passion in his voice was strong, magnetic. "We'll go to Madrid first. I have a villa there that my sister maintains. After the fight, if I—" He stopped short.

"If what?" she asked, and turned in the circle of his arms.

"If everything goes right, we'll head to Menorca in the Balearic Islands. I have a place on the water."

She sank into his embrace, wanted to escape him, but couldn't find the strength. His breath was warm and moist against her cheek. "This is crazy."

"Love is a little crazy." He brushed his lips against her cheek.

Her upper thighs and belly pressed against his, and his mouth hovered somewhere near her own. She tried to think, yet coherent thoughts fled and hid behind her confusion, as the sun now hid behind the clouds. Her hands were pressed against his backside. The heat from his body warmed her palms. She closed her eyes for a moment and took a deep breath. Instead of her head clearing as she'd hoped, his mystifying scent unsettled her further.

"Love?" she whispered. "I'll never love anyone again." She pressed her hands against his back, memorized the texture of the jacket he wore, closed her eyes, and let the rest of her senses take over— the scent that was his own.

He made enough space to look into her eyes. "We will see, *querida.*"

She became captive in the green depths, pulled

into a world of exotic sensations and delicious agony. Her simple world, a place she understood, became as foreign as the man who held her in his arms. She closed her eyes again, rested her head on his shoulder, and let herself drift with the blissful moment.

"I'll come," she said in a breathy whisper. "But only to do the story. I could use the money. Don't expect anything else!" *How stupid a statement!* As soon as she'd said it he gathered her up, and she met his mouth willingly, parted her lips when his tongue probed gently. How could a man taste like a country? He did, or what she imagined Spain would taste like—dark wines, sandy beaches, evergreen oak trees, and laurel leaves.

"I never expect anything," he whispered into her mouth, sliding his fingers up her back to her neck, where they massaged her flesh.

She put her hands on his chest and gently pushed him away.

Stephanie decided she would get even with Miguel for toying with her comfortable, dependable life. The following morning, she plotted his fate at the Los Angeles International Airport while waiting for Ray Johnson, staff photographer and a good friend, who had gone to check on their flight. She sat on an orange plastic chair with her elbows on her laptop computer case, staring out the window at the pouring rain, trying to unravel the events of the past two days. She wanted a cup of coffee. She'd been up most of the night packing, and what little sleep she'd gotten had been fitful.

She fished out a copy of *Fodor's Madrid & Barcelona*

from her purse and flipped through the guide book she'd purchased at a bookstore on the way over, then tucked it away, unable to concentrate on anything but her conversation with Richard.

She expelled a long breath when she remembered the phone call. Adria thought her trip with Miguel sounded terribly *romantic*, but Richard wanted hard, fast answers. Why was his sister off to Spain with his client? She told him she was going to Spain to write Miguel's story, that Miguel had hired her and Ray through the *Variedades* for an exorbitant amount of money. Richard didn't believe it, and warned her not to jeopardize his relationship with Miguel.

Stephanie focused on her reflection in the window. Her hair was frizzy from the downpour they'd encountered in the airport parking lot, and mascara ran under her eyes. Her seventy-dollar beige cotton pants and the black angora sweater Adria had given her on her birthday were already wrinkled. She used her fingers to rub away the smudges under her eyes, and searched her purse for lipstick and a comb.

Pride had her declining a limo ride to the airport with Miguel. She and Ray carpooled, and now waited for Miguel to show up with their tickets.

Ray returned, out of breath, his tall, lanky body loaded down with camera equipment, his long brown hair damp and tied back in a rubber band. His tapestry shirt and blue jeans were just as wet as her clothes.

"The plane's on time," he said. "I'm glad because I hate waiting around in f'ing airports. I spend half my life waiting to catch planes."

"I still can't believe we're going to do this story," she said as she pulled up her hair and secured it with a clip she'd found in her bag.

"Neither can I. Miguel Rafael doesn't accommodate the press unless he has a reason."

"Do you know anything about him?"

"A little." Ray seemed to be studying her face. "He's never been married."

"I didn't ask that!" Stephanie felt her face redden.

"No, but I could hear something in your voice. He gets around, Stephanie. You're no match for him."

"Oh, really? Since when do you know my match?"

Ray struggled. "Miguel's an international playboy."

"Then what on earth would he want with me?" *Yes, what in the world?* Images of the beautiful Jenna Star loomed before her.

"Don't know. But something's up. You guys doin' the dirty?"

She snorted. "I just met him two days ago! Give me a break." *Okay, I got naked with him, but that doesn't count. It can't count. Okay, he tries to kiss me every chance he gets, but that doesn't mean anything. Nothing counts!*

Stephanie jumped up and found a restroom, needing a little diversion. After relieving herself she fiddled with her hair some more, unable to get it under control, and applied a little lipstick. She gave up on repairs, and went back to Ray, who was now rummaging around in one of his equipment bags.

"You know how he got that scar on his face?" Ray asked out of the blue.

"No, how?" She remembered tracing it with her finger, and Miguel saying he hadn't gotten it from a bull but something more unpredictable. That was about the time they'd started to get intimate, and she'd never found out.

"Ten years ago he was engaged to a Spanish socialite—caught her at a party getting it on with Juan Aguilar, one of Spain's most beloved *matadors*, and tried to pull her off. She clawed him in the face."

Stephanie was appalled. "How do you know so much?"

"I'm something of an *aficionado*. I've even seen Miguel fight down in Mexico. But wait, there's more."

"Why are you telling me all this?"

"You're going to write an exposé about the guy, right?"

Stephanie scowled at Ray. Something told her the that exposé had nothing to do with Ray's sudden fount of information on *El Peligro*. "Right. So, tell me the rest."

"Miguel called Juan out for a *mano a mano*. Juan was a few months from retiring, too old to face the kinds of bulls the young *matador* was fighting. He took a horn and died. The public turned against Miguel." Ray opened his case, pulled out a camera, peered through the viewfinder, and focused on Stephanie, who held up her middle finger. "Miguel knew the reception he was going to receive at his next bullfight,"—Ray continued clicking pictures, unconcerned with her gestures—"and when he walked out onto the sand, to cruel catcalls, boos, and rotten fruit, he was very drunk. The bull hooked him in the thigh, and he almost died."

"That's horrible. But he survived, and rose to the top of bullfighting."

"He is one of Spain's greatest bullfighters, but he isn't much loved. He came back stronger than ever, but with a big attitude. Juan Aguilar was more than a Spanish hero. He was also the *matador* who took

Miguel under his wing. Essentially, he challenged his mentor, and the mentor died."

Stephanie leaned back against the chair, crossed her legs, wondered how this information would affect her current relationship with Miguel. What *was* her relationship? she wondered.

"Just so you know, all that happened at *Las Ventas*. He hasn't been back since. That's the big deal about this fight. It's going to stir up a lot of memories, memories Miguel's fought hard and paid a lot of money to make the public forget."

"So the hype about this fight is true?" She felt her mouth go dry.

Ray shrugged, fiddled with his camera. "Bullfighters are a suspicious lot. If he thinks he's going to die, he just might." He focused on a something in the distance, and his camera whirled.

Stephanie turned and saw Ray's subject. Miguel stood at a ticket counter, looking casual in jeans and an oversized white cotton sweater, talking with a pretty redhead who seemed to be enjoying her new customer. The sweater enhanced his dark hair, and the tight jeans accented the strength in his thighs.

He looked down at something on the counter and his hair fell forward. It was thick and shining. Pushing it out of his eyes, he tilted his head back, laughing at something the woman said. She laughed with him and touched his hand in an intimate way.

Playboy!

Stephanie put her elbows on her knees, her chin in her palms, and wondered what had caused their amusement.

"I didn't tell you all this so you'll feel sorry for the guy," Ray said, and lowered his camera to his lap. "I'm telling you this so you'll understand he's hardened and experienced in things you and I couldn't begin to understand. He'll do whatever he has to do to stay on top of bullfighting. He has an agenda if he invited you. He hates the press. Something's up, and if you aren't banging him, then what could it be?"

Stephanie socked him in the arm. "*Ray!* Maybe he's just impressed with my fantastic abilities as a journalist."

"Right. He'll manipulate you to serve his needs. Just be careful. Protect yourself until we can get a clear idea of what he really wants."

Brushing a stray curl out of her face, she took a deep breath and turned again in the direction of Miguel. A small child tested new legs just a few feet away. The boy tumbled backward onto his well-padded bottom and raised his arms for his mother, who held several suitcases and struggled not to drop them.

Stephanie helped the woman with her bags, then returned to her seat. Miguel still busied himself down the way, but waved to her when she glanced once again in his direction. She waved back.

"I don't know how I'm going to communicate with anyone in Spain," she said to Ray. "And I know zip about bullfighting."

He passed her a heavy canvas bag. "I packed you some research material. I figured you'd never think of it in your current state. You'll be okay with me."

She shot him a hard glance. "What *state* is that?"

"The state in which you've been acting as if you're facing a firing squad instead of a trip to Madrid. Or is it the thought of attending a bullfight?"

"Bullfighting is not civilized."

"Neither's football."

"I don't like football, either."

Ray sighed.

Miguel finally disengaged himself from the red-head and walked over to Stephanie. He introduced the man who now joined him as his brother, Galleo. Solid and unsmiling, 220-pounds-plus, Galleo took an unflinching stance. Dark, steady, brown eyes stared at Stephanie, narrowed with disapproval.

"You're wet," Miguel said to Stephanie, holding out his hand and helping her rise from her make-shift seat.

"And you're not," she replied sarcastically, with a tight smile.

He put his hand on the small of her back and led her toward the gate. He whispered in her ear, "I have enough sense to get out of the rain."

"Oh!" She twisted out of his reach. "But not enough sense to stay out of a bullring!" She'd meant it in jest, a witty comeback, but Miguel's altered expression suggested she'd hit a nerve. *Good,* she thought.

They boarded the plane and took seats in first-class. Galleo sat with Ray, and Miguel, after tossing their flight bags on the racks above, sat with Stephanie. After the plane was at cruising altitude, she reached for the bag Ray had given her. She tried to ignore Miguel at her side, who busied himself with the *Los Angeles Times.*

She examined the material, but discovered that some of it was in Spanish. This puzzled her. She twisted in her seat to ask Ray why he'd given her things she couldn't read, but he was talking to Galleo, half turned in his seat, and she was unable to make eye contact with him.

She settled back and found Miguel peering over his paper at her.

"Spanish magazines? Brushing up on the language?"

"No," she clipped. She tucked the magazine back in the bag and pulled out a biography about Miguel, in English, titled simply, *The Danger.*

"Is this a good book for learning something about my captor?" she asked.

He laughed. "I don't see any chains!" He took the book from her. "This is not an authorized biography. I've never read it." He handed it back.

Stephanie opened the book and flipped through the pages.

> . . . *any* other matador *in modern times . . . he came from nowhere . . . impatient crowds fighting for tickets . . . regained consciousness . . . a geyser of blood spurting from his left thigh, spreading a dark stain over his suit of lights . . .*"

She snapped the book closed and reached for one of her own magazines, but she couldn't concentrate; she was tired. She leaned her head back and closed her eyes, but they popped open when Miguel took her hand and brought it to his lips.

He held her gaze. "Are you glad you came?"

She took a quick breath when he kissed the palm of her hand. "I'll be happy when I figure out why you wanted me to come." Everything that Ray had shared with her now tumbled around in her thoughts.

"You are coming to write a story."

Sure, and hell just froze over. She turned toward the window with a start, as if to be rescued by the same sky spread out before her, but she found no salvation in the thick clouds—maybe, she thought, because she knew a storm raged below them.

She looked at Miguel again, found herself studying the scar.

He had an agenda. What could it be?

His eyes were on her mouth, and then his head inclined toward hers until their lips met. Her mouth seemed oversensitive, keenly aware of the feel of his wet flesh on hers. Her tongue met his. *How good you taste,* she thought. Her hands wove in his hair, the cool, coarse strands slid between her fingers.

It was a clanking that brought her out of this new-found bliss. Their lips separated, held together for a split second by their mingled wetness. She followed the noise and saw in the next aisle the same child and the mother from the airport. The baby was pounding a spoon on the tray pulled out to hold his jars of baby food.

Quickly looking back, she saw that Ray had observed the kiss. Miguel released her hand and retrieved his newspaper, which had fallen into the aisle.

She felt possessed with unmet, unknown longings. She was miserable. Many hours passed before Miguel's kiss was nullified, or Ray's warnings.

FOUR

They were over eight hours into an eleven hour flight, and had long ago finished dinner as the plane followed the dawn over the North Atlantic Ocean. Most around them slept. Pillows were propped up on windows, seats leaned back to their breaking point, and light snores and hushed chatter filled the first-class section.

Stephanie adjusted the light above as she read about the Spanish fiestas and folklore of Madrid.

"La Villa, *the village, is what the inhabitants of Madrid call their city, and in many quarters there are still traditions alive of a time before all those villages had melted together into Spain's capital. . . .*"

She flipped through the pages of her guidebook:

Corrida del Toros: *Bullfighting is certainly one of the best known, although polemical, Spanish customs . . . for the fans,* La Corrida *is an art rather than a sport . . . the challenge of man fighting against beast.*

Polemical? Stephanie thought about the word used to describe Miguel's occupation. Polemic meant aggressive attack on the opinions of another, or some form of controversial dispute. No doubt there were two camps surrounding the *art* of bullfighting—those for the continued tradition, and those against the death of innocent animals.

In an average year twenty-five thousand bulls are killed before an estimated thirty million spectators. The industry supports one hundred fifty thousand employees and toreros.

A real cash cow, she thought. *Or is that cash bull?*
At the moment she leaned against the brutal killing of innocent animals.

Sleep continued to evade her—and, apparently, Miguel, who read from a book he'd earlier pulled from his flight bag.

"What are you reading?" she asked, curious about the worn, leather-bound book he held tenderly.

"A little book of prayers—my missal." He looked over a pair of stylish reading glasses and held her stare for a moment, as if he waited for her amazement that he could read at all.

"Really?" *Prayer book? Okay.*

"I see you continue to have a narrow opinion of bullfighters. I suppose you can't imagine that I might also have an economics degree from the University of Madrid."

"You're putting words into my mouth," she said, *but no, she* couldn't *imagine.*

"I don't have an economics degree from the University of Madrid." He winked at her. "No time to study when you are a young man chasing the bulls. I studied at *Escuela de Tauromaquia de Madrid.*"

"Sort of a college for bullfighters?"

"Sí."

"It isn't that I have a narrow opinion of bullfighters. It's that I've *no* opinion."

"Maybe you will have a bad opinion when this is all over."

"Probably."

Miguel laughed so loudly that the child who'd earlier broken up their kiss stirred in his young mother's arms, and the mother screwed up her face in disapproval. He took off his glasses and smiled at the woman. She hesitated and shyly smiled back. Stephanie watched the exchange between the two and realized that Miguel had an innocence that hung around him. It could disarm his enemies. *And maybe his bulls and lovers,* she thought.

"But you'll write a good story, because I am going to tell you what to write."

"Final approval? Did you arrange that, too?"

He slipped his glasses back on, opened the book, and said, "Of course."

She wasn't surprised. "You'll tell me all about the origins and history of bullfighting?"

"If you like."

"And will you tell me why you were really in California?"

"To meet you." He winked at her, which he seemed to do a lot. "It was fate—I never argue with it."

"I'm serious."

"So am I."

"Remember, I'm trying to write a story about you. I need to know what drives you to face a bull every

Sunday when you don't need the money, and why you'd travel to the States when you have an important bullfight coming up."

He closed the prayer book again, and now his face clouded over. Taking off his glasses, he rubbed his face with both hands as if he could rid himself of some worry. "*Señorita,* I don't know why I still fight the bulls when I have millions of dollars. Part of it is because my public will not let me go. And I went to California just to get away. Reporters and fans all the time dog my heels over the dusty roads of Spain. *Dios mío,* you will see when we get to Madrid. There, I am *El Peligro.* A god to my people, but a god with no powers to save himself."

Drama! He dripped with effect!

"Isn't it true modern *matadors* don't die as often now that they have modern drugs to inject the bull with, or modern saws to shave down their horns?"

He shook his head in exasperation. "Where have you heard these things? The owners of the bulls take pride in their animals. They wouldn't allow them harmed."

She considered what he said, then remembered his picture in *People Magazine.* "You weren't alone in California. You were doing the Hollywood scene, even allowing interviews, not behaving like a man who thought his days were numbered."

He scratched his head. "I was not *doing* the Hollywood scene. Someone invited me to a party, so I went. And that was not an interview. Someone took our picture together, and did a little research to find out who was on Jenna's arm. Next thing, they have an unauthorized story."

"Did you have *sex* with her?" Stephanie wasn't sure where the question came from, and felt strangely embarrassed that she'd asked it while he rested a prayer book on his knee, as if the book stood in judgment of her question.

"No, *señorita,* I did not have *sex* with Jenna Starr . . . but I could have."

"I'll bet."

Miguel's little book slipped out of his grasp. A flight attendant happened by and picked it up and handed it back to him.

"That looks well-read," Stephanie commented, still surprised that he was religious. The leather-bound copy had the look and texture of a wrinkled brown paper bag.

Miguel put it against his heart. "My *madre* gave it to me when I was twelve. She said, 'Son, I know you would rather have a sword or a cape, but those things cannot comfort you.' She was right. After she died, I found it in a cupboard. Long forgotten by the child, it was soon revered and treasured by the man. I don't go anywhere without it."

"My mother died, too—last year—cancer." Why had she blurted that, she wondered, frustrated to have shared something so painful. Twisting her fingers together, she stared down at her hands, reminding herself to think before she spoke in the future.

He reached over and took her hand consolingly. "And you have not found any comfort in a cupboard, eh, *querida?*"

When he smiled again, she felt herself wrapped up tight in his devastating appeal. Ray's words came back to haunt her: *He'll manipulate you to serve his needs. Just be watchful. Protect yourself until we can get a clear idea of what he really wants.*

"Excuse me," she said, and jumped up, squeezing past his knees and making her way to the restroom.

Once inside, she stared at her reflection for a long time. *What am I doing on this plane going to Spain with this man? What? What? What?*

A gentle rap on the door brought her out of her musings. The OCCUPIED sign was on. Whoever knocked could wait. *How rude! And in first class!* She relieved herself, washed her hands, and opened the door. Miguel leaned against the restroom exterior, the obvious intruder.

"Can't you wait your turn?"

"Ah—" He pushed his way into the restroom and pulled her back in with him. Locking the door, he turned and swept her up into his arms. *"Querida,* I wait for nothing," he whispered, his hot breath against her ear, her cheek. Then his lips claimed her mouth. "I take what I want."

"Miguel—" She could do no more than whisper his name into his mouth. His ardor held her more captive than his arms.

His kissing was urgent, demanding, deep.

The next knock at the door was hard and insistent. Miguel made enough space to look at Stephanie, and wiggled his eyebrows.

"Please open the door," a tight, female voice demanded. Stephanie was mortified, put her hands up to her mouth to stifle a giggle.

He gave her one last kiss, glanced in the mirror long enough to slice his fingers through his dark hair, and opened the latch.

Two older female stewards stood sentinel on either side of the entrance. One said, "We do not allow the Mile-High Club on this airline!"

Miguel glanced back at Stephanie, raised a conspiratorial eyebrow, and took her hand. "We have been found out, *querida."*

All those who had once slept now seemed focused on the activities in the cabin, including Ray and Galleo. Stephanie couldn't look at either of them. Settling into her seat, she turned to Miguel and whispered, "You're crazy!"

He reached for her hand and put it in his lap, pressed her palm into his erection. "Sí. You make me crazy."

She managed to reclaim her hand, and some dignity. He chuckled at her consternation and picked up his book, which he'd tucked into the pocket of the seat in front of him.

Miguel's hurricane passion at ten thousand feet had lit her entire body with desire, burned up the momentary sadness brought on by the memory of her mother. Her thoughts whirled around in new bittersweet confusion. If he showed no restraint about ravishing her in the restroom of a plane, what protection would she have against him in his villa?

She'd better get a room with a strong lock!

She reached up, flipped off the light, punched her pillow a few times, and tried to sleep. She was completely unsuccessful.

Dawn seemed to break endlessly over the heavens, and with the yielding light Stephanie gazed out the window at the lofty mountains, white plains, steep cliffs, and snug sandy beaches that passed beneath them. Once in awhile she looked over at Miguel, who had fallen asleep. In slumber his hair had diffused across his forehead, his features relaxed, his breathing even. She could almost see him as a child, hopeful that his mother had brought him a sword or cape, only to be disappointed with a little prayer book.

All the hardness of *El Peligro* was gone. The scar on his cheek didn't seem so severe.

His sweater was pushed up, and she studied the gold linked bracelet around his wrist. Around his neck she could see a chain tucked discreetly under the knit fabric. She reached over, gave it a gentle tug, and easily freed it. A little cross bounded out and rested in her palm.

A strange shudder quaked through her body, starting from her feet and reverberating up to her head. Miguel affected her with his passions and his spirituality. There was a disarming naivete about him. Perhaps this was what made him so fearless, or so sexy.

She fished under the seat for the biography of Miguel, now sandwiched in her carry-on bag with all the other material Ray had so generously provided.

Miguel Antonio Rafael grew up in Barcelona, which is the capital of the Spanish region of Catalonia, a vivid and accessible metropolis. The boy Miguel lived in the poorest areas. He came out of nowhere. One day his face appeared on the advertising panels of the city's double-decker buses. . . .

Too tired to read from a book, she tucked it in between her leg and the armrest, fished deeper into the bag, and pulled out a newspaper, yellow from age, inside an exposé about the cruelty of bullfighting.

There is a dark side to bullfighting. It's barbaric. It should be regulated to the past. . . .

She looked over at the modern day *matador,* someone trapped between the past and the present, wondering about his world and how different it was from her own.

Did he seriously believe he would die? Ray's airport council about Spanish superstitions seemed a hard pill to swallow.

Something had caught her eye on the paper:

Bullfighting Trivia: *Number of* matadors *killed in the ring: More than 500. Average number of times a* matador *receives last rites after being gored during his career: Six. Last* matador *to be killed in the ring in Spain: Juan Aguilar at* Las Ventas.

Juan Aguilar—the *matador* Miguel had challenged to a contest. Interesting, or eerie?

She tucked the paper away and leaned her head against the vibrating window. A sprinkling of wild passions and moments of ecstasy was nothing to build dreams upon, especially with a man who took pride in the torture of innocent animals and seemed to live by his own set of rules.

She crossed her arms over her chest and wondered about the Spanish socialite who nearly destroyed Miguel's career. He must have seriously loved that woman.

The idea gave Stephanie's heart a little twist.

Why did he want her—not just around him, but obviously as his lover—when it was pretty clear what kind of women he normally surrounded himself with? *Socialites. Movie stars.*

The question ate at her, made her want to shake Miguel out of his slumber and ask him. Instead, she reached over and touched his hair, let the shiny, coarse strands slip between her fingers, then brushed her fingers across his cheek.

He sighed in response, but didn't wake up.

All he needs to do is smile at me and I am palpitating with desires, she thought, turning back to the window, certain another night wouldn't go by before she became his lover. What woman could resist? Who would want to?

Throw caution to the wind. Live a little.

Eat drink and be merry, for tomorrow you may die.

A city peered over a distant ridge—*his world,* Madrid.

In the Barajas Airport terminal a mob of reporters descended upon Miguel, all firing questions in Spanish. Galleo, Miguel's massive brother, made a perfect defensive block and pushed them aside. He barked out orders, shouldering Miguel and his small entourage toward a waiting limousine. It was just morning in Madrid, but the air-conditioning inside the limo couldn't keep up with the torturous heat outside. Beads of sweat slipped down Stephanie's chest in response to the sweater she wore, and she felt groggy from jet lag.

The flight had been over eleven hours, and they lost nine with the time change. What she needed was a bed.

Though Miguel wore a sweater, too, he seemed unaffected by the heat, cheerful and full of energy.

After some time, Ray pulled off his sweatshirt and settled across from Stephanie. "It's great to be back in Madrid! I know some hot nightclubs, Steph. Look! The statue of Miguel de Cervantes! The first time I saw that, I broke down and cried."

Stephanie leaned over and looked out the window at the monument speeding by, catching just a glance of the *Plaza de España* as they sped on *Gran Via,* a congested main artery, through old Madrid.

"I spend my life on the road," Miguel said, adding to their conversation. "When I have any real free time, I go to my place in Menorca, where it overlooks the waters of *Cala Turqueta.* After this fight, perhaps you can both come to visit me there."

"Cool," Ray said emphatically. "I'm there. Don't you spend a lot of time at your *granderías?*"

"No. The ranch reminds me of the plazas, and when I want to really get away I prefer the sea. We'll be going to my bull ranch tomorrow for a few days—in Southern Spain."

Bull farm? Stephanie thought. *Oh, joy.*

"Madrid is still my absent home. My sister maintains my villa and lives there with her husband Jacko, my strongest, meanest *picador.*"

Galleo gave him a gentle smack on the arm at the insult. Miguel punched him back. It dawned on Stephanie that Galleo could understand English, though he seemed to pretend otherwise.

"Theresa always welcomes me home. I have a big family. Many will be at the villa to greet me and then drive out to *La Libra.*"

Traffic was horrendous, but the driver beat some of it by turning off the main thoroughfare. They passed small bars, cafés, and people milling about the streets as they sped through the city under a flawless blue sky.

A few more tricky turns and they drew up to a modern, two-story complex surrounded by thick, lush trees. There was no sweeping driveway to whisk them away from inquisitive eyes. A crowded lane awaited Miguel's arrival.

Again, Miguel shouldered his way through a horde

of reporters and photographers, some of whom had tailed the limo from the airport. *Aficionados,* some who had been waiting for him since the day before, cordially received him.

Miguel grabbed Stephanie's arm and propelled her forward just in time to save her from being squashed by a wave of human beings. She welcomed the rescue, since the combination of heat and bodies made her feel worse, light-headed, off balance, but the rescue came too late. The world tilted, someone said something, and then blackness.

There was more confusion when she opened her eyes. A woman held a glass of water up to her lips. Another fanned her frantically. Miguel said something to them in Spanish, then he asked Stephanie with concern: "Are you all right?"

For an instant his words drifted in the chaos around them. She struggled to understand why there were two Spanish women tending to her immediate needs. "Yes—I think." She tried to focus on a group of men who were embracing each other with affection. Someone helped her to a sofa, where a glass of ice water was produced. She looked around the wonderfully cool villa.

White walls. White furniture. White carpets. White tile. An El Greco hung over a modern fireplace of white stone, the first splash of color to meet her eyes. A Goya took space above a well-stocked wet-bar. A few other exquisite art specimens graced the corners, adding a little more contrast to the room.

Outside, the colors abounded. A picture window revealed the morning sun, and beyond a small patio, pool, and spa, were dazzling potted flowers, dark cypresses, and stone walls were woven thick with fern and aged ivy.

Stephanie was left in the company of Miguel's sister, Theresa. The other woman hurried off to some unseen location and returned later with a platter of *tapas*: snacks prepared of seafood, meats, and chicken.

Miguel stood at the wet-bar with his bullfighting entourage. They all seemed anxious about his return. At least thirty men talked at once, and soon a light cloud of smoke laced the room. Children also ran around, their clatter as loud as the adults'. More food appeared, along with bottles of wine and beer.

Stephanie couldn't eat, but she thought she could handle a *cerveza*, a beer. She read the label: San Miguel, lager.

Sure, get drunk.

A big, fat man, with expensive but ill-fitting clothes came up to her. In the middle of his arrogant, dark face were two small eyes. He sized her up, filling her with nervous apprehension. He took her free hand in his massive one and said something in Spanish which didn't sound like a greeting.

"No hablo mucho español," she said, and forced a smile.

He turned quickly away from her and pounded on his big feet straight to Miguel. Ray came over long enough to tell her she'd just met Miguel's manager, Domingo.

The *cerveza* couldn't go down fast enough!

The *matador* now smoked a cigarette as he leaned against a cold fireplace with a knot of men. Domingo said something in Miguel's ear, but he shook him off and glanced over at Stephanie. She met his gaze, lifted the lager bottle to him, and struggled to keep her expression placid, not revealing her true feelings. A Ferris wheel of emotions warned her in no uncertain terms that she would never be welcome here among his family.

Obviously, Miguel hadn't informed anyone that he would be having houseguests. At first, they glanced at her with curiosity, but as the day grew longer, the hostility was almost palpable. She began to wonder if she would survive this assignment emotionally intact.

She set her empty bottle on a tray moving by, and took another.

Ray busied himself taking pictures, but after some time he plopped his gangly body next to Stephanie and reloaded his camera.

"You must be okay if you're drinking beer."

"Miguel's turning me into an alcoholic." She heard her voice slur. "Maybe I can find some tequila over there at that bar, and can you get me a cigarette? I've taken it up."

"I guess you're not taking my advice about going slow." He popped a *calamares fritos* into his mouth and made a *"Mmmmmmm"* sound.

"Nope. Tripping the light fantastic, baby."

"Shit, these are the best *tapas* I've ever had." He munched a few more. "Want to tell me about what happened in the restroom on the plane?"

"Nope. Who do these people think we are? Houseguests?"

"As far as I can tell, Miguel isn't saying *who* we are."

"Rather rude that he hasn't introduced us to anyone. Domingo introduced himself—I think."

"He asked you to leave, actually."

Stephanie made a small noise. "Great."

"Maybe you'd better go lie down. You look as if you're going to drop."

"I—" Stephanie stopped talking, as did everyone, all attention now on the foyer. Two men blocked a young woman's entrance into the villa. They would die of exhaustion before she gave up trying to get around them.

She saw her target—Miguel—and she literally ran into his arms. Logical deduction said this wasn't one of his sisters. With painful, acute perception, Stephanie realized once again that Miguel meant something to her. In this foreign land, though, surrounded by sacred traditions and Spanish women who took the breath away of every man present, how could she compete?

The young woman seemed to have an energy field around her, and it spoke of youthful sensuality. Her dark brown hair danced around the bends of her knees as Miguel spun her around. Her black leotard and full red skirt spoke of Spanish history, and it hiked up her youthful body as she slid down Miguel's. A lacy shawl draped recklessly around her neck came to a loose knot between her full breasts.

Stephanie turned to Ray. "Who's that?"

Ray pushed the advance on his camera and it whirled, cocked and ready. "That is Paloma Aguilar, the very grown-up daughter of Juan Aguilar."

"The *matador* Miguel challenged at *Las Ventas?* The last matador to die in a Spanish bullring?*"

"The one and only."

"Juan's daughter doesn't blame him for her father's death?"

"Doesn't look that way."

Paloma sauntered toward Miguel again, her great velvet brown eyes on him. Her cheeks grew bright crimson and lovelier when Miguel put his arms around her waist and whispered something to her.

She laughed and dropped carelessly onto the leather sofa, and patted the seat for Miguel to join her. Then she looked over at Stephanie, with nothing more than curiosity in her gaze.

Trunks were suddenly produced and opened. Miguel passed out gifts he'd apparently brought back from the United States. Everyone received something, from designer jeans to American cigarettes. Stephanie watched the exchanges with fascination. He was a very generous man—taking a short, unplanned vacation to escape, and still finding the time to remember his family and friends.

On her honeymoon in Hawaii, Steven wouldn't let Stephanie buy more than refrigerator magnets for her friends, and barely let her purchase things for herself, all the time complaining about the marked up prices and how the tourists were ripped off.

From the looks of Miguel's gifts, he couldn't have cared less about expense. Many of the bags were from South Coast Plaza, an upscale shopping mall in the Newport Beach area of Southern California. Miguel handed Paloma a large beautifully wrapped box from Nordstrom, Stephanie's own favorite store. She ripped through the tissue paper and, laughing like a little girl, held a sexy, black silk dress up for everyone to see. Catcalls bounced off the walls in approval.

After the gifts were distributed, Galleo picked up a guitar and began strumming. Paloma jumped to her feet at the sound of the music and offered Miguel her hand.

"Encantado, gracias," Miguel said, and took it.

At first their steps were simple and unaccented, but their glances grew more provocative and they

danced in closer contact. They linked hands, and
then hips, and finally, Stephanie realized, they were
dancing the steps of the national flamenco.

Paloma pressed against the length of Miguel.
Then he suddenly spun her around. Her skirt un-
folded like a blossoming flower, her legs the shapely
stem. Miguel pulled her to him for a quick kiss that
ended the dance. Cheers exploded.

Watching Miguel with Paloma was Stephanie's undoing. She needed sleep to forget what she'd seen,
that their dance spoke of familiarity and tradition,
things of which she could never be part.

Suddenly those who were laughing and carrying
on as if they could do it into the night sobered and
filed toward the door. A few more pats on the back
were delivered, and more kisses, as last minute stories were told. It didn't take someone who spoke
Spanish to understand Paloma didn't want to leave
with the rest of the group.

She stood with her thin arms akimbo, face-to-face
with Galleo, who spoke to her in harsh tones. Each
time he took her arm she jerked it free. Miguel finally got her to obey. Her eyes flashed back at
Stephanie before Galleo escorted Paloma out.

Miguel came over to Stephanie. "Feel better?"

*Oh, sure, after watching you dance with Paloma, I feel
just great.*

"She didn't want to leave," she said of the young
woman.

"Paloma?" He looked over his shoulder, as if to
see if she were still there fighting with Galleo. "She
wants to talk to you—she's very interested in the
United States, especially the fashion. I told her you
were too tired. She can visit with you another time."

"Is she your girlfriend?" Stephanie wasn't sure

why she asked the question—it just popped out. Maybe being tired gave her more initiative.

"No. I am her guardian."

That was some kiss for a guardian. "I'd like a bath and bed."

He showed an understanding smile and turned to his sister.

Theresa showed Stephanie her bedroom, but she was too tired to notice the accommodations. She searched her suitcase for a nightgown, then padded to the bathroom. The solid black of the marble and gold were the only colors that registered in her state.

She stripped off her crumpled traveling clothes and stepped into the hot running water.

Miguel hadn't told her anything about his personal life. It was unrealistic of her to think he didn't have women tucked away in Spain—all over the world, for that matter. The thought caused more weariness. Now wasn't the time to analyze her divergent emotions.

After her bath, she slipped into the pink cotton nightgown, closed the shutters against the sun still high in the afternoon sky, adjusted a veil of thin white curtains, and slid between cool crisp sheets. It was only mid-afternoon, but she didn't care. She hoped oblivion would whisk her away for a long, long time.

The door opened.

It hadn't occurred to her that Miguel might barge in whenever the mood struck him.

"Are you awake?" he asked, and seemed to hesitate at the door as if he'd realized too late he was an unwelcome intruder.

"Yes."

"Do you need anything?" The door shut, and he came to stand by the bed.

"No—"

The bed moved under his weight when he sat next to her.

Stephanie tried to yank the sheet up, but it wouldn't budge under his mass. She heard his hard intake of breath when, so close, they almost touched. Her own breath dragged in across her lips, and she could almost taste him on her tongue—a faint mix of *cerveza*, smoke, *tapas*—something else, like bricks dried in the sun.

Here was her golden opportunity to go for it. Walk on the wild side. Do the dirty.

Why not shake off the baggage of a bad marriage which had left her empty, let Miguel make her sexually active again? A *woman* again. The thought drifted in her mind as she lost herself in his beautiful, languid green eyes.

His hand traveled up her bare arm, up her neck, and his long, thin fingers wove through her hair, tangling it in a knot around his knuckles. All of the intensity she felt for him returned, saturating her.

He drew her face closer to his until their breaths mingled, warm and wet. His lips moved over hers, covered them with soft, warm, moist flesh, and then his tongue slipped between her teeth until it met with hers. She slid her fingers into his hair and held him closer, ran her tongue silkily across his front teeth and around and down his lips, and opened her mouth to accept another deep, hungry kiss.

She would totally yield to him, she thought. *I'm his.*

Then something incredible happened.

"Sleep, *querida*," he whispered, and slid off the bed, out of her lunging reach.

It was a long time before she could.

FIVE

As Miguel came down the stairs he took a few deep breaths, trying to quell his tormenting erection. If Domingo weren't waiting for him, he wouldn't be struggling with that, but making love to Stephanie.

He found Domingo waiting in the living room, a big cigar clamped between his lips. He could see his manager was angry—boiling—but Domingo would still be respectful of his famous *matador*. If it were not for Miguel, Domingo would still be selling used televisions in a business that went sour when the people he left in charge ripped him off.

Domingo could not sell televisions, but he could sell a *matador*. He had a way with everyone, a shocking forwardness lacking in all social graces that people liked for some strange reason. Domingo had made lots of friends over the past fifteen years, keeping the bullfight judges and the press happy with cases of expensive wines and Cuban cigars. Most important, he'd smoothed the way after Juan's death, when no one wanted Miguel in their cities, let alone their bullrings. He viewed this booking at *Las Ventas* as his biggest failure to his *matador*. But even Domingo couldn't conquer *El Peligro's* greatest enemy, Pacote Aguilar, Juan's brother and a powerful Spanish newspaper reporter.

"¡*Matador!* Have you lost your mind, bringing a woman back from the United States? A reporter! You're playing with your fate, dancing on traditions! *Dios mio,* you have a death wish!"

"She's beautiful, eh?"

Domingo snorted, and relit his cigar. Great bellows of smoke swirled around him, almost hiding him from Miguel's view. "Your cock is going to get you killed."

"It isn't that way with Stephanie."

"It should be *no* way, *Matador!* All of Spain is watching your every move! Reporters camp out on your doorstep. They saw the woman come in with you, and not come out. There are questions and speculations! They think she is a movie actress. Why did you allow yourself to be photographed with Jenna Starr?"

Miguel lit a cigarette, and tossed the used match into an ashtray, of which Theresa kept plenty. "I did not have my manager there to smash the camera."

"But you had Galleo. No doubt you kept him locked up in a hotel room! He called me every day, frantic to get you home and back on *La Libra!*"

"Tell the press whatever you want about Stephanie." He crushed out his cigarette as a great weariness came over him, and his leg began to hurt again. "Make something up."

"They want to hear you are going to marry Paloma Aguilar. Everyone wants to hear it."

"No." He sat down. "I will not make the announcement."

"You want cheers in two weeks, not jeers! Besides, think of the anguish that you will cause her lover boy. He will not be thinking of the bull's moves, but yours—on his woman!" Domingo laughed.

"Francosis is already running scared. I will not play the hand Pacote awaits me to play. It's very distasteful."

"Bahhh!" Domingo took a long drag of smoke. "You have the kid by the short hairs. So what if Pacote forced him into this challenge because he has something on him? Since when does the great *El Peligro* care about such things?"

Miguel's eyes narrowed, and he felt a little sick thinking of what Juan had on Francosis. "I told Juan on his deathbed that I would take care of Paloma. I have seen to her health, her education, everything in accordance to the death wish. Now you ask me to abuse her happiness to gain popularity? How can I do that and not have the fates frown down on me?"

Domingo's great, fat face grew red. *"Matador,* what do you care about her happiness? She will do as she is told. You are her guardian, and the fates know that!"

"And as her guardian, I say no to this publicity scheme. Nor will I use this kid's heart to gain my own victory."

"This kid might see to your death!"

"No. Something is in the air—a change."

"Shake this up. Change the odds! Besides, you can send Paloma away for a few years, and then break off the engagement as it suits you. Francosis can prove his love—stick around for her—though I say he'd never wait for your rejects."

Miguel jumped up, winced when a sharp pain blasted his hip. "My public demands my blood soaking the sands of *Las Ventas*. Nothing less! I've seen this all in a dream. I've seen myself die. Domingo, I've seen the rosette on the bull—the mark. Making this announcement is not going to change a thing, but that American woman sleeping upstairs will." Miguel paced a few times. His sister walked in, sized up the situation, turned, and left them alone.

"Don't worry, *Matador,* I will personally be at the ring for the *sorteo.* I will make sure we do not draw the bull you've seen in your dream."

Miguel shook his head. "You cannot change fates by a *sorteo!*"

"It's been ten years since a senior *matador* died in the ring in Spain," Domingo said practically.

"It makes no difference if it's been twenty years. My death is imminent unless I follow my heart."

Domingo looked stricken by Miguel's statement. *"¡Matador!* Do not say these things."

"When I was in California I had a vision—from God, I think—that this woman reporter would somehow change my terrible fate, without all this interference you and Pacote cook up."

"Matador, you wound me, referring to me and that dog Pacote in the same breath!"

Miguel sat down and put his head in his hands, rubbed his face hard.

Domingo puffed on his stogie for a few minutes, then took it out of his mouth. He seemed to be reflecting on Miguel's state. *"Matador,* you are in bad shape," he finally said in a worried tone. "Make plans to go *La Libra* in the morning. You can rest out there. Maybe get in some practice. I will go tell the press something, but it is going to cost more than a box of cigars to keep them from reporting what they saw today, Pacote among them."

"Pay them what they want, and that includes Pacote. I am tired. Tomorrow meet me in my Madrid office. There are paychecks to sign."

Miguel left Domingo, took the stairs two at a time, and nearly ran through the hall when he reached it, his leg suddenly better. He passed the room Stephanie slept in, passed his own bedroom, turned down several more corners, and found himself in the most private of places within the villa walls.

Sweet incense permeated the room. He went down on his knees and, there before the statue, lit a candle. Theresa kept the altar for him. Whenever he fought the bulls the candles burned until his safe return.

The statue of the *Patrona of Palma del Río,* his mother's patron saint, stared coldly at him. He found no comfort in her eyes today. He touched the cross around his neck, put his hands together with the gold cross between them, prayed to face death without fear, and prayed for forgiveness. He should not have brought Stephanie to Spain, and he should not want her in such a completely physical way.

Stephanie opened her eyes and focused by degrees on the high-beam white ceiling. She rolled over and snuggled up with the feather pillow, its covering crisp like those her mother used to iron. Gradually the full realization came. *I'm in Spain! This isn't my pillow!* Bolting up, she looked around the room, tried to remember everything that had happened since leaving LAX—a long flight, a mob at the airport, a mob at the villa, a goodnight kiss, and sweet dreams.

Thin, wispy white curtains blew gently in a warm breeze. The shutters had been opened wide and the windows lifted, to let in air and the morning sun. She could see that her clothing had been unpacked, the empty cases neatly stacked in a corner. A crystal water pitcher glistened with condensation on the side-table, and a tray bearing doughnuts and steaming hot coffee sat patiently on a small conversation table.

Doughnuts! No bagels here! She couldn't remember the last time she had sunk her teeth into something so high in calories.

Who had come into her room while she'd slept and done these nice things without disturbing her? She hung her legs over the side of the bed, still disoriented from time changes and travel. A charming anniversary clock read eight o'clock.

She must have slept like the dead in the beautiful four-poster bed, finely crafted from blond wood, with a wrought iron, laced-up top. A matching armoire and side-table graced either side and, in front of the bed was a full-length mirror, intricately detailed in the same kind of wood.

The disheveled woman staring back didn't bear a resemblance to the woman she'd left in California. Here was someone whose eyes were bright, her hair thick against her neck, a rosy hue on her cheeks— someone who looked to be in love!

How can I be in love with someone I just met! Get a grip! How am I going to write this exposé when I'm so emotionally—and physically—stirred up? Don't waste your energy. You, girlfriend, are undeniably going to get your heart fried by more than this Spanish sun!

Somehow she had to pull together a story about a subject that was as foreign to her as global capitalism—prove to her boss and that tightass editor from the *Variedades* that she had the *huevos* to do it!

Finish the story with a bullfight finale, presumably in which the star *matador* will be gored to smithereens by a raging bull. Then be on her merry way, with her heart completely unaffected by use of extra layers of super-duper vital organ emotional sunscreen.

End of story.

Writing is what I do, she thought logically. *This is just an assignment, albeit an unusual one.* She'd written unusual stories before. Of course, the information had been gathered and written in a language she understood. *Don't dwell on your shortcomings, or the inconvenience of being in Spain!*

Exactly two glorious weeks ahead in the middle of the Iberian Peninsula. Art collections to see, the palace of *Escorial,* the *Paseo del prado, Retiro* Park, tons and tons of shopping. *Stop acting as if this is the Spanish Inquisition!*

She made a mental note to call the *Variedades* with a fax number. They'd promised to forward her some additional research materials; not that Ray hadn't done an outstanding job on his own. A phone line would be nice, too. She needed to modem in to get her E-mail. No doubt there were plenty of messages from Adria wanting *details, details, details,* and just as many from her brother wanting *answers, answers, answers.*

Pulling off her nightgown, she watched it flutter to the floor and then shook out her hair. Squaring her shoulders with new determination—vowing to focus on the task at hand and not get wrapped up in a love affair sure to sour, she went to the window.

Her eyes snapped shut against the assaulting Spanish sun. The smell of jasmine drifted up from some unseen garden, and applause rang out from down in the street. She held her hand over her eyes and squinted into the blinding sun trying to determine the excitement.

A group of reporters stood in a knot gaping up at her nakedness. A cheer and a few catcalls floated up to greet her.

Oh, my God! She dropped to the floor, horrified, and crawled out of their view. Her hearted pounded as more jeers drifted up. *Perfect!* she fumed. *Add a little humiliation to your whacked out emotional state!*

She found her robe—thoughtfully hung on a hook in the bathroom—and went back to the window. Stealthy peering down into the street, she was amazed at how many reporters still loitered in front of Miguel's villa. No wonder Miguel hated reporters—and must have really enjoyed the freedom of California! Movie stars made such a big fuss about paparazzi, but being in the newspaper business, she'd never had much empathy for their cause. *That might change,* she mused.

She unpacked her laptop and the materials Ray had supplied, and started to work. Mornings were always productive for her, and many found her still in her pajamas by noon. Of course, she had no idea what time it *really was*, and thought it better not to try to calculate it.

The coffee went down, and so did all three doughnuts. Ideas for the exposé began to come to her, and the diversion was welcome, validating that she would be okay—she could handle this assignment.

The outline began to take shape. She would start with a short but thorough history of bullfighting, then do a transition into Miguel's childhood in Barcelona, his *vision*, as he called it, to become a *matador,* the obstacle to and challenges of rising from poverty to an icon in Spain, and Juan Aguilar's influence. The woman who came between them—

Wait a minute.

Stephanie flipped through the unauthorized biography.

> *Lucia Benitez, the daughter of a Spanish shipping magnate, loved bullfighters—but Miguel Rafael, a green novillero rising in the ranks, didn't know how many until she sealed his fate with her betrayal.*
>
> *Nothing is more dangerous than a Spaniard with an injured ego. When Lucia slept with Juan Aguilar, she publicly humiliated Miguel. He had no choice but to call out his mentor, his boyhood idol—now his tormentor.*
>
> *The sordid details were splashed across newsstands in the Spanish speaking country and were openly discussed on street corners. Everyone knew that when Miguel discovered the lovers secluded in an upstairs bedroom he pulled Lucia off Juan, and in the tussle she clawed him in the face. This led to a scar he still carries.*
>
> *It took two of Miguel's strongest picadors to get him off Juan, who many believe he would have killed.*

Stephanie set the book down. She felt as if she had betrayed Miguel by reading these unauthorized, disparaging accounts of his life.

She and Miguel had one thing in common, she thought, watching the sun change its course across the white wall. Both were betrayed, both humiliated by someone they loved. But to have it be public knowledge—Stephanie couldn't imagine the added pain.

It seemed to her that virtually everyone was at one

time hurt by love, beginning with family relationships. She had an absent father; Miguel had the untimely death of his mother. She had a husband with a motive; Miguel had a woman with a motive.

She closed her eyes for a moment and let a warm breeze play over her arms and ruffle her hair. *Yet we still reach out for love,* she thought, *despite the inevitable hurt.*

Had ambivalence replaced Miguel's desires for love, as it had for her? Since meeting him, she had felt a transformation was taking place, operating somewhere in the back of her mind, arousing her— intensifying her feelings for a new relationship. Was it the same for him, or was she simply today's diversion?

Remember, he'd been seen with Jenna Starr before you.

She took a deep breath of sultry Spanish air, shut down her computer, and took a long shower. Slipping into a pair of jeans and a white, scoop-neck T-shirt, she bounded down the stairs, feeling a lot more grounded. Most of her reluctance to see anyone, especially Miguel, was gone.

No one had come up to bother her, and the villa was very quiet all morning.

She looked around—no Ray, no Miguel, no Miguel's sister, Theresa, or her husband. It was eerie being alone in someone else's home, and she felt every bit the intruder.

A pot of coffee steamed on a white tile counter. Suddenly a Spanish woman appeared almost silently from a side door, startling Stephanie. The woman, obviously a housekeeper, dressed in a white starched dress, eyed her warily. Both were unable to do more than nod in greeting.

While pouring another cup of coffee, Stephanie

saw a note propped up on a floral vase on the table. It was from Ray.

Good morning, Steph. I'm visiting some friends in Madrid. Thought you'd want to sleep late. Here's my pager number—just got it activated this morning. Maybe we can do lunch later. Miguel was gone when I woke up. So was Theresa, and her hubby. Have a good day if we can't meet up later. Ray.

Stephanie frowned. Have a good day with whom?

She tossed the note down, poured more coffee, and eyed a new arrangement of doughnuts with interest. She left them untouched and started her exploration of the villa.

The two-story, white stucco building sat recessed under deep awnings and shuttered windows, to protect the occupants from the heat. The housekeeper now walked around shutting windows, and Stephanie heard an air-conditioner kick on.

There was a loft above the living room area, with its own set of intimate spiral stairs. She took them, her hand slipping across cold wrought iron as she inched her way up, wondering what treasures existed in the unique garret.

A mountain of chambray plaid pillows littered the floor here, more pillows than she'd ever seen in one place, and a low table, but no other furniture. An entertainment center was built into the wall, with a giant-screen television. She sank into thick, velvety white carpet and admired the lofty retreat.

There was a huge poster of Miguel dressed in a suit of lights—*traje de luces*, she corrected herself. It depicted him from the side, his back arched, a whirling cape flowering out and around him, and a huge bull sliding by, its withers pierced with *banderillas*. The poster was old, dated five years ago, but beyond the date and location—*Plaza del Toros Mexico City*—her Spanish was too rough to interpret.

Miguel dressed in the garb of a *matador* was astounding, embodying all of Spanish tradition. The tight pants were molded around his taut butt, and the cape swirled in poetic motion around his lithe body. He was so tall, handsome, and beautiful. She almost staggered. A small picture in a book didn't have the same effect as one of these posters.

She left the loft, her heart pounding and her emotions raw once more.

The villa grounds, though not extensive, were carefully nurtured with overflowing exotic plants and thick trees. Several flowering blue jacarandas soared high above the walls of the villa.

She tried Ray's pager. He returned the call and told her he couldn't meet her until later, said that she might want to take in some shopping if Miguel weren't around.

"I think we can interview this challenger of Miguel's," he said. "My friends here have all kinds of connections with bullfighters."

"Do you think Miguel wants us talking to him?"

"He's the one who called the *Variedades,* not you. How can you do an unbiased story without some background on Francosis Gaona?"

Ray had a good point. "Set it up. In the meantime, I'm going to take your advice and do some shopping."

"Try the *Galería del Prado.* You'll find anything you want there. But watch out when you leave the villa. The place is crawling with reporters. There's an alley in the back that I slipped out of this morning with no problems."

"Thanks." She hung up, ran up to her room, and found a floppy hat, a big bag to carry her treasures, and a map of Madrid.

With the help of an English-Spanish dictionary, she managed to make the cab service understand that they needed to send the driver to the back of the villa. When the taxi arrived, she stepped outside the gates into the alley, and thought for a moment she was home free. Suddenly, reporters swarmed around her.

One came to her rescue.

"Can't you leave the *señorita* alone?" he hollered, taking charge as he opened the cab door and slid in with Stephanie as if they were the oldest of friends. When he saw her surprise he smiled and said, "The name's Pacote. May I ride along?"

"I—I guess." She slid up against the far door, warily eyeing the intruder, who wore far too much cologne.

"You were a pleasant sight for us weary reporters this morning."

She stiffened, momentarily humiliated. "I was blinded by the sun!"

"So you're the *Variedades* reporter from California." He boldly looked her up and down, and she felt color creep into her cheeks. "We had hoped you were really Jenna Starr."

"Sorry to disappoint you!" Stephanie huffed. "How do you know so much about me?"

"I know everything about Miguel," he said, waving a big hand in the air as if dismissing her thoughts. "Where are you going this fine day?"

"Shopping, *Galería del Prado,* but—"

"Good!" He shot off rapid-fire Spanish to the cab-driver.

They soon strolled through the elegant shopping complex, where they browsed in a few of its upscale stores. She hated to admit it, but she rather liked Pacote's company. The handsome man in his forties lavished her with stories about Madrid and advised her about what to see and what to avoid.

He insisted that she let him purchase the dress she found in one of the many trendy shops, a summer number of multicolored cotton. He wouldn't take no for an answer. Then he invited her to lunch, his treat.

They ate at *La Plaza,* a self-service restaurant, and shared a bottle of *Penedès* white wine.

"The *matador* did not say who you were," Pacote offered, then held up his glass to admire the wine.

She lifted the glass to her lips and took a few sips, thinking it tasted wonderful. Then she said, "Then how did you know I work for the *Variedades?*"

Pacote turned down his face into a twisted smile. "Ah. A few phone calls."

"You're the only one who knows?"

"So far."

Stephanie considered his words, wondered where they would lead. What did he want from her? "I'm sure Miguel would like to keep it that way."

"Here is our waitress. Do you have a favorite *tapa?*"

"No. Anything, really." The wine went from her now empty stomach to her brain. She felt light, relaxed, a little too comfortable with this interesting man with the black, bracing eyes.

He openly studied her. "You're beautiful, but different than the others. Maybe you've bewitched *El*

Peligro, eh?" Pacote popped an olive into his mouth. His dark eyes never left Stephanie's face. "Miguel doesn't talk to reporters—he has Domingo for that. Maybe this *corrida* will be even more interesting if Miguel is in love."

"I'm here as a professional," she reminded him, but she could see he wasn't buying it.

"There must be something else between you two. *El Peligro* does not bring women to his villa where his sister lives."

Stephanie couldn't seem to hold his gaze, and she looked out over a passing crowd, many laden with shopping bags. "No, there's nothing else between us."

Pacote poured himself another glass of wine. "Juan Aguilar was Spain's greatest living *matador.* He had just announced his retirement when Miguel called him out. I'm sure you know the rest—why this *corrida* is so significant."

Stephanie wished she'd brought along her small tape recorder. Instead, she fished through her purse for a notepad. "Do you mind if I jot down some notes?"

He shrugged. "No. But this is common knowledge."

"Juan didn't have to take the challenge."

Pacote pushed his lips out, and twisted them. "Of course he had to, *señorita.* "

"You were obviously at this bullfight—" A question popped into her mind. "Were you at Miguel's next *corrida* at *Las Ventas*—where he was seriously gored?"

"Ah. When Miguel walked out onto the sand during the *paseillo,* no one suspected he was drunk, but when he came out with his *capote,* everyone knew.

We all watched in a sick kind of awe. Every cold heart wanted to see him die."

Stephanie shuddered at the cold brutality.

"His goring left the crowd in mourning," Pacote continued, "and the feeling was almost as if the very sport could no longer exist without *El Peligro* to hate. Then something miraculous happened. Miguel recovered, got his reflexes and timing back. The rest is history. When Miguel should have been defeated, he was instead victorious. Some say he signed a pact with the devil to live that day. It's then that he took the name *El Peligro*—what *matador* in his right mind would use such a bad luck name?"

She could clearly see Pacote's resentment. "You were a fan of Juan's?"

His lips thinned, and he took a long drink of wine. "*Señorita,* there are those who will always remain faithful to Juan Aguilar. We will not rest until Miguel takes a horn in the heart."

This guy really didn't like Miguel, she thought. Maybe she shouldn't be sitting here in broad daylight chatting with him.

"Miguel must prove himself in the *Plaza Del Toros,* where Juan's ghost haunts the very hot and unforgiving sand," Pacote said. "Francosis draws enthusiastic ovations from the crowd, and his taunts have found their way into Miguel's pride. No *matador* before Francosis has been able to draw Miguel back to *Las Ventas.*"

"No doubt with a little help from the press?"

He smiled wide. "Sí. You are learning. Miguel is going to try to manipulate them now—try to bring them around with the help of Paloma Aguilar, Juan's poor orphaned daughter."

Paloma looked like anything but a poor orphan.

Stephanie clearly remembered the beautiful young Spanish woman, and the flamenco that she and Miguel had danced like lovers. The memory, buried until now, pierced her heart.

"How will he use her?"

"Bullfighting isn't like a sport where you collect points. The crowd and the judges rate the *matador's* performance. He can be brilliant, but if the crowd turns on him it makes little difference. Miguel doesn't want the crowd remembering Juan's death. At *Las Ventas*, they will not only remember, but relive their horror."

"And you are helping them remember?"

He smiled, showing his very large teeth. "Miguel will have Paloma there in his box, showing her support—and maybe more—to the man who murdered her father." Pacote rubbed his chin again. "Interesting that you don't know, *señorita*, what most of Spain is speculating about these two, yet you share the *matador's* villa?"

Stephanie suddenly didn't like Pacote, wanted to get away from him, didn't want to understand to what he was eluding.

He leaned back in his chair and seemed to be enjoying the intrigue. "All of Spain talks about Juan's daughter, but they do not yet talk about the woman reporter living in *El Peligro's* villa—maybe sharing his bed."

A chill crawled up Stephanie's spine. "That's a libelous statement."

"Do not worry. The other reporters will not break a story before *me*, even though they saw you yesterday. They watch and wait—to see what Pacote does. Ah, enough talk of bullfighters. Tell me about Laguna Beach, California."

Later, in the cab back to the villa, Stephanie wondered long and hard about Pacote's references to Paloma and Miguel, and his innuendoes about breaking a story about her. He was no secret keeper. Someone was going to pay to keep the man quiet, and she knew it would be Miguel.

He wouldn't be happy about her lunch date. She should have kicked Pacote out of the cab.

She fought to shake off pangs of jealousy. Paloma meant more to Miguel than guardianship—but what?

SIX

It was dark before Miguel returned to the villa. He quietly entered and saw one light on, the one in the loft above the living room. Was Stephanie up there? He'd sent Theresa and Jacko to *La Libra*, and planned to join everyone there tomorrow. He wanted to bring Stephanie, but he had a ticket in his pocket to send her home, generously purchased by Domingo.

Everyone who barged into his office today had protested the American woman's presence in his villa. Paloma was the only one who remained silent, sitting in a corner, her eyes downcast.

Miguel knew now he must send Stephanie home before this story broke on its own energy. Domingo could be controlled to a degree, but who knew what Pacote might do now that he'd had access to Stephanie, or any one of those low bastards who dogged his heels for a story?

After *Las Ventas*—after—*Dios Mío*—if I live—I'll go back for Stephanie.

He blew out a long breath, tossed his keys on the side-table, walked over to the wet-bar and poured himself a shot of tequila. It went down easily, and so did the next one. *Stephanie . . . why did I bring you into this madness? Why do I listen to my visions?*

She was the only person in his world who didn't care that he was *El Peligro,* or understand what it meant to be such a great killer of bulls. Would she see the pageantry of the *corrida,* the bravery, or would she only see the cruelty, the blood, and the death?

Dios mío, but his leg hurt again today, and he'd had that nightmare again last night. A very, *very* bad sign. His death seemed certain now. If a bull didn't get him, something would fall out of the sky and crush him and put an end to his miserable life.

Since returning to Spain he had felt himself dangerously seesawing between tradition and breaking away—to be his own man—with Stephanie. She was toppling his equilibrium, and he was very superstitious about this, and about the vision he'd had in California, unable to understand its meaning when he continued to have the nightmare.

He stood at the bottom of the stairs, looked up. Could she give his life meaning beyond the bullring, perhaps meaning beyond this fight? Could he retire and enjoy his millions, perhaps live in Newport Beach, California, or on that canyon in Laguna? *Dios mío,* how could he live in California? Spain was his home, his everything.

He found Stephanie nestled in the middle of the pillows reading that damn unauthorized biography someone had given her—putting him in a bad moral light. She listened to Spanish music, a rich flamenco guitar with contemporary rhythms.

She didn't hear him come up the stairs so he observed her for a moment, felt love warming his heart and desire filling his groin. *I am in love with this stranger. How has this happened? She sits under my image, in these dim lights, with the music . . . Santo Dios, help me.*

He remembered how long he'd struggled to get to the top in bullfighting and stay there. The thousand passing towns and million passing faces, every day the smell of bull's blood, sometimes so strong a hot shower for hours couldn't rid him of the smell of death.

Jesús, Jesús, he thought. *I'll never enjoy my millions. Juan and I have twin fates.* A blaze of fear ignited in him. The terror rose so fast and so suddenly that he felt his balance sway. *I'm going to die. I know that bull is sharpening his horns right now, and Juan's ghost is supplying the file.*

Stephanie glanced up and was startled to see Miguel standing in the shadows at the top of the spiral stairs. *It's about time he got home,* she thought, annoyed she'd spent her first night in Madrid alone. Even Ray had never come back.

Miguel wore a red cotton shirt and faded blue jeans. One finger was caught in a belt loop, the other hand fidgeted at his side, and his expression was dark, furrowed, and different than any she remembered. He crossed the small space and stood before her. He trembled, and his dark green eyes seemed glazed over, filled with some private pain.

"Miguel, what's the matter? What—"

He dropped to his knees, moved over her, and silenced her questions with his mouth. The kiss wasn't familiar to her. It wasn't gentle, but demanding, almost suffocating. She twisted out of his grasp, confused, but he was quicker, stronger, and caught her up in his arms, pressed his mouth to hers, and pinned her down under his weight.

Suddenly, Miguel rolled off and sat next to her, visibly shaken. Both struggled to catch their breath. He ran one shaky hand through his hair and leaned against the pillows, then pulled something out of his pocket and tossed it to her. It landed on her foot.

"Your ticket home," he said thickly. "I'm breaking my contract with the *Variedades*. Go home before it is too late."

"What?" she cried, immediately stricken. She picked up the ticket and stared at the departure time through tears. *Oh, my God, tomorrow.*

He ran his hand through his hair again. "I am sorry."

She struggled to make some sense of this. "Is it Pacote? He pushed himself on me! He forced his way into my cab!"

"Pacote?" He raised an eyebrow. "Go home, *señorita*, before you come to hate me—I will come for you when this is over, if you will still have me."

The jasmine came thickly through the open loft window. She struggled to breathe, to understand what he was saying.

"Why do you want me to go? What happened today, if it isn't Pacote?"

He looked at the floor, and she thought he looked old and tired. "I am a selfish bastard. Ask anyone." He chuckled, but there was no mirth in it. "The ways of the *corrida* are not for the faint of heart." He stood up and walked to the stairs, and she saw that he limped.

Miguel stopped on the second step and turned toward her. "Spain wants me to marry Paloma Aguilar," he said thickly. "But my great country does not realize, nor will she understand, that I am in love with another woman."

He disappeared down the stairs.

Stephanie sat on her bed, thinking about what had just happened. She'd almost cried—almost. Her second urge was, *fine. F.U. I'm out of here. You're all bonkers anyway.* Then dignity began to sink in, first on a personal level. Yes, he was a *hunka, hunka* gorgeous Spanish icon with whom she wanted to fulfill her every sexual fantasy. But Miguel was no simple man to just fill a need, no low-maintenance type who would be happy with a sixer and a remote.

Besides being a male Spaniard with a strong sense of masculine pride, Miguel surrounded himself with people who made his decisions for him, both in the ring and out. Domingo must be behind the airline ticket. She knew Miguel hadn't bought it. Everyone wanted her out of his life—out of Spain, fast.

He might be genuinely in love with her—*in love with me*—his words still rang in her ears—but duty would come first, last, and always, over an unsanctioned relationship. If his fans wanted him to marry Paloma, he'd marry Paloma.

The deal was closed, done.

Personal feelings aside, Stephanie thought of her professional life. She could just see the smirk on Bob's face when she showed up for work in a few days. Not to mention the *Variedades* editor, Marc Garcia, who'd pretty much spread it around the Hispanic staff that she'd fallen flat on her face in a Spanish-speaking country trying to write about a subject too vast to learn in a crunch.

And she had a family to consider in all this. How

would she explain to her brother that his star client *"kinda"* kicked her out of his villa?

What should she do? she wondered. Run home and never know what might have been, or take a stand and risk a wounded heart? She could stay in Madrid, get a hotel room (after all, she still had tickets for the bullfight) and write an unauthorized story.

Or, she could confront Miguel tonight and tell him she wasn't going anywhere, that he'd have to throw her out of the villa—which he might very well do, or enlist one of those massive *picadors* lurking around to do the dirty job for him.

Who would believe this mess she now found herself in? Going back home, burying her feelings, wouldn't make them go away. She knew the most painful relationships to give up were the ones that were never fully realized. Since meeting him she'd felt hypnotized, intoxicated, on the edge of discovering ecstasies she'd only heard about.

I love him. Wow! I don't know why, or how I know that already. Don't care, just do—he can't make me leave. I won't go. I'll become a stalker. Spain—that's a whole country, babe—wants Miguel to marry Paloma. Well, too damn bad. He's mine.

She left her bedroom, ready to draw the line in the sand. Theresa had never showed up, and Stephanie wondered if Miguel had sent her and her husband packing. That would mean they were alone. Ray obviously flourished in the Madrid nightlife, and wouldn't make it back before dawn.

"Miguel?" she called, but nothing. Silence. *"H-h-hellooo?"*

He hadn't even bothered to find out if she'd eaten, which she hadn't. The pangs now made themselves known. *Some hospitality,* she thought. The kitchen was empty, so she made herself comfortable and found some leftover *tapas* from the other night. A bottle of white wine helped adjust her attitude.

The ticket home was still in her pants pocket, folded in half, bulging like a man's wallet. Did Ray have one? She pulled it out and laid it on the table.

I'm not going home, she thought. There was nothing, and no one, waiting for her, just two cats.

After eating and finishing two glasses of wine, she was ready to cross swords with Miguel—provided she could find him. She hadn't heard him leave, but that didn't mean anything. He moved around like a Stealth Bomber.

She ran up the stairs. No one behind Door Number One, or Door Number Two.

"Hello?" Her voice echoed. "Miguel? Anyone?"

She opened another door. Incense touched her nose. The room looked like a shrine. A low-lying bench sat before an elaborately carved oak table on which here sat a large wooden crucifix and a statue of a beautiful woman, her angelic face illuminated by a votive candle. *Mother Mary?* She wondered. A pair of rosary beads was draped over a picture of Christ, which hung on the wall behind the woman.

The prayer book! At first Stephanie thought this room must be Theresa's, but there was Miguel's little prayer book next to the statue. She felt intrusive, and a little confused at discovering another layer of Miguel.

What was that noise? She cocked her head to one side. Running water? Backing away from the altar, as if to turn her back would be disrespectful, she followed the sound.

Another door opened, and she carefully peered

into the *matador's* bedroom. Closet doors were pushed back, and a rack of men's clothing hung there. A dark blue brocade spread covered the bed and contrasted vividly with more white walls. The bathroom door was shut. From there she heard rushing water.

As she opened the next door a faint smell of eucalyptus hung on the heavy mist, and as it cleared some she saw Miguel up to his chin in frothing, whirling, hot water. His eyes were closed, and the sounds of the spa masked her intrusion.

Cobalt-blue glass tile with green grout lent tranquillity to the room, an almost mystical place. The massive white tub was nestled in the middle of a three foot counter of the same tile, and it wrapped around the entire unit. Neatly stacked blue and white towels and other bath items took up part of the space.

This room was designed for a man who needed to soak his tired, perhaps wounded, muscles—a place to rest, reflect, to be alone. Hot steam rose and swirled and clung to everything and now to her, as her fine blond tendrils danced into new curls. Her clothing began to stick to her back.

He lifted his arms out of the water and rested them on the sides, exposing his well-maintained biceps and triceps. Steam lifted off his skin. A leg came out and relaxed on a step, revealing a deep, abrasive scar. It twisted like a coiled snake, starting from his knee, slicing up his thigh, and disappearing into the water's foam.

Las Ventas. Oh, my God. How had he survived that?

All else was perfection. The golden cross glistened wet in a few dark, matted chest hairs. Beads of sweat gathered on his cheeks and nose. At that moment she wanted to rip off her clothes and do a swan dive into the swirling, frothing tub, run her hands over those scars, and follow that up with her tongue, put an end to this torturous sexual tension that existed between them.

Dignity reared its head again, warning her that a lap in that water with him tonight would mean dry dock in the morning.

Save it, girl. Make him wait.

She walked up the three steps and stood looking down on him.

Ladies and Gentlemen, this is your pilot speaking. I'd like to welcome you aboard the biggest mistake of your life.

He opened his eyes, and the green orbs focused on her, didn't blink, and didn't seem surprised, just drank her in, weakening her earlier resolve not to join him.

"I'm not leaving," she said, trying to stand with poise and dignity on the ledge of the slippery spa countertop. She fished the mangled ticket from her pocket and tossed it into the foaming water.

He blinked then. Dark lashes fanned down to his wet cheeks and flashed back up to study her. A slight smile came over his full, soft lips. "Tomorrow we leave for *La Libra.*"

"Fine, *Matador.* I've always wanted to see a bull farm." Carefully, she went down the steps, stopped, turned, "Tell Domingo he's wasting his time."

His hands grasped the sides of the tub, and he hoisted himself up. Volumes of water and steam rolled off him. Her gaze moved down over his flat belly, to the dark hair that started just below his navel and blossomed out and around his full erection. She looked back into his eyes, smiled, and closed the door.

* * *

The next morning Stephanie sat at the conversation table in her bedroom before a steaming cup of coffee and a half-eaten doughnut. One leg was propped up on the other chair, and the phone was plastered to her ear. The windows were open, and sun patterns filtered through the lace curtains and played on her legs. Her computer was on. She'd been working on the story since dawn.

Ray had been up several times trying to help her get an Internet connection, but something wasn't working. She needed to talk to the editor at *Variedades,* but the time difference made standard communications difficult. They were nine hours ahead of California. She hadn't been paying close attention to the clock this morning, and time got away from her.

After the scene in Miguel's bathroom, sleep had seemed impossible. She couldn't get the image of his beautiful, naked body out of her mind. It took extreme willpower not to seek him out in the night, and secretly she hoped he'd seek her out. But he hadn't, even though she'd left her door ajar.

"Stop worrying, Richard." Her brother had been giving her a verbal, seemingly non-stop warning about her involvement with Miguel, or what he could deduce about it.

"I'm not going to remind you how important my business relationship is with Miguel."

She scratched her head. "And I'm not going to remind you that you keep saying that, over and over again."

"Miguel is worth millions. If I keep him happy, our relationship can be very fruitful for both of us.

If you and he have some kind of *misunderstanding,* I don't want him thinking of you when he's trying to do business with me."

"Ouch." *Change the subject,* she thought. "How's Adria feeling?"

She heard her brother take a deep breath. "Fine. Well, not really. The doctor thinks the baby is coming earlier."

Stephanie lowered her foot to the floor and sat up. "Why? Is everything all right?"

"As far as we know. She just had her first sonogram and found out the fetal dating was wrong in the beginning."

Stephanie desperately wanted to talk to Adria, who'd run an errand just before her husband called. Stephanie suspected Richard wanted to talk alone. Adria, no doubt, wanted to encourage Stephanie to have a fling.

"I'm supposed to be in the delivery room," she said.

"You *should* be *home* in time. Two weeks, *right?*"

"About ten days." *Ten days, and back to my cats.*

"Stephanie, one last warning. I hope you're not more involved with Miguel than you're saying. He lives in a different world than us. He's not right for you."

Nobody's right for me, bro. "Don't worry."

Someone knocked at her door. She was expecting Ray. He seemed to think he could get the right kind of cables for her computer, and had gone out looking.

"I have to run. Tell Adria I'll E-mail her once I get my computer working. The setup is different here, or something technical that I don't understand. Love you!"

After she hung up she did a quick check in the mirror. Jeans again today, her signature, and a blue plaid western shirt. Going to a bull farm, she might as well look like a cowboy. She'd pulled her hair up into a small knot and skipped makeup, other than lipstick. Ray said the ride to *La Libra* was several hours and to dress comfortably.

Señor *Matador* had not made an appearance yet. That changed when she opened the door.

Miguel was wearing a white cotton bathrobe, his hair wet and slicked back. The scent of soap followed him into the room. Her heart squeezed in her chest. How could a man claim such good looks, such perfection, even in a robe?

His gaze skittered across the room and stopped on the chair, on the shopping bag that contained her new dress, purchased yesterday by Pacote. Miguel went over to the bag as if he'd come into the room looking for it, reached in, pulled out the garment, and examined it.

"I did some shopping yesterday," she said, trying to read his expression. His eyebrows were drawn together, as if he disapproved of her choice.

"So I heard," he answered. He folded the dress up and slipped it back into the bag. "Take it back."

"Why?"

"I forbid you to *ever* talk to Pacote again," he said harshly, new anger evident in his eyes. Another layer had just revealed itself—hot temper.

"You must ask permission to talk to anyone outside my family and *cuadrilla.*"

"I thought I came here to do a story," she said, holding back an injured look even though his words stung. "I can't get it cloistered in a villa while you traverse around God-knows-where, leaving me alone!

I told you last night that Pacote pushed himself into my cab. You should have told me who to stay away from on that long flight over."

Miguel's nostril's flared as he took a deep breath. He raked a hand through his wet hair before his eyes came back up to hers. "Maybe you didn't realize *yesterday* that I have responsibilities here. Over three hundred people work for me. I had business in my Madrid office."

"I don't know anything about you, Miguel, except what I've read in unauthorized biographies, and what I discover by accident!"

"I *donn* want to fight with you—"

"Then stop telling me what to do!"

"The terms of your stay are different. No story."

"I won't accept those terms." She crossed her arms in front of herself.

The stalemate hung in the air between them.

He watched her with steady scrutinizing eyes, the muscle in his jaw twitched and the scar on his cheek looked whiter.

"I don't want you to leave," he said finally. "But you must try to understand my life here, and respect it."

She felt blood rush up to her cheeks. "I've understood nothing since I met you!"

"And you may never understand this life of mine."

"Let me write the exposé, Miguel. Don't forget I have something to prove, not only to myself but to that editor of the *Variedades*. *¿Por favor?*"

"*Sí.* You can have your way. But stay away from Pacote, and talk only to those I approve. If you want dresses, I will buy them. I will buy the whole department store."

He came over and wrapped his arms around her and she let him, despite the fact that she wanted to find a quiet corner and lick her wounds. She felt amazed and bewildered that he could comfort her when he was the cause of her discomfort.

She rested her head on his shoulder, relaxed in his embrace. For a long time he held her there, with the morning sunlight flickering off their bare feet and the scent of jasmine drifting on the breeze.

He kissed her forehead and broke the spell. "Hurry and pack. We leave soon."

Stephanie came down the stairs before Miguel, carting a small suitcase. Domingo waited at the bottom. She remembered his unflinching, rock-hard eyes, and his gaze now traveled up and down her body with a hostile expression.

"You must leave today," he said in clear, concise English, pointing a finger at her. "Where is your ticket? I have a car waiting now."

"I'm not leaving. Now if you'll excuse me, I think I smell coffee."

"You're leaving if I have to take you to the airport myself!"

"That—would be kidnapping." She came to a jarring stop when he blocked her passage.

"You could have done the *matador* great harm by associating with Pacote. You don't belong—"

"*Domingo!*" Miguel's voice broke through the air. He took the stairs down two steps at a time. "I told you I'd meet you at *La Libra.*"

He came to stand between Domingo and Stephanie, dressed now in white jeans and a green cotton T-shirt. The rest of their nose-to-nose, heated conversation was in Spanish. Domingo slammed the door when he left.

Ray emerged from the kitchen with the wide-eyed housekeeper peering around his body, both curious about the entire ruckus. Miguel was visibly shaken, and barked out something to the woman in Spanish before finding the stairs and disappearing.

Ladies and Gentlemen, this is your pilot again. We'll be cruising at about ninety-million miles per hour, so expect a hell of a lot of turbulence.

They raced along in a Jeep sport utility vehicle, passing foothills, pretty villages, orange groves, olive trees, and grapes darkening in the glorious shining sun. The drive toward Southern Spain was breathtaking—peerless beauty, with sharp contrasts forming hills and peaks.

Miguel drove, while Stephanie sat in the front with him. Ray and Galleo sat in the back. Spanish music filled the car, chosen earlier from a selection of CDs. The windows were down, the wind warm, and Stephanie could smell orange blossoms in the air. A laptop and disposable camera rested in her lap.

Earlier, she'd written some questions for Miguel, and she planned to ask them on the way to the farm.

They hadn't spoken privately since Domingo had charged out the villa door. For now she had to be content to steal glances at Miguel once in a while, and know that he once in a while stole them back. She read nothing in his expression as to what he might be feeling about her coming along, or Domingo's sudden appearance at the villa causing trouble. She dreaded the thought of seeing Domingo again, and she was certain he'd be at *La Libra*.

Stephanie looked down at her laptop and read her first question. "What do you think of Francosis Gaona as a *matador?*" She saw Miguel's fingers tighten on the steering wheel, the knuckles go white.

He glanced in the rearview mirror, then at her.

"He has no form, no style, and uses circus tricks to incite the crowds. He'll likely get himself killed before he makes a real name for himself in bull-fighting." Miguel chuckled. "Unless, of course, his name is associated with my death. Then he would be guaranteed a place in bullfighting history!"

She read her next question, then asked it: "Would you compare yourself with any other *matadors?*"

"Do you want to know who I'm like in the bull-ring? Me. I am *El Peligro.* Listen, no two *matadors* are the same, except that we are all a little crazy."

She chuckled this time. "You must be crazy, to stand before an animal bred for centuries to kill man."

"The bulls don't bother me. I'm talking about be-ing crazy enough to stand before a crowd of thou-sands screaming at you to give them more, and when you've given all but your life they complain about your performance!"

Stephanie reached for her purse on the floor of the Jeep, and searched the contents for her lipstick. Her arm accidentally brushed against Miguel's. In-evitably their eyes met.

His quick, warm smile warmed her. She returned it and applied lip gloss, her heart tripping with ex-citement.

She kept remembering his naked body, and the magnitude of his erection.

"There's a lot to learn about bullfighting," Stephanie said with genuine interest.

"Yes, *señorita,*" Miguel agreed. "A lifetime to learn it all—and still there isn't enough time."

They drove in silence for a while, with just the sounds of the Spanish guitar floating on the warm breeze.

"Look," Miguel said, pointing out the window. "My pastureland. Do you see the bulls?"

The animals dotted the brown hillside like black mushrooms. They munched grass, oblivious to everything but their food and the sun baking their backs.

"The fighting bulls are a special breed," he explained. "They live like kings for four years."

"And then—" Stephanie sliced her hand across her throat.

He took his eyes off the road for a second and shook his head with a smile. "I kill the bulls very fast. They do not suffer."

"*Hummm.* Okay." Stephanie took a deep breath of the pastureland scent.

Miguel kept glancing over at her, smiling, as if he knew some secret to a quick death. "If you can forget about the animal, and view the *corrida* with the splendor and beauty it provides, you might find yourself an *aficionado* soon."

He continued to smile over at her.

"Would you pay attention to the road!" she cried when he swerved the car.

He shrugged, slapped his hands in the ten and two position. "The bulls you see here are from the *Vistahermosa* caste." Miguel reached down for his car phone and punched some numbers. He spoke in Spanish, and hung up. "I let them know we are very close," he said to no one in particular.

Within the next hour they stopped at a fenced

gate which Miguel opened with a plastic card he slipped into a mechanical device. Before they drove through, several young boys scurried to the Jeep, crying, *"Matador! Matador!"*

Miguel rolled down the window, said something in Spanish, and left them in a cloud of airborne dirt and gravel as the Jeep slid down a long drive.

"Fans?" Stephanie asked, craning her neck to see them disappear with the last curve.

Miguel sighed. "No. Poor boys who want to be *matadors*. The best I can do for them is send out food and drink and a little coin. Maybe bring one in to help me today."

When Stephanie turned back around she saw the adobe ranch house, surrounded by well-kept gardens, tall century-old oak trees, and rose beds that lined the drive. There was a quaint windmill off in the distance. A group of men stood on the drive.

Miguel pulled on the emergency brake and the Jeep door was suddenly jerked open. He was pulled into a ring of men, who all talked at once.

SEVEN

Stephanie took a long drink of cold ice tea, then looked around as another layer of Miguel peeled away. The ranch house embodied his career, and was the complete opposite of the villa in style and decor, starting with walls painted in dark, muted tones. Every available space displayed electrifying pictures of *El Peligro*.

"So Miguel goes to Mexico?" she asked Ray, who reloaded his camera while sitting on a brown leather sofa. "This poster says *Plaza Monumental de Tijuana*, and I saw one at the villa that said Mexico City."

"I told you at the airport I saw Miguel in Mexico. It was for some charity event. The proceeds went to the *matadors'* hospital fund."

Stephanie scanned the posters and photos as she moved down the wall. Miguel swirled capes, held swords ready before swaggering animals, executed graceful passes, and stood in flowers blanketing the ground after a kill. In one pose he stood holding a *muleta* in one hand and a sword in the other. Much younger, his hair longer, he looked off into the crowd. Yet another photograph showed Miguel splayed out in the dust, his face twisted in agony, a massive bull pouncing on top of him.

This picture held her attention the longest. This is what kept the crowds coming back, just like at car races. The spectators denied wanting to witness a crash, but secretly the *aficionados* wanted to see a *matador* gored.

She moved to another picture, a framed cover from a Spanish magazine—*6 Toros 6*. Miguel was turned away from the camera, and a bull, its horns just inches from his body, stood defeated, its massive black head bowed. Miguel's skintight, red silk *talequilla*, with blinding gold flashing down his legs, framed his sexy butt. He obviously wore nothing underneath his bullfighter pants.

This picture was both sensual and disturbing to Stephanie—the beautiful man, the wounded animal.

Trophy cases brimmed with odd things like human hair pigtails—the badges of the *matadors'* profession, called *coletas,* and worn during the bullfight. Earlier pictures of Miguel showed that his ponytail was his own hair. Several pair of bullfighter shoes, heelless slippers called *zapatillas,* and odd, wide-brimmed beaver hats were on one shelf.

Another supported a built-in glass case displaying beautiful bullfighter swords. Each was of the same length, over thirty inches long, with a slightly downward curve at the razor-sharp end. Each rapier had a different handle. Some were encrusted with precious gems, others with engravings. Wooden swords hung there, too, used instead of steel to save the matador's wrist until the end of his *faena.*

Less ominous were the magenta capes, blue or yellow on the inside, carefully folded in a glass case, along with glittering, colorful *traje de luces* heavily encrusted with embroidery. There was a temperature gauge on the case to control humidity.

"These are priceless," Ray said, taking a few pictures. "These once belonged to some of Spain's greatest *matadors.*"

Past the glitter and the sparkle of the costumes, death was evident everywhere. A pair of sharp *banderillas*—the barbed sticks wrapped in colored paper used to place in the bull's withers—hung between two very old posters, one announcing Manolete and the other Belmonte.

Stephanie looked away from the fighting images and around the ranch house. Highly polished wood floors, brown leather furniture, oak tables and chairs, and the smell of leather, smoke, and masculine items. Windows offered sweeping views of red brick walkways leading this way and that; fences were covered with bougainvillea, hibiscus, and wild jasmine. In the distance, green hills, pastures, and olive groves undulated over the graceful hills.

Miguel could be heard through the open window talking and laughing in the drive. His Spanish cadence pleased Stephanie's ears. Everything about him pleased her but his occupation.

She knew better than to float around on happy helium out here on the Ponderosa, thinking none of *this* mattered, when she couldn't even seem to deal with men who had *normal* jobs.

Her string of bad relationships before and after Steven now competed in her mind's eye for attention and reminders. Still, Miguel had a way of making her feel like the most desirable, most exciting woman in the world. It was just going to cost her a lot to enjoy the feeling. She'd come up with the funds, she thought. She felt herself smile, remembering Miguel saying something similar on her brother's balcony.

Was this really love? She almost scoffed out loud. Steven was the man she'd come closest to solidifying that emotion with. If these feelings for Miguel were indeed love, and not some vain hope of her love-starved ego, and the two of them *couldn't* work out traditions, chauvinism, logistics, and Paloma, then this Spanish fantasy was going to bankrupt her emotionally.

A large bay window faced beautiful Moorish gardens, and in the not to far distance there were stables, corrals, and barns. There were people milling around, and women setting up picnic tables.

Miguel was animated about something.

Any woman who dares to love this man must not only accept this way of life—but live it, Stephanie thought. She'd made up her mind last night that Paloma couldn't have him, yet how could *she* have a man who was prisoner of his own fame?

Ray took pictures of a bull's head above a fireplace. He poked its nose. "Can you imagine staring this thing down with a little cloth and a sword? It gives me the *willies.*"

"Your own shadow gives you the willies."

He turned the lens on her and focused. *Click. Whirl. Click. Whirl.*

She blinked each time a flash hit her eyes. "Put that camera away!"

Ray obliged her. "You doing him yet?"

"You're lucky I'm not holding one of those swords right now. *Nada.* We are not having sex."

"Define sex."

"Mr. Special Prosecutor, we are not touching genitals."

He chuckled. "Lips?"

"I appreciate your concern, but so far, Miguel's taken. You know about Paloma Aguilar?"

"I wondered if you did. I heard about it yesterday."

"He claims he's not going to marry her."

"Maybe he won't, but he'll still announce the engagement, string her along for a few years, and after the public forgets, or he retires, he'll break it off."

"Sounds incredibly cold and heartless, doesn't it?"

"It is incredibly cold and heartless."

She sat down and opened her briefcase, which someone had set down with her overnight case. She pulled out her laptop computer. "I really need a modem hookup. Did you ever get what we needed?"

"No, but Miguel said there's a computer here at the ranch with Internet capabilities."

"The editor of *Variedades* wants to see where I'm going with this story. I'd rather not hassle with overnight delivery services."

"You don't seem very upset that your work is being questioned. Is this a growth moment?"

"Funny. No, it's 'here's your *f'ing* story thus far, leave me the *f* alone'. Besides, Miguel's going to have final say over everything that's written. I wish I were working with Bob on this, and not Marc Garcia."

"Marc has wagers going that you're going to screw this up."

"Which way'd you bet?"

"I'm with you, cuz you're with me, and we've always made a great team."

Galleo came in and broke up their love huddle. Miguel wanted them at the corral.

They had a hard time keeping up with Galleo. Stephanie suspected he wanted to ditch them, not lead them to his *matador* brother. He took them across a good acre of manicured lawn, through symmetrically clipped hedges, a formal garden with a bubbling fountain. Flowering plants grew up one side of the whitewashed stable in a melody of color, and potted plants lined the walkway from the gravel drive to the barn. Roses and dahlias surrounded a small patio to the left of the building. They found Miguel there.

Family members, and some of Miguel's team, leaned against the corral fence, including Domingo. They smoked, and drank from cold bottles of beer.

"Do you want to learn how to do some cape work?" Miguel asked when she came up to him.

"Sure," she said, thinking he meant to demonstrate for her.

Ray readied his camera.

Miguel pointed to a calf munching its lunch. "See that little cow?"

Stephanie glanced over at the beast. "That would be a calf," she corrected him.

"She's yours today."

"Mine?" She looked at him incredulously, allowing herself the freedom to laugh, even though she felt Domingo's disturbing glare focused on her. "Why?"

"Come, I'll show you."

Miguel called a young boy named Renaldo into service. The child looked scruffy, his clothing tattered, his face and hair dirty, but his appearance didn't seem to phase him. He was obviously a happy child, and beamed every time Miguel asked him to do something.

Ray leaned over and whispered to Stephanie, "That's one of the kids that ran up to our Jeep earlier." His camera began to whirl, focus on the boy, and stop as he leaned close again. "Miguel's very generous with everyone, in case you haven't noticed that already."

"I noticed," she whispered back and slipped on her sunglasses. "But a day spent on the farm with Miguel, even a little food and a few pesos to take home, won't change that child's situation."

"That's what you think. Renaldo is going to be telling this story for the rest of his life. His family, friends, and probably the constable of this fine province will be having him over to hear all about how he spent his day helping the great *El Peligro*. His lot in life was just elevated considerably."

Stephanie made a mental note to do a little research on these boys who lived out of bundles to get near the *matadors*, and why it was equivalent to a benediction when they did.

"Is this where Miguel practices before his fights?"

"No. This is just a corral. There's a practice ring on the ranch, but according to Galleo it's about a mile from here, tucked in the middle of an olive grove. I understand we're going to get a private *corrida* tomorrow."

Stephanie wasn't sure she wanted to see Miguel actually kill an animal.

Miguel gave orders to Renaldo in Spanish. The boy enthusiastically scurried off and returned shortly with a cape. Miguel took it and walked to the center of the corral, then called to Renaldo to open the gate where the calf waited.

Stephanie left Ray's side and climbed up on the corral fence to get a better view. The sun was high in the sky, and the heat shimmered around Miguel, who was still dressed in his white jeans. The scent

of flowers and manure mixed in the breeze, and a
curious bee flitted around Stephanie's hair.

The little heifer charged forward and skidded to
a stop, creating a good deal of dust from her entrance. She looked around as if to acquaint herself
with her new surroundings, then gazed at Miguel.

A bigger crowd gathered around the fence.

"What now?" Stephanie asked Miguel from her
safe position.

Ray's camera hummed next to her ear.

"Remember, we must provoke her to charge,"
Miguel explained patiently. "This is not a fierce
fighting bull, but a bashful little calf who would
rather eat than play this game with us." Miguel
moved closer to the animal and waved the cape before the calf's nose. The animal didn't budge, and
continued to watch Miguel with indifference.

Suddenly the calf charged, and Miguel slid
through a dozen beautiful passes. Stephanie and Ray
joined the others in crying *ole!* each time the animal
catapulted by him.

Miguel moved with the grace of a ballet dancer,
fluid and ethereal at each turn, each pass, a flash
of magenta and yellow satin. He swiftly shifted his
stance and, snapping his cape with his wrists, called
to the calf again.

Stephanie was mesmerized, a real excitement
building within her as she watched the cape unfold
and swirl around Miguel's body, connected to him
and suspended on the breeze.

Miguel folded his cape over his arm, his little calf
now dazed, and went down on his knees, defenseless
before the creature in either a show of bravery or
stupidity. Stephanie felt sorry for the little animal

now that it was the butt of a joke, but everyone else seemed to love this part, and cheered.

The calf was corralled. Miguel waved Stephanie down off the fence. "Your turn," he said, brushing off his knees.

"Me? I—" Her gaze jumped over to Domingo and the crowd now watching. Several men had smirks on their faces.

Miguel saw where her gaze rested. "Don't mind them. They are still from the old country, where women cook and clean and leave the bulls to the men."

"I wouldn't exactly call you Mr. Modern," she said teasingly.

He chuckled. "Now pay attention."

She listened to Miguel's instructions, half in anticipation, half in dread.

Miguel anchored himself behind her and slipped his arms around her waist for a more precise demonstration. He exuded reckless passion, she thought, even now with everyone watching them.

Renaldo returned with a *muleta*, a stick and red cloth. Miguel placed it in Stephanie's hands, and his fingers curled possessively around hers and the stick.

"First," he began, "you must learn to hold the *muleta* in order to perform your *faena*."

"Why not a cape?" she asked, wondering what it would feel like to twirl it around her body.

"Too big and heavy for you to manage. The *faena* is the work done by the *matador* during the last part of the bullfight. Here is where you show your mastery to dominate the bull."

He released her hands and promptly took her hips and drew her closer, then repositioned her hands on the *muleta*. He showed her how to sweep it back and forth.

"Ah, a natural!" he whispered in her ear. "But you are too tense. The animal will know this."

She gave him a side-glance that collided with his sultry, green eyes. For a few seconds their gazes locked, and a tremendous joy cascaded over her. *I can do this*, she thought. *I can do anything with his arms around me.*

"You're not paying attention," he said gingerly, showing a skewed smile.

She dropped the *muleta* to her side, and turned full circle to face him. "How can I concentrate with you leaning against me?"

Renaldo came rushing into the corral carrying a board with bullhorns tacked to it.

"Now what are we doing?"

"He's going to be the bull."

She watched Miguel patiently explain to the child how to use the horns, pretend to be a fierce fighting bull. Renaldo laughed at something Miguel whispered to him, and began chasing Miguel around the corral with the horn-board, much to everyone's delight.

Miguel, a little breathless, ran up to Stephanie. "Never let the *muleta* drop in front of your body like that, or the animal will see you."

"What about my calf?"

"Later," he answered. "First the boy."

Stephanie eyed the child resentfully and waved the *muleta* at arm's length, a little less sure that she wanted to participate in the lesson now, feeling somehow demoted.

"Call to the boy," Miguel instructed patiently.

"But remember he's supposed to be a mean and angry bull."

She let the *muleta* drop to her side again and said in a mocking tone, "What do I say?"

"Get that cloth up! And say something like, *La toro, ah, hah!*"

Stephanie skewered her mouth into a frown and jerked the cloth back up. *"La toro—"* She looked at Ray, who had a stupid grin on his lips and his camera ready. *"La toro, ah, hah!"* She shook the *muleta* with not much conviction.

Domingo snorted, and until that moment Stephanie had temporarily forgotten about him.

"You couldn't get a raging bull to charge with those limp wrists," he hollered, kicking some dirt with his boot. The men around him joined in raucous laughter.

Stephanie pressed her lips together and shook the cloth with more determination. *"Hey, bull!"* she cried.

The boy pawed the sand with his crusty bare feet and started to rush past her, but instead of planting herself as instructed, she backed up and smacked into Miguel, squashing his toes.

"Watch it!" Miguel cried, and hobbled back a few steps.

More scattered laughs.

"No!" Miguel, said, less patiently. "Look, the bulk of the bull will hurtle under the cloth." He took the *muleta* from her and demonstrated the beginning of a *faena* with the human-bull. "He may even skim your legs," he said as the boy flew by, "but the animal's momentum will take him several feet beyond you before he realizes he's been duped and skids to a stop." Renaldo stopped and spun around. "You can't move suddenly like that or the bull will see your body movement. You want him to see only the cloth."

"It's this stupid *muleta!*" Stephanie protested like a disappointed child. "I want to try the cape! If I have to wave something in front of that animal— child—at least let me decide what I'm going to use!"

Miguel shrugged complacently. "A cape is very heavy, but if you want to try—"

After a few moments the cape was produced. The magenta silk and percale article was perfectly round and—if laid flat on the ground—about six feet in diameter. It was much heavier and bulkier than Stephanie expected, and she fumbled with it until Miguel came up behind her and showed her how to hold it properly.

Stephanie leaned against him, her body within the folds of his for a moment. The small crowd watched them with faces of disapproval and scorn, invad- ing—extinguishing—a second of sensual escape.

Miguel pressed himself into her backside, and she felt his hardness rub against her bottom.

"I would rather teach you how to use *this.*" His words were murmured in her ear, his breath hot on her cheek.

She gave him a side-glance and whispered back, "It's too big for me to handle."

"Hmm. I think you can handle it."

"Why don't you find out tonight—"

"Matador!" someone called. *"La vaca! La vaca!"*

"The crowd is going to start a riot soon," Miguel said, smiling, lifting his eyebrows in acknowl- edgment that he got her message loud and clear. "Let's give them a performance. You go back to the fence." He elevated his voice, calling, "let's get Ray down here to face the cow."

"Wait a minute!" Ray protested, lowering his camera lens.

"Give me your camera," Stephanie demanded, her hand outstretched.

I just gave Miguel the okay to come to me tonight. Okay. Breathe.

Reluctantly, Ray handed his camera to her.

Miguel tossed the cape to the boy and handed Ray the *muleta*. He reluctantly strolled into the center of the ring.

As soon as the gate opened the calf ran full tilt straight at Ray. He stumbled backward, managing to not get hit, but still landed on his backside. Stephanie got the whole thing on film. The second pass wasn't any more graceful as beast flew by and knocked him off balance. Ray threw down the cloth, and in a show of total defeat, he ran and jumped up on the fence, the calf hot on his heels.

"Chicken!" Stephanie hollered, thinking it didn't look *that* hard. After all, she did have a way with animals.

"Well, hotshot, you try it!" Ray said, dusting off his blue jeans.

"I think I will!" She jumped back down into the corral.

Miguel retrieved the *muleta* for Stephanie. She took the stick and cloth as the calf again took its rightful place center stage. She walked toward the animal, thinking, *How cute, with its big brown eyes.*

"Spread the *muleta* with the stick," Miguel advised from his post on the fence. "Now, call to her."

Stephanie spread the cloth. "Hello there, little cow."

The calf peered around, looking almost as bored as Domingo. Stephanie swept the cloth back and forth, moving closer as she called a little louder. After a few minutes she frowned, turned back to Miguel. "What's wrong with this animal?"

"*Look out!*" Miguel cried.

She glanced over her shoulder just as the cow made contact and landed her on her butt with a dusty *thunnnk*. Everyone laughed, but it was Domingo's loud bark that made her steaming mad.

She scrambled to her feet and aggressively approached the calf again, determined to show Domingo she wasn't about to run away in the face of danger—and yes, she wanted him to get the metaphorical meaning!

The little beast again looked at her, disinterested, but she wouldn't be tricked twice.

"Pretty cow," she said, fluttering the *muleta* back and forth. "Come here, pretty girl. Do that again and you're going to be someone's veal dinner!"

The animal dropped its head and flew past Stephanie, going smoothly under the *muleta* with a *whoosh*. There were shouts of *Ole!*

A sudden elation came over her, not because the people watching approved, but because for an instant she had controlled the wild creature. So caught up in the applause, she didn't notice the calf wheel quickly around for the next charge. This time when she hit the ground, she saw stars.

Miguel grabbed the cape off the fence and distracted the calf. After getting the animal back in the pen, he ran over to Stephanie. She pressed her palms to her temples, trying to shake off the dizzy sensation.

Miguel dropped to his knees. "Are you all right?"

"I—I think so."

"You were pretty good," he said, taking her hand and helping her to stand.

Stephanie brushed dirt off her jeans. "Then why did I land on my ass twice?"

Miguel gave her the once-over, from her disorderly golden blond hair to her dust-covered bottom, which he tenderly brushed off for her. "Both times you forgot about the calf, but you learned that she didn't forget about you."

Testing her legs, Stephanie walked over to the fence and retrieved her own camera.

Miguel came up behind her, and she caught her breath when his arm slipped around her shoulder.

"Now, are you hungry for something besides me? You can see a feast has been laid out."

She felt out of place, and stayed close to Ray during lunch. When Ray left to take pictures, she sat down on a wooden bench that wrapped around an oak tree, gazing out at some distant mountains.

Several boys had saddled up horses, and were now mounting. She watched them ride down the gravel lane and disappear, Renaldo one of them, his little tummy and pockets now full.

Miguel was still eating, sitting between Domingo and Galleo.

Every once in a while he'd look up and make eye contact with her. Even across the stretch of grass, she could feel his eyes on her. *He's thinking about tonight,* she thought. *I've filled his head full of sex.*

One year and three months since she'd been with a man, she calculated. Would she be inferior to his lovemaking skills? She worried a little bit about it, then remembered she'd read somewhere that macho Spanish men were *wham-bam-thank-ya* men. Maybe she wouldn't have to do much, but that idea didn't give her much comfort.

Did he have condoms out here on the ranch? She didn't have any.

He was looking at her now, and she smiled back. *He isn't a wham-bam type,* she decided. He was too full of sexual promise—he dripped with passion. In her experiences with men she'd never met a one who exuded such powerful pheromones, robbing her of a sense of self even in the most mundane places. Since when did she play the seductress?

She decided not to worry about tonight until it came. Besides, she was a little sleepy from all the fresh air and exercise, and didn't have much mental energy left.

The sun shone through the oak branches and leaves, sprinkling her with oblique patterns. They danced over her legs, and for a moment she drifted with the designs, back to her childhood.

She and Richard had once played in an old oak tree in the backyard of their home in San Diego. Their father had built them a tree house. He'd laid old green carpet on the plywood floor, and their mother had made pretty, blue flowered curtains. Richard hated those curtains! Stephanie wanted a playhouse, and he wanted a fort. This difference of opinions caused trouble.

Peace was finally found when they divided the structure with masking tape down the middle. Only her side had the curtains.

She'd kissed her first boy up there. Billy Landers. His family had moved from Kentucky the year before, and he had latched onto Stephanie before the moving vans had pulled away. One day, with the shadowy leaf patterns playing across his face, it dawned on her that he was kind of cute. She leaned over and kissed him.

Billy asked her to marry him when his mouth was still wet from the kiss, and promised he'd give her whatever she wanted. He said he was going to be a preacher, and preachers always kept their promises. He gave her a little silver cross for her tenth birthday, and announced they were going steady.

Three weeks later Stephanie's father left home. Jim Madison, who'd made the tree house and taught them how to throw fast balls and believe in the wonderment of fathers, went to work one morning and never came home. Stephanie and Richard waited with their mother at the kitchen table until the sun came up the next morning.

A few days later he finally called to say he wasn't coming home. He'd run off with a woman he'd met on a business trip. After that no one ever talked about him, as if he'd never existed, but their mothers sobs in the night were proof that he had.

Stephanie and Richard slept in the tree house until the weeping stopped, huddled together in one sleeping bag on the line that would never divide them again.

Jim Madison's child support checks never came. Their beautiful mother lacked any formal education. She found a low-paying job and could barely support her children. She settled at a young age for vague hopes that her husband would one day come home.

He never did.

Stephanie couldn't help comparing her own marriage to her mother's. Steven had left her for another woman, too, but unlike her mother she'd never settle for vague hopes about her future with one particular man. *Would she?*

She looked over at Miguel again. The rules always got thrown out with men like him.

As if he'd read her mind, he stood up and walked over to her, still holding a crumpled napkin in his hand. He looked beautiful under the leaf patterns. If she kissed him now, would he ask her to marry him while his lips were still wet?

"Hi." She yawned, stretched. "I could use a nap."

"Go back into the house. Ask Lydia to show you your room. She's my youngest sister, and probably in the kitchen."

"You don't mind?"

"No. I want you awake tonight."

She made her way over the gravel path, then turned to look over her shoulder. He was watching her, smiling.

She would be wide-awake.

EIGHT

It was dark when she finally opened her eyes and focused on a huge oil painting of a bullfighter. Someone was knocking at the bedroom door. After seeing her appalling reflection in the mirror, she found Miguel on the other side of the door. He wore tan linen slacks, and a dark green, short-sleeved silk shirt. His hair was damp, and he looked and smelled wonderful, so wonderful that she almost grabbed him and threw him on the bed, but he seemed distant.

"Let's go for a walk," he said in a serious tone.

"Let me freshen up. I just woke up."

"With all this noise? I'll wait for you."

The commotion coming from the house registered. It sounded like a party. People talking all at once, music blaring, and the strong smell of tobacco were all evident now that her door had been opened.

It also registered that Miguel wanted to *walk*.

Did that mean, *talk?* As in, *Sorry, Stephanie, I'm going to go through with this engagement to Paloma?* Or, *Yes, I'll make love to you, but just so you know, I can't promise you a long-term, committed relationship.* Or, *I can't have a relationship with a woman my family and friends—my country—can't accept. You understand, eh?*

Stephanie pushed her troubled thoughts aside, showered, and slipped into a light blue linen summer dress. She tried not to think too far ahead, or expect too much from this relationship. She applied makeup and lipstick and lots of perfume, clipped her still damp hair up in a loose knot, and joined Miguel. He sat on one of the leather sofas, and when he saw her he jumped up, grabbing a basket that had been resting next to his feet.

Ray was busy cleaning his camera equipment. A half a bottle of wine sat in front of him. He glanced up at Stephanie, but said nothing as she walked by with Miguel. Others stood around in knots, smoking and drinking. Galleo quietly strummed on his guitar, but stopped when she entered the room. Domingo wasn't around, but he didn't have to be. Everyone in the room watched them leave.

The moon was high above them when they stepped out into the night. It cast the ranch in a pale, gray light—*almost surrealistic,* Stephanie thought. Jasmine was carried on the warm breeze, and the smell of orange blossoms, as they walked up the gravel path toward the barn.

"It's barely one week since we met," Stephanie said, trying to quell the strange worry building deep in her belly, "but it seems longer." *Almost forever.* "You don't know how old I am or my middle name, but here we are in the middle of Spain walking under her moonlight."

"You worry too much about time, and the significance of it. You're twenty-nine-years-old, and your middle name is Anne."

Stephanie stopped and looked at him, surprised. "My favorite food?"

He grinned, winked. "You've got me there."

They continued walking.

"You can go back to Madrid if you want," Miguel said in a steady voice. It lent Stephanie no clue as to his feelings, but she felt as if he'd taken one of his swords and plunged it straight into her heart. She didn't know how her legs carried her across the gravel path.

"I just got here."

"I know, but you don't have to remain. Ray said he'd go back with you. I'm staying until Tuesday or Wednesday to avoid the crowds and the press, to try to get it together mentally."

"Do you *want* me to leave?" she asked, confused by another turn of events where he was trying to get rid of her.

"No, *querida*. I want you to be where you will be the happiest."

That was a breakup line if she ever heard one!

"Do I look unhappy? Did I say or do something today that makes you think I want to leave?"

"No. But my family is very hostile toward you, and this hurts me deeply. I can order them to be nice to you, but I cannot order their hearts."

Stephanie took a deep breath, struggling to hold in her tears. His family was rejecting her presence there, putting pressure on him, and he was committed to following their wishes. She shouldn't have come—she should have taken that ticket and gone home.

He led her to a little glass table and two very fine wood chairs nestled next to a fountain in the center of the garden. It was a good distance from the house and secluded by tall hedges. Miguel set his basket on a table and pulled out a candle, fished in his pocket for his silver lighter and lit it.

"We'll be alone here." He retrieved a bottle of dark wine from the basket. "Sit," he said, pointing to a chair.

The sky was a riot of stars. Stephanie glanced up at them, wondering how she could have gotten such a wrong impression about their relationship. He didn't want to be her lover tonight. He wanted her back in Madrid—or back in California. She suddenly felt shy and insecure, and a little miserable.

Miguel handed her a glass of wine.

"I shouldn't have come," she said, having difficulty with this new chasm between them. Perhaps her offer had embarrassed him, and he struggled with a nice way of declining. "I thought it would be different."

Miguel leaned back in his chair, took a sip of his wine, and glanced around his property, at the harmony of plains, mountains, and vast sky.

There was an enormous sense of isolation there under the Spanish stars, Stephanie thought. The heavens seemed different in Spain, as if she had not only left her country, but her universe.

"I have hurt many people lately," he began, then fished out a cigarette. He lit it and smoke caught on a new breeze and defused. "But I didn't set out to hurt anyone. Not you."

Here it comes. He's going to end this.

"Can I have one of those?" she asked.

He gave her a faint smile, picked the pack off the table and shook one out. "You're getting bad habits around me."

She leaned over for him to light it, and looked at

his long fingers, wished they were tangled in her hair.

"I shouldn't have brought you to Spain," he said as he leaned back and tossed the lighter on the table with a clank.

Her heart tripped, then slowed to a hard, painful beat.

"Why?" she asked, and blew out some smoke, liking the feel of the cigarette between her fingers. It gave her a sense of focus, something besides the ache in her heart.

She tried to read his gaze over the table while she waited for his answer. It didn't come. A warm breeze moved her hair. A bird was startled somewhere. Miguel looked celestial under the moon, from another planet—one that belonged in this new universe. *He is the essence of Spain,* she thought, *all contrast.*

"Are you still having the dream?" she asked, needing to change the subject, no longer able to wait for him to tell her he'd lost his feelings for her.

"Yes."

"You shouldn't believe so much in dreams. Mine never come true. Sometimes I dream Steven and I still are married. Sometimes I dream my mother is still alive." She took another deep breath of the warm, night air, wistfully staring at her cigarette. *Why am I smoking? Why am I sharing such painful things with him? Why am I trying to keep him talking—keep him from saying it's over, this madness between us?*

She looked up at Miguel, who continued to watch her closely.

"I didn't know you were divorced," he said.

"Oh, well . . ." Stephanie felt her equilibrium af-

fected by his statement. Divorce was such a distasteful word, a badge of failure.

"Tell me about it," he said, and stretched his legs,
crossed his ankles.

"I couldn't. I mean, there's not much to say." This
topic seemed too personal, too painful, a tangle of
unresolved emotions.

"Did you leave him?"

How could she tell Miguel, who had seemed completely fascinated by her until now, that Steven had
run off with one of her girlfriends? The scenario
didn't cast her in a very good light. She couldn't
keep her man.

"Steve was a little deceptive, and I was a little
blind," she said, thinking she might as well just tell
the truth. It would make her sound desperate or
petty to lay blame.

"He had an affair?"

Ouch. That statement still sent resentment through
her.

"He wanted things he didn't have to work for,"
she said honestly. "He thought my brother was going to financially back his harebrained business
deals. When he found out that wasn't the case, he
found a woman with a little more cash of her own."
Stephanie shrugged her shoulders. "So much for
happily ever after."

"You blame yourself?"

"Only that I married him without understanding
what his real needs were. He didn't want a wife. He
needed a meal ticket. I think deep down I always
knew that, but at the time I didn't want to examine
it too closely."

Stephanie picked up her wineglass and took a
deep drink, surprised that she could be so honest

with Miguel. Richard and Adria were the only two who knew how she really felt about her failed marriage.

"You and I are the same in some ways."

She'd thought the same thing.

"What really happened to you and Lucia?" Would he now open up to her about his own failed relationship with the beautiful socialite?

"She used me to get to Juan," he said flatly. No pain registered in his tone.

"Yes, I heard that."

"Everyone tried to tell me, but I wouldn't listen. Her glamour and sophistication bewitched me." He touched the scar on his cheek, then reached for his wineglass.

"You found her and Juan together?" she asked, trying to imagine it. Knowing Steven had an affair was a lot different than stumbling into a bedroom and seeing it firsthand.

"At a birthday party. They slipped upstairs into a bedroom." Miguel racked his fingers through his hair, closed his eyes, and sat very still for a moment. "I naively went looking for her."

Now Stephanie could *see* the pain. Miguel's entire body took it on—changed, sank. She wanted to get up and go to him—put her arms around him, comfort him somehow, but their own relationship still sat on a ledge.

"Dios mío, everyone was there, everyone important in bullfighting. The next day the terrible details were splashed on every newspaper in town."

"But you couldn't let it go?"

"I only meant to humiliate Juan for humiliating me. I had no visions—premonitions—that the great Juan Aguilar would take a *coronado.* Not Juan. He who never took a scratch in his career—it's what made him a god. Every *matador* is gored sooner or later—superficially, seriously, or fatally."

The warm breeze blew out their candle. Miguel lit it again.

"I knew he was in trouble with his first bull. *Dios mío*, he was letting the bull get too close, he was covered in blood—and then he faltered, stepped into the animal."

Miguel swirled his wine around in his glass, as if he could see an instant replay there in the liquid. "The bull clipped his leg, knocked him down. I ran out and tried to distract the bull, but the beast whirled around like a cat and took Juan in the gut before I could save him."

Stephanie stared down into her own wineglass, digesting his words. It was distressingly obvious that Miguel had not forgiven himself.

"Whatever happened to Lucia for causing you so much pain?"

"She could not show her face in the plazas. Last I heard she married a retired *picador* and had five babies, one right after another, and she is fat as a cow."

She saw the twinkle come back into his eyes.

"You're teasing now."

"No. No. Two hundred pounds!"

Glancing down at her glass again, she said, "Personally, I'm glad she's not in your life anymore." Admitting this to him was like taking a step closer to the ledge and looking at the vast possibility of falling over.

He arched an eyebrow. "Are you?"

She looked up and showed him a tentative smile. "I'm sure women have always chased after you."

He laughed. "No. I was a skinny poor kid who smelled bad. The girls of my town called me *El Oler—The Smell*."

"Oh, how mean." She stretched her legs out in front of her; the longer blades of grass ticked her ankles.

"After my father died, I worked on the docks of Barcelona cleaning fish to help support my family. Fish has a permanent signature. I reeked of it for years."

She laughed, and it felt good. Then she poured more wine, refusing to count how many she'd already drunk. "When did you have time to become a great *matador*?"

Miguel finished the bottle, tossed it down into a thicket of grass, and lifted out another from the basket. "On my days off I played with other boys a game of *corrida*. Like American boys who play football in the streets, I played bullfighter. Sometimes I would be the *matador*, other times, the bull."

"Were you like Renaldo, chasing after *matadors*?"

"No great *matadors* lived in Barcelona, because none came from there. I waited for them to come to me."

His smile faded, and he seemed to slip away again. "Did they come?"

He snuffed out his cigarette and promptly lit another one. "I was fifteen, and still reeking of fish. I saved my precious *pesos* from long hours on the dock to buy a seat to see Juan Aguilar. He was my idol. Not a good seat, but a seat just the same. While I was making my way into the plaza, a beautiful woman, wearing the biggest white hat I had ever seen, told me she'd been unexpectedly called away. Did I want her seat? And she handed me the ticket."

"Who was the woman?"

"Juan's wife. The seat was in the shade in Juans box. Juan looked up from the *callejon* as he entered the ring and saw me sitting in a seat reserved for his wife. He approached me, demanded I get my skinny, smelly ass out of his wife's seat. I showed him the ticket and told him how I came by it. Then, I told him I would one day be the greatest *matador de toros* to have ever lived, greater than him."

"Oh, you *didn't*."

"He told me to stay after the bullfight. For reasons no one will ever know, Juan took me into his entourage and began to train me personally."

Stephanie let the implications of this story sink in. "Where is Paloma's mother now?"

"Dead. Killed in a car accident on her way to Seville, just one year before Juan died. Some say he hit the bottle after she died, but I never saw him drink. Paloma had no one after that."

"So what happened to her?"

"Juan asked me with his last breath to take care of his *niña,* and I have."

A deathbed wish!

"Did you try to commit suicide after Juan's death? Is that why you got drunk before a bullfight?"

"I wanted to die for killing Juan. I could not face the angry crowds. I could not face myself."

For a long time neither spoke. Stephanie listened to the night sounds. A bird changed branches above them. A breeze moved the leaves. There was a bellow out on some hillside, and a dog barked in the far distance. Cigarette smoke drifted between them.

"What are you going to do about Paloma now?" she asked because she needed to know, and felt herself edge even closer to the ledge.

He took a deep breath, but said nothing.

"Do you love her?" The power of the wine gave her the strength to ask the painful question.

"I told you at the villa that I'm her guardian. She is like a sister, and she does not love me, either. She has a lover."

"Oh—what will you do? Just get engaged? A publicity stunt?"

He drained another glass of wine, but still didn't answer her. Then it dawned on her, and the realization stabbed her heart. "You *are* going to marry her!"

"No." He shook his head. "I am going to marry *you.*"

Oh, my God, he's serious! What happened to ending our relationship?

Stephanie stood up with no direction in mind, confused, afraid to let Miguel get so deep into her heart with his obscure pronouncements. Nobody in Spain was going to let him marry her. He caught her up in his arms, ran his fingers through her hair, knocking her hair clip out. It hit the gravel path and made a *kkkkksht* sound.

"I am selfish, even cruel, to ask this of you, but say you will marry me. Say yes. Then promise me you will not believe what you hear or read in the newspapers this next week. Promise me you will wait until this is all over. Promise me, *querida.*"

How could she make such a promise? "What can you promise me?"

"That I'll always love you."

She clung to him, melted against his body, filling the moment with memories of what he felt like, how he smelled and kissed, because deep down she knew this was all she was going to have left when the final bull bit the sand.

He took her head in his hands and held her gaze. *"Promise it to me. Prométemelo, por favor."* His mouth crashed down on hers, smothering her with unyielding, wet pleasure. She clung to the outer edges of her reason, but her body betrayed her, responded completely to his seduction in the garden under his universe.

Stephanie pulled away and looked into his eyes. They were pools of green moss, intense beauty. "I promise."

I am not like my mother. I am not like my mother. I will not settle for vague hopes.

They returned to the house and went straight into his bedroom under the watchful, disapproving eyes of his family. The room was large, with a bed pushed under a window and a carved oak writing table next to it. Moorish artifacts were tucked in corners—a warrior's helmet, a sword propped in a corner—obviously priceless treasures. A rich, thick tapestry covered the floor, and her feet sank into it as she walked across the room. A Picasso hung on the wall. The room felt musty—dark, sensual.

Stephanie sat on the edge of the bed and glanced around at her surroundings while Miguel produced yet another bottle of wine and turned on a stereo. Spanish music flowed through the room, an up-tempo but seductive song. Several candles twinkled in selected areas before he came over to her with two new glasses of wine.

"Since I met you, all I do is drink." She could

hear her heart pounding, pushing the two glasses already consumed through her veins.

"This will make it easier for you."

"Easier?"

"To do as I say." He sat down and the bed sloped. "Stand over there and take off your clothes—very slowly."

No swooping down on her and ripping off her dress, like the night at her house? He wanted her to strip for him—while he watched? The idea mortified and excited her at the same time.

Miguel's eyes suddenly sparkled with mischief as he waited for her to do his bidding. If this was fantasy hour, she had a request of her own.

"Go change into a pair of those matador pants—*taleguilla*. Nothing else. Then I will strip."

A smile rose on his lips, and something very sensuous lit his eyes. "Any particular color?"

"Red and gold."

He jumped up and left the room.

There is no way on earth that I'll strip in front of him. It suddenly occurred to her that she was white as a lily flower. Though she lived in Laguna Beach, she never found time to make it down to the sand. Having gained a few extra pounds this past year now weighed heavier on her mind than her thighs. How could she participate in this erotic adventure and expose herself so completely?

What happened to wham-bang, in the dark, with the lights out?

Waiting for him to return was torturous. When the door opened, it quietly closed behind him. Casually leaning against it, he pressed his head to the wood. He didn't have much hair on his chest, but a pack of muscles and a few scars. Red tight pants with gold brocade spiraling down the sides now clung deliciously to him like a second skin, the sensuous bulge of his erection delineated. His hair had fallen across his forehead, and in one hand he dangled his wineglass.

"*Señorita,* let me say I have never had this odd request before." He took a drink of his wine, and motioned to the center of the room.

"Neither have I," she said, trying to find a ray of humor in all this. With him looking at her seductively, though, she felt anything but amused.

"I have hungered for you all week. Now, I want my fill. All good meals start with *tapas*—take off your clothes. I am a very visual man."

Visual man? She set her wineglass down and moved to where he pointed, definitely turned on, her knees a little weak. Though she tried to look calm and poised, as if she stripped for men every day of her life, inside she was boiling with an unexplainable desire.

He continued to press his backbone against the door, one bare foot propped against it.

Her fingers trembled as she slipped the straps of her dress off and let the fabric flutter down to her belly. Sliding it around, she released the buttons and let it fall to a pile around her ankles. In the shadows, his gaze followed the fabric all the way to the floor. Then she watched it move back up again.

She lowered her head, and her hair fell forward, hiding her face from his close inspection, certain it was bright red. She wet her lips with her tongue and reached back and unclasped her bra, intoxicated by more than the wine. It slipped down over her waist and dropped to the floor with her dress, releasing her breasts. Her nipples were hard, erect, even though it was warm in the room. Now, with just her panties, she stood before him, let him gaze at her from his tight corner.

"Take them off," he whispered thickly.

Wetness now gathered in the fabric that he wanted her to shed. Her thumbs slipped between the lace, and she tugged the panties free. Lifting her head back up, she opened her eyes and her gaze met his. It seemed as if he looked at her nakedness for an eternity.

He pushed himself off the door with a little shove of his foot, went to the closet, and pulled out a bull-fighter's cape. He unfurled the fabric and spread it out before her on the floor.

"*Sientase*—sit," he ordered. She lowered her body onto the cool, blue satin.

The candle's light bounced off the sequin of his pants and flickered around her, the same way the leaves had played their patterns under the oak tree earlier.

He went back to the closet and retrieved another cape.

Sparkling red and gold starbursts seemed to fly from his pants, sparkling, almost hypnotizing her as he twisted the cape in small circles until they grew larger, stretched wider, began opening up like blossoming flowers. A cool current soon moved her hair when the cape swirled over her head.

He had incredible control over the large, bulky cape. It touched nothing in the room but what he wanted it to touch—her.

The soft, gentle current undulated over her body as the cape's edge gently tickled her just below her neck and slid slowly down her chest. Her eyes were closed, and she drifted on the erotic sensation of satin sliding down flesh.

It stopped. She opened her eyes. He stood in the center of the room, the cape clenched in his hands and hanging limp at his side, his breathing labored.

"Lie down," he said thickly. "On your back."

Stephanie stretched her arms back and began to slowly lower herself, her heart hammering in her ears.

The cape swooped over her again, spiraled over her nakedness. The breeze it created ruffled her hair. Lower it came, a spinning yellow topaz, tingling across her breasts, her stomach, fluttering down her pelvis.

He executed the cape one last time, and while the cloth was suspended above her he moved down onto his knees and let the fabric slide across the entire length of her body and then fly up into the air, so high it almost touched the ceiling. It slid around his body one last time before it fanned out around him like an offering.

His breathing came hard, and his eyes seemed to bore into hers with violent passion.

A hot ache rose in her throat, and wetness now dripped from her and onto the beautiful cape. How could she control herself? He had lit her brighter than a comet, hotter than the sun, and she throbbed for him.

He tossed the cape, and came over to her.

Of course he was capable of torture! This was evidence!

He kissed one of her knees, lifted her leg and kissed the inside of her thigh, made his wet attention all the way up her body until he pushed her legs open. His tongue grazed her center, and her reaction made him moan deep in the back of his throat.

A tidal wave of ecstasy washed over her as his coarse dark hair tickled her inner thighs and his hot, textured tongue flicked at her womanhood, lapped with a gentle rhythm and great attention.

His eyes met hers from between her legs and pinned her helplessly to the satin cape.

She arched up, raised herself to his greedy mouth, all inhibitions forgotten. With her eyes shut and her head thrown back, she let him give her pleasure.

Oh, my God, I'm going to . . . Swear . . . Now—

He moved up on his knees just before that happened, ready to open his *taleguilla,* but she moved up, too, stopped him from undressing himself. They faced each other on their knees. Fingering his gold cross, she traced the scar on his shoulder, followed it with her tongue, tasting his salty flesh, inhaling his musky scent, down to one nipple. The bud grew hard under her gentle punishment. Exploring his rock-hard belly, her hands gingerly slid over the bulge in his pants. His eyes closed, and his breathing came rapidly.

He stood up as if to shed himself of his pants, and she stopped him by taking his hips, held him there before her. Still on her knees, she cupped her hands around the bulge and took a deep breath of fabric and man. His fingers were tangled in her hair, and held her pressed against him. Looking down at her, he watched as her tongue moved across the fabric along the entire length of his erection.

"Quiero que seas mía," he whispered.

"Soon . . ."

She opened the clasp and wriggled the *talequilla* down over his hips, over his protruding penis. The moist, pink head slid between her lips. Earth, olives, musk, sex . . . all these things registered as she took him into her mouth. The twisted fingers in her hair tightened when she began to move with long, slow, sucking strokes.

His knees began to tremble, and she wondered if he were close. Coming to his own realization, he pushed her back onto the cape and pulled the pants the rest of the way off, tossed them behind him into the dark.

The *Las Ventas* scar still shocked her, but not enough to take her out of her fantasy.

From somewhere he produced a condom, and she watched him slip it on, wanted to do that for him. His head snapped up and his gaze captured hers.

She reached for the now sheathed penis and opened her legs to him. He moved over her, this solid, hard, Spanish man, and into her, slowly. She heard him make a small noise—*"Ghhhhhhh."*

When he propped himself on his elbows and his fingers slid through her hair, their lips met in a kind of madness, of thrusting tongues, no longer gentle but almost cruel. He moved within her, slowly, at first. She didn't want *slow.* She wanted hard and fast, something punishing and dominating to extinguish the heat burning between her legs.

Don't ever stop. . . . she needed more and more of him.

A fine layer of perspiration now covered their bodies. Time disappeared. Everything disappeared.

He picked up the tempo, and each time he slid into her a different sensation was building and burning, taking her to places she'd never been. Crying out his name, she felt him shudder in her arms and tremble from head to toe, as she, too, accepted wave after wave of ecstasy.

For a long time she heard his breathing in her

ear, first fast, then slower, as his heart rate calmed. She didn't know how long had passed before he rolled over next to her and threw his arm over his forehead as if he'd just realized something. Stephanie moved on top of him, framed his face with her hands, crushing her mouth against his for a long, deep kiss. His arms came around her again.

"How am I going to live without you?" she whispered. "I'm so much in love with you."

Miguel's hands moved up and down her back. "You are never going to live without me, *querida*."

He rolled her over and began exploring her body all over again.

NINE

Her father told her a silly joke and made her laugh, and she made him laugh with one of hers. His broad smile stretched from ear to ear, and then he leaned down with his hammer and put another nail into the playhouse. . . .

Something brought her to the surface of wakefulness, and she struggled to keep the dream, but it slipped away, and one hell of a pounding headache said hello.

The morning light spared nothing. Miguel was still asleep and naked next to her. A sheet snaked around his midsection. His breathing was slow and even, and healthy dark stubble showed on his face. Two empty wine bottles and two empty glasses, one turned on its side, explained her headache. A red and gold pair of *corrida* pants and a linen dress rested in heaps, and both capes were crumpled on the floor. The musty scent of lovers clung to everything, and her.

She put her nose to her arm and inhaled this blending of bodies. Squeezing her eyes shut, she willed for sleep to return so that she could wake up from this new dream and find herself back in Laguna Beach, California, surrounded by the familiar smell of eucalyptus and the demanding cries of her cats—a life she understood.

This was not the reality of Stephanie Madison, who planned her days down to chamomile tea before bed. What experiences did she have to draw from to help her understand this new relationship? She remembered reading somewhere that romantic fantasies didn't just happen, that you turned them into reality through your own efforts. Now that the fantasy was over, what reality did the morning hold? What effort could she put into making things run smoothly between them from this point on?

What would he now expect? What would she expect?

Besides her head pounding, every muscle in her body ached, especially her hip, where she'd taken the tumble with the calf.

Girlfriend, you're in deep now, way deep. God, he looks like a child sleeping, with no traces of the man, vulnerable. I don't want you to be a matador. *I want you to have some innocuous job.*

Don't rationalize what happened. Don't analyze it. Just let it be. But sex with Miguel had been close to a spiritual experience. How could she not analyze it, pick it apart, and arrive at some conclusion—solution? She had to do *something*.

Get up.

She rubbed her temples. She needed water to drink, and a toilet, desperately. Slowly, she sat, shaking from the wine and the physical workout. In the bathroom, she relieved herself, then washed her face, rinsed her mouth out, and tried to recognize the woman who stared back.

Red-rimmed eyes and her hair in total knots. *I am never going to recognize myself.*

She smelled her forearms again, remembering how the past two years she'd worked hard to eliminate men from her life—the countless private mental sessions where she'd convinced herself that she would never again let a man into places she treasured—getting to know a man *that way.*

As soon as *it* happened things became dangerous and frightening, and new risks came into play. Like the risk that she'd fallen deeply in love, so deep now that she'd drown before she ever found the surface of reality. This man who asked her to marry him, and then took her to the heights of unbelievable passion, was a *bullfighter. He's totally committed to his family and his country, and he thinks he's going to die because of a dream.*

Here is the line. She used her toe to draw an imaginary line on the floor's tile. *This is reality.* She made an X. *This is la la land. You are here.* She made another X. *Jump over. Come on, girl. You can do it.*

He's asked me not to believe what I hear or read this week.

Could it get worse? Of course it's going to get worse.

Stephanie looked up at the clear glass shower stall, remembering Ray's words at the airport so long ago: *"He'll do whatever he has to do to stay on top. . . ."*

His family wanted her off the ranch, and last night he had told her to leave—in a nice way, but told her just the same.

"He has an agenda . . ."

Regardless of his wishes, he couldn't continue to have her there at the ranch, not with so much obvious hostility, and decisions to be made.

But he wants to marry you!

If her head didn't hurt so much, she thought she

might have started laughing hysterically. *Marry me? When hell freezes over!*

Send her back to Madrid. Make promises he can't keep. He is a prisoner of his own fame.

She sat on the toilet for a long time, with a wet rag on her forehead.

Miguel was still asleep when she sat back on the edge of the bed. *I can't stay here.* It would be better to wait for him in Madrid.

He opened his eyes, peered at Stephanie through heavy, sleepy lids as if he, too, were a little confused. *"Buenos días."* He stretched like a cat after a long nap, yawned, and rubbed his eyes. He looked at the clock. "I have to get up—" He fell back onto the pillows, his first attempt to get out of bed a total failure. He flung an arm over his eyes.

"I'm not staying," she blurted, and heard the petulance in her tone. "I think it's a good idea if I head back to Madrid right after breakfast."

He didn't move, didn't take his arm off his eyes, didn't say: *"Don't go. I need to you here with me now that we've shared this incredible, intimate experience."*

She watched his chest rise and fall. The silence was deafening to Stephanie, and told her more than she wanted to understand. It reinforced her insecurities and fears that this relationship was a total fantasy, created by a woman who wanted to believe. Last night Miguel had spoken of love and marriage, but she reasoned they were in a different universe then, and they'd both drunk a lot of wine.

He knew he couldn't marry her. *He knew it.*

"You'll miss a private *corrida*," he said to the ceiling. "I must remember to pick up Renaldo and his family, which I am sure has grown since he went home yesterday."

"I don't want to see you kill an animal," she snapped, new hurt invading all the other confusion, because he could only think of bulls when her heart was breaking.

He dropped his arm, turned his head on the pillow, and looked at Stephanie. "You're going to see me kill three next Sunday."

"I'll deal with it then," she said, running fingers through her tangled hair, able to read a little passion stirring in his sleepy eyes.

His hand moved down her arm and back up again, and she knew the signal, remembered with vivid recognition what they'd shared the night before. When he came up on his elbows the sheet slipped back, exposing the dark V of hair just below his belly button. She averted her eyes, but his hand caught her chin, and turned her head gently back. He kissed her tenderly, eagerly, as if it were the first time their lips had ever come together.

Some part of her said to stop, not to encourage any more lovemaking.

He looked into her eyes, and must have seen her hesitation. "What, *querida?*" he asked, and tried to tip her chin his way again, but she pulled back.

"I'm going to take a shower." She left him on the bed. Before she shut the door she heard him whisper something. It sounded like, *"promise."*

Miguel chewed on his doughnut and took a sip of coffee, watching the reaction of his family on this otherwise beautiful morning. Everyone knew what had happened the night before, and from their cold silences he understood their disapproval. For the first time in his life he was not comfortable with his family, and he didn't know what to do with the experience. He was nothing without his family, but he would also be nothing without Stephanie. His new fate was sealed by the dream.

Last night, while he was wrapped up in her arms, a new dream had come. In that version he saw his own salvation.

Instead of a thousand pound bull plunging its horn into his body, it sailed past him in several beautiful passes that had the crowd on its feet.

Olé! And again. *Olé!*

A thousand times *Olé!*, in the most beautiful *faena* ever witnessed in the history of bullfighting. *Whoosh. Whoosh.* The duped bull sailed by, trying to get him. Then the bull stopped. Miguel shook the *muleta,* but the bull's gaze slid off the cloth and onto him, the most dangerous thing that can happen in the ring. Miguel shook the *muleta* harder and faster, felt his heart hammering in fear, but the bull only laughed and said, "*Matador,* your fate has been changed." Then the beast staggered and fell dead at his feet.

Roses scattered over Miguel from the *barrera* seats, and when he turned toward his box he saw Stephanie, wearing the biggest white hat he had ever seen. She waved a handkerchief at him, and then tossed him a single white rose.

He woke up with a start, his body covered in sweat. The moon's light had made a grid across Stephanie's naked body. He had slipped back down next to her, drawn her close, felt tears burn his eyes, and drifted back to the carpet of roses that awaited him at *Las Ventas.*

Now he watched her. She picked at her food and

would not look at him, could not look at him and remember what they'd shared last night. His body still ached from it, craved more, but she had shut him out—perhaps denied it even happened.

Instead of being filled with joy this morning, he was filled with anger and sorrow. He'd told her that he loved her and that he wanted to marry her, but he was certain she wouldn't keep her promise. Women never kept their promises to *El Peligro*. Why should she be any different?

And the bull was laughing. . . .

He wanted a smoke. He wanted a drink. He fingered his cross. *¡Dios mío!* He needed to go to church, to confession. Too many things weighed down on him. He needed to release some of the burden.

She is like a drug. I'm addicted, and everyone in this room knows it—

Domingo chomped on his cigar, his big lips working the tobacco into a wet rag, a nasty habit he normally reserved for late afternoon. He sat next to him with the morning paper open, said something about the bulls Miguel would fight next week. He knew he should listen, that his men spent a lot of time studying the bulls in advance, but his thoughts were full of Stephanie.

Domingo wanted to talk about what Pacote had written in today's paper. Miguel didn't care to hear it.

"They are saying *El Peligo* is washed up. *Matador*, Pacote is trying to rile the crowds before the gates even open."

Stephanie needed to go back to Madrid, Miguel thought, barely hearing Domingo. There, she could shop, relax—be away from this negative environment. He should have listened to Domingo and not brought her to the ranch, but to watch her go would have caused physical pain in his heart.

She looked very beautiful to him this morning— properly ravished, yet very sad. He wanted to convince her not to worry, tell her about the new dream, but his words held no conviction to this American girl who thought his dreams were silly and of no importance.

He had to make her promise again.

Domingo had big plans to make the announcement in a few days, even though Miguel had warned him not to use Paloma in any publicity stunts. Domingo respected his *matador,* but might still do as he pleased if he thought it was for the better, and Miguel worried about this flaw in his manager's otherwise trustworthy character.

Miguel knew that he and Domingo were going to have a big fight, and he didn't want Stephanie to see it. He did want her in his box at *Las Ventas,* and he didn't care if the entire world knew it.

She doesn't want to watch me kill a bull. Well, this was going to be a problem. Killing bulls was what a *matador* did. There was no *corrida* without a death at the end.

She is not going to keep her promise, he thought, painfully. *None of this makes any sense to her.* It was beginning to make less to him.

And the bull was laughing. . . .

They ate breakfast with his family. Stephanie felt their hostility as they looked from Miguel to her, and back to him again. Being his lover hadn't cemented her in their hearts—it definitely made matters worse. They made her feel like a leper, unclean. Their problem had just turned into a crisis.

The only time she and Miguel had after breakfast was when he walked her out to the Jeep. Ray, obviously giving them time alone, said he'd be along in a minute.

The sun was already brutal at seven o'clock in the morning. Birds chirped in the oak trees, protesting, perhaps, the sudden heat wave.

"I guess this is good-bye." Stephanie leaned against the Jeep, squinted into bright sun, and wondered how she would survive without him for even a few days.

"No." He reached out and touched her hair. "Nothing is different in the morning sun. I love you, *querida.*"

Her heart squeezed, and she shook her head in disagreement. "Everything's different, Miguel."

"You no longer love me, eh?" He touched her chin and tilted it up to receive his kiss.

She responded, kissed him back, his words ebbing in her consciousness. Last night had been like a dream. They had drunk ecstasy together. Now, though, the sun was cruel.

"I love you, but—"

"I want to marry you," he said, putting his hands on her shoulders. "I *will* marry you."

Her eyes came up to meet his, and in them she saw tumult.

She could only show a small smile. *It doesn't matter what you want—these people around you will never let you have your way. I'm not going to cry. I'm not going to cry.*

"You will sit in my box on Sunday? I am going to show the world who I really love. You must believe me. Somehow keep your promise. Promise again."

Ray appeared, loaded down with their suitcases. He tossed everything in the back and slid into the driver's side.

Stephanie backed away from Miguel, unable to give him his promise, and he opened the car door for her. When she slid in, Ray handed her a cold bottle of water. They pulled away, and after a few hundred yards, Stephanie turned and saw Miguel standing in the driveway. She hung her hand out of the window and waved. He waved back.

"There's going to be a press release," Ray said. "Galleo told me this engagement is going to happen."

Stephanie took a deep breath, closed her eyes, and rested her pounding head against the car seat. "I know. It isn't what he wants, but he doesn't seem to have much say in his life."

"You okay, then?"

"He has enough to deal with without me playing the jealous girlfriend."

"Is that what you are, Steph?"

"I guess it's official. I'm the jealous girlfriend." She swallowed something hard in her throat. Blinked back the tears.

"You okay?"

"Sure. Great." More swallowing. More blinking.

"You want to talk?"

She shook her head.

The future seemed deep and wide and very far away, in Laguna Beach. She inhaled strong-smelling mountain herbs: rosemary, sage, lavender, and thyme, but the hot, punishing heat forced her to roll the window up. Ray pushed a button, and cool air filled the Jeep, bringing relief.

The smells had reminded her of Miguel's scent—

and her initial reaction to it at Richard's last Saturday—a *million* years ago, when Miguel had entered her life and turned her world on its axis.

Ray took his eyes off the road for a second and glanced at Stephanie. "I hate to see you hurting, Stephanie."

"Thanks, but you warned me." *Yes,* she thought, *you warned me.* She was crying now, and wiped her cheek with the back of her hand. The floodgates opened, and she cried so hard that her shoulders shook.

"Feel better?" Ray asked once she'd stopped.

"Vastly." She blew her nose unceremoniously in a tissue she found in her bag.

"I'm going to get some proofs developed," Ray said, wisely avoiding comment about her tears. "And if you're up to it, we can meet with Francosis later. My deep throat connection set something up. How about it? Can you handle it tonight?"

"Sure, why not? I'm a professional. Bounce right back. See?" She gave him a big fake smile. Miguel's warning about talking only to those he approved of rang clearly in her head, but she discarded it. The rules had changed. The only thing still tangible was this story.

He shook his head. "Have any other plans for the rest of the week besides working on this story?"

"Sightseeing." She stared at the road in a kind of daze.

"I'd love to get some pictures of the city."

"It'll be fun . . ." she said, but she wasn't thinking about fun.

The beautiful Spanish scenery sped by, but she hardly noticed as her thoughts remained full of Miguel. She slept most of the way back. Later, the skyline of Madrid came into view. A smoggy haze settled over the city.

"I heard about your lunch date with Pacote," Ray said as they inched their way through downtown afternoon traffic.

"Who hasn't?"

"Pacote's the one who keeps Juan Aguilar's memory alive in the minds of bullfighting fans."

"What difference does it make what Pacote says?"

"He's a popular writer with the Spanish *aficionados*. He can make or break a man in the bullring. And you know he's Juan's younger brother. Some say he's the one who started the trouble between Francosis and Miguel."

"I didn't know that. Why didn't Miguel tell me?" Ray shrugged. "I don't know."

"How did you find out?"

"A little investigative journalism?"

"Oh, you mean *my* job?"

"There's more you should know," Ray continued. "Domingo gave Pacote some cash to not write anything about you staying at Miguel's villa—or to publish a picture of a naked woman in his window." Ray cleared his throat.

"Oh, my God!" *He'd taken her picture?* "How much money?"

"About ten thousand American dollars."

"Oh, my God. Does Miguel know?"

"I'm sure he does."

Stephanie struggled with this new information, and the implication that Miguel had kept it from her. Humiliation raised its ugly head.

"Domingo pays reporters to write what he wants reported," Ray added. "If Miguel has a bad day in

Seville, there's no reason for the fans in Barcelona to know, unless it's televised."

"You should be writing this story! You know more than I do!"

"I can't write. I can give you the information, but you have to put it into words. What are your plans after the fight?"

"Back to my cats."

"You could use a *real* vacation, Stephanie. Why don't you come with me to Càdiz for a few weeks? I got an invitation from friends of mine to stay in their villa at the sea. The only downside is they have a gaggle of kids running around. The noise level can be earsplitting at times."

"I'll think about it."

Theresa was waiting for them at the villa, mysteriously returned before them from the ranch. She had a message from Miguel. He wanted Stephanie to call him when she arrived. Her thoughts were still too scrambled, wounds too fresh, for her to talk to him. Besides, she didn't want to be at his beck and call just because they'd been lovers.

Later, she and Ray met Francosis downtown at a place called *Café Gijon*.

Miguel's challenger was surrounded by hangers-on, including several beautiful women. Besides being very young he was handsome, Stephanie noted, with long, dark brown hair and chestnut-colored eyes. He often flashed his big smile to his admiring entourage.

In sorry English, he wanted to know right away who they were, and why they wanted to talk to him. Ray explained they were American journalists doing a story about the upcoming fight. A dawning came over his expression, and he asked if Stephanie was the Jenna Starr staying at *El Peligro's*.

This statement shocked Ray and Stephanie. Hadn't Miguel shelled out a lot of money for silence? How had Francosis heard? He wouldn't say. Suddenly, he paid closer attention to Stephanie, as if he were seeing her for the first time. She squirmed under his *knowing* inspection, wondering if he'd seen Pacote's photograph.

Several bottles of wine were produced, but Stephanie declined, thinking that if she were not careful she'd end up in AA after this assignment was over.

Ray pulled out a list of questions prepared by Stephanie in advance, and she turned on her little tape recorder. She also took notes when Ray broke down the language barrier, which wasn't often enough in her opinion. She glanced up from her scribbling just as Paloma suddenly walked up.

The young woman was dressed in a modern, short, blue suede skirt and a skimpy tank top, nothing like the *señorita* Stephanie remembered from Miguel's villa her first night in Spain.

She plopped down next to Francosis, and a wave of strong perfume engulfed them all. He greeted her with a long, familiar kiss, and settled his arm around her slim shoulders in a very territorial gesture.

Ray glanced at Stephanie, and Stephanie glanced at Ray.

Okay. What's this all about?

Was Paloma *involved* with Francosis? Was this her lover that Miguel talked about? *Holy smoke!*

Stephanie couldn't understand any of the conversation firing around the table. She leaned toward

Ray and asked for some consideration, but instead Ray said he and Francosis were leaving to take some pictures of the *matador* around Madrid. They would meet up with them later.

Stephanie watched as her interview and his retinue walked away with Ray. Confused, she looked back at Paloma. Big brown eyes studied her. They were large and animated, and seemed filled with curiosity.

"Are you really a reporter from America?" Paloma asked in very good English. Then she reached up and yanked a clip out of her long, thick hair. It cascaded down her shoulders.

"Oh, you speak English!"

"Yes. I speak several languages. You really a reporter? Pacote says you are." She rearranged her hair, and clamped it back in place.

Pacote sure gets around! "Yes, I work for a Spanish language newspaper in California."

"How can you do that when you don't speak Spanish?"

"It's a long story."

"And no doubt Miguel is behind it."

"No doubt. Tell me, does he know you and Francosis are *friends*?"

Paloma shrugged, seemly unaffected by Stephanie's direct question. "Oh, no!"

"I think he'd care to know," Stephanie found herself saying. "There's a lot riding on this bullfight. It won't look good if—" It suddenly dawned on Stephanie that perhaps Paloma didn't know her own fate. "What do you know about the engagement?"

"*Señorita,* Stephanie, you must help me. I do not want to be engaged to Miguel. He will never marry me. He will ship me away for a few years, and when he retires he will break it off. It will be too late for Francosis and me. You must *please* help me. *Us.*"

Stephanie felt as if she'd jumped on a carnival ride. "How can I help you?" *I can't help myself!*

"Francosis does not believe the rumors. He thinks I will have a press conference of my own and call Miguel a liar, and declare my love for him. I can't do that to Miguel. *Señorita,* I can't humiliate him before *Las Ventas.* He is sure to die, then. But Francosis will die of a broken heart."

"All this talk of dying! I don't—*won't* believe it!"

"You do not understand. I know to an American it sounds very fantastic."

Very fantastic!

"My heart belongs to Francosis. But what can I do when I am bound by duty and honor to do as Miguel says?" She sighed very loudly, and Stephanie couldn't tell if it were sincere or for effect. "I cannot tell Francosis the truth—that this is only a publicity stunt." She shook her head violently back and forth. "But *you* can tell him."

"Me? You should talk to Miguel. Leave me out of this."

She shook her head. "Miguel would be very angry if he found out about me and Francosis. Besides, Domingo, that fat pig, will make Miguel do what he wants."

Stephanie didn't want to laugh, but hearing Paloma call Domingo a fat pig sounded really funny, and mirrored her own private thoughts.

"Domingo gets fat on Miguel's money," Paloma added. "Come. I am too jumpy to sit."

"Where?" Stephanie grabbed the tape recorder and her purse.

"Let's shop, eat, and drink a lot of wine."

Paloma took Stephanie's hand and they left the café looking like school chums, and later like best friends. They walked through the streets of Madrid and chatted about styles, American movies, and California.

Stephanie spent far too much money, so did Paloma, and soon they were both loaded down with shopping bags. It was dark by the time they stopped long enough to eat. During a light meal of sandwiches, Stephanie learned that Paloma had been in a boarding school until she was seventeen. She attended a university in Paris, and at twenty-two she now worked in Miguel's business offices in Madrid.

"Do you blame Miguel for your father's death?" Stephanie asked her.

"No. My *padre* loved Miguel. He loved him even on the day he died. He told me. He said, '*Niña,* Miguel *had* to call me out. I dishonored him.' My *padre* was a big man. He could admit when he was wrong."

"But he still accepted the challenge."

"*Señorita,* Stephanie, there is so much you cannot understand about the *corrida.* Men like my *padre* and Miguel, they are born *matadors.* Everything they do is for the bulls. Francosis is no different, but I love him, anyway. My *padre* had to take the challenge, just as Miguel had to take it from Francosis. These things are sent down from God."

Or from Pacote's pen!

Paloma fished a cigarette out of her purse and lit it. She blew out a long stream of smoke. Her dark eyes were on Stephanie. "Miguel has made love to you, hasn't he?"

"W—what?"

"I can see it in your eyes." She shrugged. "He

has a way with women. You know, he has had a lot of them. But he never loved anyone after Lucia."

Stephanie felt her cheeks burn red. How could Juan's daughter talk so casually about the woman who indirectly caused her father's death?

"Miguel said Lucia got fat."

Paloma laughed, put her small hand over her mouth. "Lucia? No." She shook her head. "She is still beautiful, even though she has four children. I saw her once in Seville. She came to a *corrida* and wanted to talk to Miguel, but he refused. People say she never forgave herself. But I think she is a witch."

"And they think Miguel made a pact with the devil after he was gored at *Las Ventas*."

Paloma smiled, smoked a little. "But he is some man, yes? Have you seen his butt in his *corrida* pants?"

Stephanie laughed.

"Women throw him underpanties and hotel keys instead of roses."

He never loved anyone after Lucia. . . .

"All I need from you, *señorita*, is for you to tell Francosis the truth. Then, no matter what happens, he will not go crazy before the fight—look there is Pacote! He is hiding behind that palm tree. My uncle is a *corrida* worm."

Stephanie didn't have time to digest Paloma's words before spotting Pacote lurking in the shadows.

"Pacote waits for me to see him," Paloma said casually. "Should I see him now?"

"I don't want to talk to him."

"Let's see what he wants!" Paloma waved to him.

Pacote rushed over, moving chairs out of his way, like a charging bull. "Ah, two beautiful Spanish roses. What luck!"

"You cost Miguel a lot of money the last time we *chatted,*" Stephanie said coldly.

"No big deal, *señorita.* He paid happily."

"Why were you sneaking around us?" Stephanie demanded.

"What sneaking? This is Madrid!" Pacote smiled at Paloma. "You look beautiful tonight. Where is your *matador?*"

"Which one?" she teased.

Stephanie shot Paloma a warning glance and stood up, scraping her chair. "Come on Paloma, let's go!" She took Paloma's arm, and they hurried from the bar.

Paloma was laughing so hard by the time they hit the street that Stephanie swung her around to face her. "What's so funny?!"

"You shocked my uncle Pacote! No one ever walked away from him like that! He is steaming mad!"

"He's trouble."

Paloma smiled. "Who cares? Let's go dancing."

She seemed to know where they were going, and pulled Stephanie along with her through the crowded streets of Madrid.

"Miguel cares," Stephanie finally said as they stopped waiting for a break in traffic to cross the street.

"He worries all the time about what his fans think. They come even before his stupid bulls, and everyone. Even you will come after."

"Where are we going?" Stephanie asked, trying to keep up.

"*Joy Eslava.* It's a dance club."

"Dancing isn't going to solve either of our problems."

"But it will make us feel better."

Ray and Francosis were found sitting at a table on the second tier of the dance club, sharing a bottle of wine, looking like chums. The music was loud, and down on the dance floor people crowded together and couples swayed to the music.

Francosis swept Stephanie up in his arms and insisted that she dance with him. He was making a scene by his presence; people were swarming around him. He chased them off and said he wanted to dance with Jenna Starr. Before Stephanie knew what was happening, Francosis led her out to the dance floor. He was a good dancer.

While Paloma and Francosis danced to the next song, Stephanie told Ray everything. He shared some new facts, too.

"Francosis didn't want to challenge Miguel. He's been forced to do it by Pacote. Apparently he's got something on Francosis—blackmail."

Stephanie shook her head in disgust. "What could he have on him?"

"I don't know, but the kid was forced into this *mano a mano* at *Las Ventas*. He's putting on a show of bravado for the fans, but he's worried and a little afraid. He claims Miguel *knows* that Pacote's blackmailed him."

"Surprise, surprise," she said, numb. "Everyone's involved! It's a conspiracy."

"Francosis also told me that he and Paloma are more than lovers. He wants to marry her. He's very upset about the rumors going around. If this announcement is made, it will just be another edge for Miguel. Francosis is more worried about losing his woman than this *corrida.*"

"Nobody knows better than Miguel what it's like

to face a bull when you've had your heart broken,"
Stephanie said. "Francosis could be in trouble."

Ray ran his finger around his beer bottle. "That's
right."

Stephanie watched Paloma sway in Francosis's
arms. They were close to the same age, and it was
obvious they were madly in love. These two young
people were reckless, dancing in a public place.
Could Miguel be so heartless—so cruel—as to allow
an announcement to be made just to put him in
favor of the fans and make his rival jealous?

It was too fantastic. If true, it would alter her perception of the man she thought she loved.

As they were leaving the nightclub, Stephanie
spotted Pacote sitting at the bar. He raised his glass
to her in mock salute. How long had he been there?

Long enough, Stephanie was certain.

TEN

In the days that followed, Ray interpreted the Francosis interview and Stephanie started to incorporate some of it into the exposé. Unlike Miguel, Francosis was from an upscale Madrid family, and both his parents were alive and well. He said the day that he decided to become a bullfighter his mother cried for one week. She wanted him to be an international banker like his father.

Stephanie spent time working on the story and on shopping, sightseeing, and sunbathing at the villa. She tried not to allow her emotions to surface, and to keep an unbiased reporter's opinion.

Why be a masochist? she asked herself again and again. No point in wearing a hair shirt about a relationship that wouldn't possibly survive after Sunday. Miguel would snap out of this infatuation for a woman from the States who had absolutely nothing in common with him and forget about his stupid fates and dreams, or whatever catalyst had driven him to get involved with her in the first place.

Serious relationships were not based on wild passions and two weeks in Spain, she reminded herself over and over again. Either Miguel lived in *la la land*, thinking he could really marry her, or he expected a miracle to take place.

Maybe *she* wanted the miracle, too.

Abracadabra. Poof! He's no longer Spain's greatest *matador.* He retires, and she gives up her career and learns to make *tapas* and pick olives. She converts to Catholicism, and smokes and drinks like a fish.

She stays pregnant and barefoot for the rest of her life, and lives in a quaint seaside villa filled with ten, dark-haired babies. Not one in the bunch looks like her. They call her *madre,* and wear long, satin white dresses when baptized in the *Catedral de San Isidro.*

Domingo is a godfather, and so is Galleo. They come to their house every night for dinner to talk about the good old days in the *corrida.*

Her firstborn tells her he wants to be a great matador, and she cries for one week. She becomes an alcoholic, and Miguel leaves her for a woman who can have lots of babies and keep her figure, like Lucia.

She couldn't find escape anywhere.

The newspapers were full of Miguel, and so were the local television stations. His picture was plastered all over Madrid—megastar in Spain, really huge—and the magnitude of his fame finally sank in for Stephanie.

A Spanish bullfighting magazine contacted her through Miguel's office, wanting her story, and then another one called. Stephanie had completely forgotten about Miguel's prediction that this exposé would sell for more money than she could ever make working for the *Express*. He'd been right; they were willing to shell out big bucks.

Ray read the newspaper accounts to Stephanie every day.

The entire nation awaited this bullfight with excitement and impatience. The cafés around Madrid overflowed with men making wagers. No one thought Miguel would really be gored. Everyone talked about his pact with the devil.

The name *El Peligro* fanned fantastic tales, and they were told over and over again in the cafés around the plaza.

No one had died in the ring in Spain since Juan Aguilar, and most didn't believe Miguel would change that record. Still, it added to the excitement.

The city of Madrid seemed proud to have *El Peligro* back in its beautiful *plaza de toros,* a real financial boon for the economy. People flowed into the city from all over Spain. Just as many foreigners arrived. Rock stars, movie stars, and a computer mogul had some of the best seats in the plaza. Jenna Starr was reported to be among them.

Stephanie learned the clubs around Madrid were on fire the week before this important *corrida.* Ray partied every night, and came back with reckless stories of wine and women.

She stayed at the villa, floating on a strange anticipation. Every day she waited to hear that Miguel and Paloma were engaged. Every night the sun went down, and nothing was reported. The newspapers were filled with other speculations, some of them very encouraging for Miguel. The polls showed that the crowds actually favored him. Time seemed to have healed some wounds surrounding the death of

Juan Aguilar, even though Pacote's articles tried to keep the hate alive.

Ray didn't think Miguel would now use a publicity stunt to face *Las Ventas,* and he didn't think Miguel would let his manager use one, either. Stephanie didn't know what to expect, but prepared herself for the worst.

Bottom line was that after Sunday she would return to California, and he would return to the plazas. They could hope to get together once in a while, but there wasn't even a red-eye flight to Madrid. And every time she saw him? Every time she said good-bye? Wait for it to be convenient for him to break the engagement, if it happened, hope he'd retire soon. Hope for something that resembled a normal life, because she couldn't move to Spain and follow him around from ring to ring? Live out of hotels, while he continued his *faenas* in the sun every Sunday and came home to her covered with—what kind of laundry detergent took out bull's blood?

Ladies and Gentlemen, this is your captain speaking. We have just passed the planet Mars. We will not be returning to earth. Sorry for the inconvenience, but now that we're beyond FAA regulations, feel free to smoke (crackle)— and send some booze up to the cockpit.

The full impact of Miguel's occupation had still not hit her, and she knew it wouldn't until Sunday. She'd watch him out on the hot sand wearing an antiquated costume, baiting an animal to its death, in which twenty-three thousand people participated. And the wake-up call would come.

Though she missed him desperately, she still refused his phone calls. If she heard his wonderful, sexy voice, she would topple. Why had she gone

down the sex road with him? She'd spend the rest
of her life comparing him to every man she met—
and they would never measure up.

There were times when she sat in a kind of stupor
up in the loft, staring at the poster, completely losing
herself in what had happened at the ranch, remembering the cape whirling over her naked body, the
lights flashing off his *taleguilla*, the many scents of
the night air cascading over her with each spin of
the cape.

Emotionally, Paloma wasn't faring any better than
Stephanie, and she spent most of her time at
Miguel's villa. Neither spoke of the possible engagement, but it weighed heavily on their minds. They
swam together, sunbathed, drank margaritas, and
started their own version of a Spanish *Ya Ya Club*.

Stephanie struggled with what she'd learned
about Paloma and Francosis and how this could further benefit Miguel in the ring— give him an emotional edge if he knew who her lover was, and he
probably did. He seemed to know everything, and
kept it all from Stephanie.

It was one thing to fulfill some destiny the fans
had hoped for since Juan's death, but entirely a different matter to emotionally cripple Francosis during this bullfight.

Ray's wise counsel at the airport continued to
haunt her. *"He will do anything to stay on top. Men like
Miguel have an agenda. . . ."*

He'd led her down a blind alley, yet had asked
her to promise not to listen to what was reported,
and to marry him. What was being reported that
she shouldn't listen to? Would fates take control of
the headlines, regardless of what he wanted? Fates
named Domingo and Pacote? Was it too late to stop

everything set into motion long before he'd made the trip to California?

The reporters had disappeared from the villa sidewalk. Apparently they knew Miguel was out at *La Libra,* and were probably keeping company with Renaldo and his friends at the gate.

This morning, after answering E-mail from her office, Stephanie uploaded some of the exposé to the editor of the *Variedades.* Ray had finally solved her Internet connection problem. E-mail flew back and forth between her and Adria, and Stephanie really enjoyed the communication. No baby yet—maybe next week. Plenty of time for Stephanie to come home and be with her during the birth.

Ray showed up late in the afternoon with the long awaited proofs. He fanned them all over the kitchen table and cracked a cold beer. Stephanie sorted through them: Her giving Ray the finger at the airport. Miguel smiling at the camera from the ticket counter at LAX. Paloma and Miguel dancing the flamenco. Stephanie holding up a beer to the camera, her eyes closed. The Spanish countryside, bulls grazing, and Miguel caping the calf. Miguel leaning against the oak tree, his arm slung around Stephanie, the pattern of the oak leaves shadowing their faces.

"These look great," she said wistfully.

"They aren't the only things I picked up." He dropped a Spanish newspaper on the table, and the *plop* blew a few of the proofs to the floor. The one of Miguel and the cow was wedged in her tennis shoe.

She couldn't read Spanish, but she didn't need to read what was obvious under the picture of Miguel and Paloma. Pushing the paper out of her way, she continued to regard the proofs, but her heart now throbbed with a mixture of hurt and anger. It swept over her, making her palms sweat and her eyes heat up as yet another emotion peaked: defeat.

"Stephanie?" Ray touched her shoulder.

"Excuse me." She ran up the stairs, but instead of going to her room she went to the one that smelled of incense and went down on her knees. She put her hands together and prayed to the little statue.

Dear God, don't let him marry her. He's not going to marry her! This is just a publicity stunt. He's mine. He's mine. And somehow I'm going to forgive him for hurting so many people for his own gain.

She put her hands over her face and cried, assailed by reality: They could never be a couple.

Paloma called her in the early evening.

"Did you hear?" she asked. Her throat sounded thick—perhaps from her own tears?

"Yes, I'm so sorry for you." *And for me.*

"Please talk to Francosis. He is going to kill someone. Make him believe this is just a publicity stunt."

"I can't—"

"Meet him at *Galerias Preciados*. He is waiting!" She hung up the phone.

Stephanie stared at the receiver for a few moments, then let it drop in the cradle. Ray still sat at the kitchen table studying the proofs, drinking a beer, when she told him about Paloma's frantic call

"I'd think twice about meeting Francosis in public again. Especially alone, and especially around the plaza."

"I'm not a prisoner. Besides I haven't seen any reporters in a few days. I need to get out."

"I'll go with you, keep the wolves at bay."

"No, thanks. I can handle him."

Ray shrugged. "Be careful. People are still saying Jenna Starr is residing at Miguel's villa, and for some reason, that's who they think you are."

"Well, I wouldn't want to disappoint them—Jenna Starr, I'll be!"

Ray shook his head, obvious concern on his face.

Time to play movie star, she thought as she closed her bedroom door and fished out one of her new dresses. Black, slinky, short, slit up the side. Nice hat. When in Spain, do as the Spanish do. Lots and lots of makeup. New stiletto heels. Velvet bag.

She'd get Francosis to take her dancing. Do the town!

Olé!

She called a cab and left the villa unnoticed. She met Francosis at the shopping mall as instructed, and they went over to *Boccacio* for dinner. The tight crowd recognized the young *matador,* and everyone seemed curious about Stephanie. Fans often came to their table and snapped his picture. He ordered a bottle of white wine and some *tapas* and tried to communicate with her in between interruptions.

"*Señorita,* por favor, mi English no good. But, ¿*Ayudarme?*"

He was asking her to help him. This she could understand.

"*Es importante.*" He released a long breath that sounded like exasperation.

"I can't help you," she said, trying to make him understand, the same way she'd tried to make Paloma understand the *fates* were in motion. She thought these people should understand this fate stuff better than she should—they lived the *corrida*. She couldn't get into the middle of this, and further jeopardize her relationship with Miguel.

"Tell me, señorita, Miguel love you? Eh? No Paloma. No marriage?"

"I—I don't know." And she really didn't. At the moment her future was unclear with Miguel, and she couldn't give this young man any hope that might not exist, or the probable reality: he would have to wait a few years for his precious Paloma. Besides, saying too much would label her a traitor to the *El Peligro* camp.

"I wish I could help. But right now, I'm just as much in the dark about this engagement as you." That was as much as she could say.

They ate in relative silence, and afterward, he took her arm as they strolled along *Calle de los Cuchilleros*, one of Madrid's oldest streets, lined with flamenco restaurants, *tapas* bars and *bodegas*. Many stopped him on the cobblestone walk, wanting to talk about Sunday, giving pats on the back, whistles, and olés!

They went into a flamenco club, and he ordered more wine. Together they sat and listened to the raw power of flamenco being performed without amplification, by a genuine flamenco guitar. Their wine disappeared, and another bottle came from somewhere, paid for by an *aficionado*.

Someone came over to their table and took Francosis's hand, and Stephanie's. The next thing she knew, she was getting a lesson in flamenco dancing! It was spontaneous and fun, the most she'd had since learning to cape the little calf. Francosis was a wonderful dancer, and patient with her as she learned the intricate steps, sliding her in front of him and behind, effortlessly spinning around her as if she were one of the bulls he'd face on Sunday. Cheers undulated through the crowd after each dance number.

She clicked her heels on the hardwood floor, accepted a rose he handed her from a nearby vase, clamped it between her teeth. More laughter, and applause.

Stephanie could not understand the whispering around the tables in Spanish.

"Who is the American?"

"She is Jenna Starr."

"She doesn't look like Jenna Starr."

"Movie stars are always changing the way they look."

"I heard she was staying at El Peligro's *villa."*

"No. He kicked her out. She is a slut. She posed for reporters in the nude. He had enough of her."

"She is a pretty slut, eh?"

"Yes. Francosis is a lucky man tonight."

The music slowed, and a romantic guitar number began. Both of them were a little breathless, but Francosis shrugged and gathered her into his arms. She drifted with him, rested her head on his strong, young shoulder. He smelled good—different than Miguel.

The music stopped, and she found her head tilting up . . . a kiss. Warm. Different.

A camera flash.

She opened her eyes. Another flash and yet another flash, then rapid-fire flashes blinding her.

"Take me back to the villa!" she cried, unable to decipher who took all the pictures. From the way they were executed, she suspected the press. "Hurry."

Francosis drove her back to the villa. Reporters

suddenly crowded around the limo, snapping more photos. Stephanie was mortified. Where had they come from? She'd thought they would still be out at *Las Ventas*.

Then she knew why they were there.

Miguel must be back!

Stephanie's fingers shook as she worked the key and entered the villa. Standing in the darkened foyer, with her hat in her hand, she caught her reflection in the mirror: Hair mussed from the hat, lipstick smeared, her cheeks flushed bright red. She turned in a half-circle and saw Miguel.

He stood at the bar looking at her, gorgeous in a pair of blue jeans and a dark indigo turtleneck. Even from that distance she could see the strong stamp of hurt and pride on his face. The reality of her crime clarified itself in that foyer. She'd been out with his challenger—and not for the business of writing an exposé, not even to help Paloma with her plight, but to assuage her own wounded ego. She had gone out drinking and dancing with Francosis, and let him kiss her.

Pictures had been taken.

Domingo and Galleo sat conspicuously on the sofa. Theresa was with them, and Paloma, who would not make eye contact with her. No doubt she too, felt betrayed.

Stephanie felt sick. An awful pressure radiated around her heart. Turning, she ran up the stairs, her hand sliding against the cool railing. One of her stiletto heels flipped off, but she didn't stop to retrieve it. The door slammed much harder than she meant it to. Once in her room, she started to throw things into her suitcase.

Miguel was soon at her door. "Open the door."

"Go away, Miguel," she said, struggling to hold back a wave of confusing emotions. She wondered if Paloma had told Miguel whose idea it had been for her to meet Francosis tonight, a night that had spun completely out of control. Flamenco dancing! Wine! Kissing! God only knew who took those pictures. They were too fast and furious to be shot by fans.

Ladies and Gents: It's yer (hiccup) captain. That would be Saturn we're passing now. . . .

"Open this door, *Señorita* Stephanie, or I am going to break it down."

Señorita Stephanie? She unlocked it and went to her closet for more suitcases. Flung them onto the bed, opened them. Broke a fingernail.

Miguel stood in the middle of her room, seeming to watch all the activity. "What are you doing?"

"Leaving."

"I did *nooo* ask you to leave."

Accent on the Spanish—oh, he was mad!

She spun around and saw that he held her other shoe.

"I'll save you the hassle."

"I *donn* want you to leave. I only want to understand *why* you can't follow my wishes."

"I'm not Renaldo, waiting around for a benediction." She hobbled over to her closet and scooped out a handful of dresses and began cramming them into the suitcase.

"You *donn* understand the problems you have caused for me tonight."

"I won't be a problem anymore. *¿Comprende?* Ask Paloma why I was out with Francosis."

He set her shoe down on the bed, fished out a cigarette, and walked over to the window. The smoke escaped through the open window. For a long time he stood smoking and looking down into the street. Did the reporters see him standing there?

"I know why," he finally said. "Did you tell him I would not marry Paloma—that the announcement was only to make him crazy with jealousy, and for *El Peligro* to win over the crowd?"

Stephanie tossed the shoe into the trunk, hopped around a few times reaching for the match, and threw it in with the other shoe. "No. I didn't tell him what a heartless bastard you are."

He took another drag of his cigarette, leaned against the wall, and looked agitated.

Stephanie refolded a sweater and smashed it back into the trunk. "Everyone is caught in this web of yours, Miguel."

She turned back to her packing, because she couldn't face him with what she needed to say. "You publicly announce that you're going to marry a woman that you have no intention of marrying so you'll make your *stupid* fans happy while they watch you sadistically torture *stupid* animals—and sadistically torture that young *matador* who's desperately in love with Paloma! You have *stupid* dreams you believe in, and then manipulate everyone in your path to make sure they don't come true!"

She threw one of her new scarves on the bed, and spun around to face him, unable to stop herself. "Bullfighting is outmoded—like cockfights, or something! And I personally can't take the dishonesty that goes with it—the deceit."

The color ran out of his face. He sat down on the edge of the bed, ran his hands across his face. "I didn't make the announcement about Paloma. I tried to tell you, but you wouldn't take my calls."

"W—what?" She walked over to him, looked down at his dark head. "Domingo?"

"No, not even Domingo. Even he could see it was not going to be necessary. Some miracle put me the favorite for Sunday."

Abracadabra. Poof!

"Who, then?" She suddenly knew. *"Pacote."*

"Sí. I came back to Madrid to give a press conference tomorrow morning and clear this up." He stood up and walked to the door, opened it, stopped, and turned back to Stephanie. "But what do I find? The woman I love pulling up in a limo with my challenger—in full view of reporters." His gaze accusingly swept over her. "And look at you. Your dress is wrinkled, your lips swollen—from what? His kisses?"

She shook her head no.

"Now I can't give a conference, because I do not know what you have cooked up with Francosis. Now, I must wait and see."

She sat on the edge of the bed, felt upside down.

He looked at the stub of his cigarette, then back at Stephanie. *"Señorita,* I am sorry you think that I am not a man and must use others to feel big—that my bulls are stupid, that perhaps even I am stupid. *El Peligo* is who I am. I cannot be anyone but this man you are looking at. I am sorry he is not enough for you."

He closed the door quietly.

She took a deep breath.

Shit. Shit. Shit.

ELEVEN

She had to go to him.

She'd gone too far and stepped on Miguel's masculine pride, and she didn't even know why she'd said such awful things. Oh, why hadn't she taken his phone calls? Why hadn't she kept her promise to not believe what was reported? Why hadn't she proceeded with caution, and never agreed to meet with Francosis?

She knew she could be stubborn at times. Still, it was impossible for her to understand the intricate complexities of a Spanish bullfighting idol while trying to understand her own wounded emotions.

Miguel didn't deserve the things she'd said to him, and she somehow had to make him understand that it had been her confusion and hurt and not her heart talking. She couldn't help thinking that Sunday would be the end of everything they'd shared. Once he regained his confidence at *Las Ventas* and Juan Aguilar's ghost was properly ushered back into the astral world, Miguel would continue with his career, and forget about her.

But Sunday would take care of Sunday, she thought with new resolve. She had to do something *now*—go to *El Peligro*.

He was probably downstairs with Domingo, getting an earful of scandalous stories about Stephanie Madison. For all she knew, Pacote could have already called tonight. Surely, he had been lurking at that flamenco club. He seemed to be everywhere at once, like an evil, omnipresent spirit.

Her clothes and suitcases were strewn everywhere, from her few moments of wounded fury. A fine layer of blue smoke still hung in faint wisps in the room. Just a few weeks ago she'd hated the smell of cigarettes, wouldn't have considered dating a man with a big attitude. And drinking? Not like a fish, and certainly not hard liquor. What a difference Miguel had made in her life! But it wasn't all bad—no, he'd made her feel more alive, more like a woman, than she'd ever felt in her entire life. She wasn't going to walk away from that feeling.

She had to tell him everything that had happened tonight. The dinner and a little dancing hardly constituted a big deal. Okay, the kiss wasn't such a good thing . . . but it could be explained.

What about the pictures? Sure as shit they'd end up in the paper. Everything Miguel and Francosis did right now ended up in the newspaper.

Stephanie thought about that for a moment. Why wasn't anything reported about Paloma and Francosis? Pacote had witnessed the two of them together firsthand. Maybe that was his ace, but how would he use it?

She stood up and went to the mirror, ran her hand down her flat belly, and looked at herself for a long time and thought of babies that wouldn't look like her.

Even one? Maybe conceived tonight?

Something to take back—a part of Miguel that would be hers forever?

Ladies and Gentlemen: There is no pilot. There is no one flying this plane.

Newspapers and magazines now littered the conversation table where she kept her laptop running. She picked one up and looked at Miguel standing in the middle of a bullring, a massive black animal sliding by. *Nothing is more dangerous than a Spaniard with an injured pride.* She wouldn't let him face *Las Ventas* with worries about her. After Sunday, it wouldn't matter, but it mattered now.

Was he downstairs with Domingo? She couldn't go down there and face all that hostility, but she had to find Miguel before she lost her nerve, before he found out what she'd done with Francosis.

It was just a stupid kiss . . . because I was thinking of you. Something warned her a simple kiss wasn't so simple when it was planted on his rival.

She slipped out of her room, made her way partly down the stairs, and crouched down to see into the living area of the villa. All was quiet and the lights were out. Had everyone left? No one was in the loft, either, or the kitchen, or out by the pool. She went back upstairs, quietly opened the room where the statue resided. No one was there, but the candles burned and the room felt warm and thick with incense, recently occupied—Miguel's prayer book was open.

She knocked lightly on Miguel's bedroom door. No answer. She tried the knob. One light burned next to the bed, and she could hear the water rushing in his personal spa. The clothing he'd worn earlier was now neatly placed on the end of the bed. The room seemed devoid of personal things—unlike the ranch, which spoke of Miguel and his occupation. Here was a neat room like a retreat. A single bullfighting painting hung above one dresser. It seemed out of place. She remembered him saying he had a villa in Menorca. Would she ever see that home?

Something propelled her to walk over to his closet and open it. Not too many things, but a few expensive suits, a leather jacket—no *corrida* clothing. The smell of him drifted out, and it seemed her undoing. Her legs trembled. Would she ever smell this again? It was so unique. She saw no evidence of colognes anywhere.

She reached over and took one of the shirts and held it to her nose. Olives. Wine. Spain. *Him.*

Turning, she leaned against the closet door. Everything with Miguel was fantasy. She closed her eyes and smiled, wondered if she should take off her clothes and slide into his bed and wait for him.

No.

Tonight she would re-create *Las Ventas,* somehow, cement him to her heart in a fantasy of her own. Fix things. Make amends. Make him *do* her—give her a baby.

She hurried back through the hall, down the stairs, and into the kitchen, and found a bottle of wine and two glasses. Headed back up the stairs, she made a detour and grabbed the two burning votive candles from the altar, then walked through his bedroom and paused long enough to take a deep breath before opening the bathroom door.

He was sitting in the spa, just like the other time—only now his eyes were open, and they were on her.

"One of these days you're going to walk in and

find me in a compromising position," he said in a flat, almost irritated voice.

"Lock the door next time," she said, trying to sound light. Maybe she'd overstepped her bounds here, she thought, suddenly not so sure he'd be easily seduced—because of what had happened tonight. She turned away and set the candles on the counter, then reached for the light switch, casting them in misty steam and flickering shadows.

"You took those from my mother's patron saint." Same flat voice. "That is very bad luck."

"For me, not you."

Stephanie turned around, took a deep breath of the eucalyptus he used in the spa to soothe his muscles. Did his leg bother him? She would remember him every time it rained and the eucalyptus trees around her house released their scent.

She touched her belly, held his eyes.

Miguel sat on the second step of the Jacuzzi, a little on one side, with his better leg propped up on the countertop. The way the shadows hit him, the way his body glistened in the candle's glow, the way his muscles were delineated and sculpted, he looked like a model posed by some fussy photographer.

His hair was wet, just washed, and slicked straight back. Sweat beaded on his cheekbones, and he looked slightly feverish.

She suddenly had qualms about this impulsive idea of hers. He didn't seem too happy to see her intruding on his bath again. His breathing, though, betrayed his calm expression—a fast rise and fall of his chest.

"Does your leg hurt?"

"No."

"Wine?" She could have sworn the rushing sound

in the room wasn't the water he sat in, but the blood coursing through her veins.

Popping the cork, she poured him a glass of the Bordeaux and set it next to him, then poured herself one. When she sat on the counter, she realized too late that she'd sat in a puddle of water. It seeped through her dress and underwear.

"I'm sorry I met with Francosis, and sorry I said the things I did."

He just watched her, and she watched his rapid breathing.

She stood up, turned and showed him her wet fanny, slipped off her dress, let it coast to the floor. Her bra slithered off, and with nothing on but her panties she turned back to him and said: "I heard that women throw you underpants into the bullring."

He rubbed his nose and smiled a guilty smile, and she knew she had him—He couldn't stay mad at her tonight.

She slipped hers off, now, and threw them into the spa. His gaze followed their flight, and then vaulted back up to her face. His erection poked unceremoniously out of the foaming water, but he didn't seem worried about its arrival. Miguel had never displayed any shame or hesitation about his body, or hers.

"Since I met you my life has been turned upside down," she said truthfully. "Our lives are very different. I'm trying to understand yours, and how I fit into it, and look at the mess I've made of things." She took a sip of her wine and thought she sounded very brave and very intellectual standing completely naked before a man with a whopping erection. "We don't know anything about each other in just two short weeks."

Swinging her legs into the water, she was submerged to the first step. It was too hot, and felt her skin flush.

He reached for his own wineglass, took a long drink, and pulled the glass back, revealing wet lips.

"I know everything about you," he said thickly. He sat up a little, reached over and took her foot, drew it over, and rested it in his lap.

He held her gaze as he moved it back and forth across his erection. "I know you as well as I know the one-bedroom house I grew up in Barcelona. I know you as well as I know the smells of the plazas. I know you as well as I know myself."

This erotic game he played with her foot filled her with solid, pure, dizzy desire.

She wet her lips, used her own volition to eddy around the hard shaft in his lap. Water, foam, eucalyptus, the candle's glow, dark green eyes, were all she could comprehend. Then his foot moved—ever so slightly at first. Then it edged its way between her legs and a new sensation started there.

"We have all our lives to know each other." He drank a little more of his wine and smiled at her as his big toe found her bud and applied gentle pressure. He lifted her foot up and slipped her big toe into his mouth. She'd heard about this kind of thing. If it hadn't felt so erotic, she would have started to laugh.

All our lives. "Mamá, mamá, *I want to grow up to be a* matador de toros, *like my* padre!"

He lowered her foot back into the water, and his hips moved slightly as she slipped it up the length of him again.

"You spend too much time trying to understand things that will never be understood," he said, pausing long enough to take a very deep breath, as if some pleasure rocked through him and knocked it out of him. "Yes, we are different, as different as the stars and moon, but we both exist in the same cosmos. Without you I cannot exist at all."

Why does he say these things? I would melt over him even without these words. Promises he can't keep.

Her eyes closed, and her legs opened wider as the flat of his foot pressed against her womanhood, the pleasure fanning out over her entire body, intoxicating her with bliss.

"Touch yourself," he whispered.

Her eyes opened. "What?"

"Touch your nipples."

He was entirely serious. Stephanie Madison didn't do these kinds of things . . . did she?

Her hands glided across her wet shoulders and down to her breasts. Never taking her eyes off his, she was filled with a wantonness no man had ever brought out in her. There was a slight smile at the corner of his lips. *He controls me. It's about power . . . use your own . . . control him.*

She moved off her step and over to him, straddled his midsection, felt his hardness against her core as she sat down on his lap. "You touch them."

Filling his mouth with wine, he pulled her up until one nipple grazed his lips. A drip of wine slipped down to his chin before he took her nipple into his mouth. The bloodred wine cascaded down her belly, and bled into the water. He licked her breast clean, then reached for the bottle, tipped it across her shoulders and let it run in rivulets down her breasts and belly, changing the water to a rose color.

She came up on her knees, arched against him. His hands cupped her bottom, held her. Fingers splayed through his wet hair, then her mouth and nose rubbed against the coarse strands, inhaling apricot shampoo, wine, eucalyptus, soap—him. She cupped his chin, felt a slight stubble, and lifted his face up so that their eyes met. He leaned forward and pressed his lips against hers, then ran his tongue across the sensitive inner flesh. Her mouth parted and tongues met in a wine-sweetness.

Everything she had ever understood about herself vanished in that moment. She never left the house on a cloudy day without an umbrella, never forgot to pack her lunch the night before, always let the person with the least in the grocery store line go first. She always had her car washed on Sunday, and would never, ever, think of having unprotected sex with a man she'd known less than a week. Now a reckless, wild, uncontrollable woman took over, someone unwilling, or unable, to stop.

Positioning herself over his swollen manhood, her knees locked, prevented the connection. *Stop. Look. And listen. You are crossing a street without a crosswalk attendant. There is no rubber stop sign.*

His eyes opened, and the color again reminded her of olives—shining—promising intoxication.

"Lo quiero. Sí, te quiero," he whispered, barely audible over the roar of the water jets. He closed his eyes when her knees gave way and he filled her completely, and she heard his breath tremble out of him.

The jets shut off and the water cleared, now a blush color. He was huge inside her, burning unseen there. Looking down to where they were joined together, she saw her hands explore him, run along his shoulder. Licking his skin across the nasty gash on his shoulder, she thought he tasted like warm soap and skin. Her hands touched his gold cross, grazed his nipples, and moved down his stomach to the black hair below his navel, became tangled there a moment. When she met his gaze again she saw a brief hesitation, as if he, too, wondered about dark-haired babies.

She smiled at him and pressed her lips to his mouth, forced her tongue inside to touch his, to slide around, taste wine, inner flesh. As he hungrily explored her mouth, his blissful assault left her breathless. Moving from her mouth, he licked and sucked his way down her chest, biting one nipple to the point of pain. Crying out, she dug her nails into his shoulders.

Suddenly, propelled out of the water, he sat her up on the counter. Water poured off them like a wave, onto the floor. She clung to him with a wet, dangerous clasp, unwilling to break the exquisite pleasure. They stayed joined, but he broke out of her clinging arms and pushed her down over the large, wet, blue tile counter, made her lie on her back and look up at him.

He stood thigh high in the water as her legs stayed wrapped around him. Lifting one, he drew it up the length of him and kissed the inside of her knee. At the same time he started to move slowly in and out of her.

How beautiful he looked, all wet and shining, his muscles straining under his skin, his head lowered a little as he watched this sensuous joining. His hooded eyes were filled with desire and fascination as he watched himself, surrounded by black hair, plunge into softness and blond curls.

I am a visual man. . . .

With each new thrust an enormous girdle of fire burned hotter and deeper in her belly. Hands played across her belly, and his gold bracelet sparkled wet under the candles. His fingers gently and expertly caressed the hair at her apex, teasing the swollen prize.

She closed her eyes.

"Look at me," he said in a ragged breath.

She obeyed, watched him push into her, over and over, keeping her balanced on that wet precipice. The rhythm of their passion seemed born for no other beings. Then it came for her—spreading outward like shafts of electricity, vibrating in scintillating spasms throughout her body.

"Miguel—oh . . . Miguel—"

His fingers dug deep into her legs, and he stopped suddenly, closed his eyes, and took a solid breath. His belly jerked a little as he came to his own edge of ecstasy and went over, crying out—*"Ahhhhh—"* when the hot fluid shot into her body.

Neither moved. His head hung down, wisps of black hair dripping with water, and she could hear him breathing, see his chest moving. His eyes were now closed, his fingers still clenched a little too tightly on her legs. Her breathing remained rapid, the pleasures still present. One of the candles sputtered and went out. The sound of water dripped around them.

I love you. . . .

Then he took her hands and pulled her against him, switched on the jets, and sank them both down into the soothing hot foam.

* * *

Miguel listened to her even breathing as she slept in his arms. He memorized the shape of her body, branded it into his mind, because he knew she would leave him forever after Sunday. This bullfight, no matter how bravely or wonderfully he performed, would send her packing.

How would he live without her? There was only one way to guarantee he wouldn't lose her, but that was not an option for him at the moment.

Domingo had pounded that fact into his head all the way from *La Libra*.

"Don't even think about announcing an engagement to the American publicly! Pacote did you a favor!" Domingo was livid, anyway, about Miguel leaving the farm a day early and returning to Madrid.

"I do not need Paloma to sway the crowd, or cripple Francosis. The fates have already changed, and favorably for *El Peligro*. I am not having the same dream."

"That is good, very good." Even Domingo knew the significance of dreams. "But you must still keep your head, *Matador*. Do nothing until after Sunday. You must come and see the bulls tomorrow. They are here now for your inspection. Forget women until after Sunday. It is time for you to be *El Peligro*."

"I want to call a press conference and denounce this engagement at once."

"What difference does it make if you wait until after Sunday?"

"It will make a difference to me."

"You're going to give up your career for an American woman you've known less than two weeks? Miguel, you've gone *loco!*"

"I won't lose her!"

"If she loves you the way you think she does, she will wait."

"I'm going to retire after Sunday." He couldn't believe he'd blurted this to Domingo, who pulled his cigar out of his mouth and stared at Miguel as if he'd changed into a bull.

"Retire? What about me? Where do I go while you enjoy your millions?"

Miguel glanced doubtfully at his manager. "You have a few million saved yourself—you can find a new man. I will retire. It's time."

Domingo had not been discouraged. "Ha! Not for a few more years, at least! You're like a son to me, so I say this as a father—Stephanie is not the woman to retire for! She's American! She's got different ideas than Spanish women. *She thinks she's an equal!* She's probably a Protestant! What do you think is going to happen when you're together all the time? You'll come to resent her for taking you from the bulls, and she'll resent you from taking her away from MTV. And do you think she's going to live happily ever after on a bull farm? Shell use birth control and prevent you an heir. Paloma was raised with the bulls, and she will have many babies. Cut Stephanie loose, and send her packing."

"I'm in love with her."

"Love? *Blah!* Love has never been good for you!"

"She just doesn't understand our ways yet. She will."

"Never! I got a call from Pacote before we left the ranch. She is out even now with Francosis—drinking—*more*. It does not sound as if she loves you."

"You lie! You will say anything to make me send her packing."

Miguel called the villa, but there was no answer. Domingo had said nothing, but relit his cigar and shook his head.

"Tomorrow night you are going to be honored. Galleo has worked hard to put this party together at *Sangria's*. I think it wise if you do not bring the American."

Now, Miguel stroked Stephanie's hair and she cuddled deeper into his side.

Everyone was going to be there. His entire retinue, judges, reporters, friends and family. Jenna Starr. Paloma. He closed his eyes, heavy with sorrows.

She never told Miguel what had happened at the flamenco club, even though she had plenty of time in the morning. They'd made love again, shared orange juice and doughnuts.

During one of their afterglow moments, while she lay in the crook of his strong arm, he said, *"Querida*, you must believe me when I say that I do not like to actually kill the bull."

Because she was so happy, and he seemed so happy, she didn't want to break the spell with the hurts and misunderstandings of last night. She looked up into his green irises. "You don't have to explain—"

"No. Listen. My style is that of a flamenco dancer. I want to dazzle the crowd with my feet and my cape. I have never enjoyed killing the bull. It is well-known that I am not a happy butcher of bulls. I hit my mark—my bulls never suffer."

Stephanie hadn't considered that a *matador* might not embrace the slaughter. "Do all *matadors* feel this way?"

He shook his head, no. "There are many who are lead-footed but handle the sword like marksmen, and enjoy the kill."

For a moment, she just listened to the rhythm of his heart.

"I promise, *querida*, that the bulls I kill on Sunday will die quick, and by my sword, not by the *puntillero*."

"What's that?" She lifted up off of him and sat up.

"Not what, but *who*. He is the man who finishes the bull off—just in case the *matador* doesn't do his job. Do not watch this. Turn away."

Turn away.

"I cannot be with you tomorrow," he said, touching her hair, her chin, tilting her face toward his.

"Why?" Did he have to practice?

"I will most likely be sick."

"Why?

"The day before a fight I always throw up, and have terrible stomach pains, and sweat like a pig. I'd rather you did not see me like this."

He was completely serious.

Stephanie instinctively knew that today would be the turning point in their relationship. Tomorrow would be Saturday, and as the clock took away their precious moments and the hour grew closer when Miguel had to walk onto the sands of *Las Ventas*, he would change. He'd just admitted it.

He would shut her out.

He'd said good-bye that morning and kissed her long and hard, maybe a little desperately. Then he walked toward the door and paused in the archway for a little longer than seemed right, yet he didn't turn around. His back had been to her, and he gave a little, violent shake of his shoulders and head, as if a chill had run down his spine.

A little later, Stephanie found Ray in the living room area of the villa. He wore shorts, a tank top, and a bandanna wrapped around his head.

"It's going to top a hundred degrees tomorrow," Ray said casually. "What a scorcher for a bullfight. Unusual for this time of year."

She told Ray what had happened with Francosis the night before, but he claimed he'd read nothing about it in the paper.

"I wouldn't tell Miguel any more than you have to. I personally checked every hotel in town and verified that there are no rooms. He's likely to throw us out into the streets if you step on his pride again."

"I don't know who took those picture last night," Stephanie said while Ray packed up his camera equipment into a little duffel he carried around. He was meeting Miguel and Domingo at the plaza to take pictures of Miguel's bulls.

"Hope they don't show up somewhere. Miguel's got a pretty big ego, and I think we'll be out in the street if he sees you in the arms of Francosis. From what Domingo told me this morning, Miguel was really pissed off last night."

"I was going to leave. I was packing. He told me not to go."

"And then what? You bang him until the sun comes up? Stephanie, I hope you know what you're doing. I've tried to keep my mouth shut . . . never mind."

"I should have let you come last night. I shouldn't have drunk so much. Ever since I've been here, I've turned into a lush, into someone I can't recognize." *I had unprotected sex.* Stephanie sat down and took a sip from Ray's beer.

"When in Spain—"

"What do you know about a *matador's* style?" She picked up a pile of proofs and looked at a picture of Renaldo, reminding herself to do the research on the kids who follow *matadors* around. "Miguel said he doesn't like to kill the bull."

"That's what I've heard—read it, too. He's what you call a dancer in the ring. He dazzles the crowd with his style, not his sword. Why?"

Stephanie just shrugged.

"Easier to handle thinking he doesn't enjoy the bloodletting?"

"A little."

Ray shrugged and wiped off one of his filters. "Are you coming tonight?"

Stephanie was confused. "Where?"

Ray zipped up his bag. "Miguel said we're going to a private party for him."

"Oh, the party." Why hadn't Miguel told her about it?

"Everyone's going to be there—at least everyone in Miguel's camp. But this place won't heat up until after midnight, so I don't think we'll leave before then."

"Midnight?" She picked up a newspaper and pretended she could read the language.

Ray stood up and slung his bag over his shoulder. "He didn't tell you, did he?"

"Sure. I knew about it." *Why hadn't he said anything?* "I'm going to finish up the story, or at least as much as I can before Sunday, take a swim, a nap. Have fun with the bulls today."

Ray stood for a long time looking at her, then turned and walked away.

Miguel came back to the villa very late. She was reading up in the loft, and he found her there. He didn't come over to her and gather her into his arms, didn't smile at her or seem like her lover at all.

This wasn't Miguel. This was *El Peligro*.

She didn't know how she knew that, but she did, and she suddenly realized that when he'd gone to see his bulls the transformation had taken place. Whoever she'd spent the past two weeks with was gone.

"We're going out," he said directly. "Dress up."

Madrid was welcoming home their prodigal son.

Hold on. Hold on. No pilot. Life vests. Christ, this plane is going down.

TWELVE

In the limo on the way to the club, Miguel said very little to anyone. He asked Stephanie how her day had gone, and if she were finished with her story up until Sunday. Galleo then took over the conversation—in Spanish, cutting her out. Stephanie had been squeezed between Domingo and Miguel's unaccommodating brother. Ray sat next to Miguel, and enjoyed a lot of extra space.

Everything seemed odd and out of focus.

She tried to think like a reporter, to be ready to take notes and make observations, and prayed her emotions wouldn't come into play.

Her red silk, strapless dress showed off her new tan, and her matching shoes added a few inches to her height. In the limo window reflection, she could see her hair twisted up in a bun and her makeup applied precisely. She'd wanted to look beautiful for Miguel tonight, but he hardly seemed to notice.

A great ruckus was made when they entered the club—a beautiful place called *Torero*. Everyone greeted Miguel—the chef, the waiters, even the parking lot attendants. His entire retinue had already arrived, along with family, friends, and employees who worked in his offices. Press, both newspapers and TV, were well represented. The live coverage was limited to Miguel's entrance. Domingo would not allow the TV reporters into the club.

Finally they were installed at a table where oceans of Dom Perignon champagne began to flow, along with beluga caviar.

Everyone talked about Sunday, about bullfighting, mostly in Spanish. Stephanie felt left out and sorry for herself; this wasn't how she imagined a night out with Miguel. People swarmed around him, crowding her out, including some very high-profile Americans.

Miguel signed autographs amid a throng and permitted his picture to be taken, while Stephanie drank her champagne and watched the pandemonium. He now stood by the table with a group of people, laughing, talking, and carrying on as if he could do it all night. He shifted his weight in a restless manner, and straightened up with a proud shake of his shoulders. This was *El Peligro*, she thought, the famous *matador*.

She didn't think she could stand another moment of the pulse-pounding music, or the turbulent strobe lights flashing around the room like raging comets. Miguel started to sit down, but clinging hands grabbed his and hauled him back up. A vividly beautiful woman—*Jenna Starr*—pulled him into her trap.

Jenna Starr!

The cameras flashed as she put her arms around him in a possessive way. His hands dropped to her bottom and remained there, and he talked into her ear as if he'd done more with her in the past. Stephanie felt herself literally lift out of the chair as raw, primal instincts took over. She was going to claw the woman's eyes out.

Then she saw Paloma.

The betrothed had arrived, and the throng now swarmed around her. She looked like a goddess in the dress Miguel had brought her from California. His attention slid off Jenna and locked on Paloma. A muscle worked in his jaw as he separated himself from Jenna.

Paloma walked slowly toward him, her hips swaying, thrusting her half-exposed breasts out, nodding at a few people as she made her way through the enthralled crowd. With a visible sigh she threw herself into Miguel's arms and parked a long, wet kiss on his mouth. Then she turned with purpose and looked straight at Stephanie with pure, unadulterated hate.

She'd found out what happened last night! Stephanie was mortified, and her stomach turned. She'd never meant to hurt Paloma. Who had told her? Francosis? Pacote? Stephanie's head swam, trying to keep up with the very active *torero* counterintelligence underground.

Paloma wrapped her arms around Miguel's neck and purred in her Spanish language, obviously trying to hurt Stephanie, and it was working. Before Paloma had arrived, Stephanie hadn't thought it possible to feel any worse.

The photogs went crazy memorializing the couple. Flash after flash burst—many from Ray's camera. *Traitor.*

Television cameras somehow crashed through the barriers, and while Galleo and a slew of Miguel's linemen pushed them back, Stephanie herself was shoved to the back of the table to make room for Paloma.

Miguel never looked at Stephanie. Some kind of

eye contact would have saved her so much humiliation and pain, but it never came. This was a public place, and his betrothed sat at his side. She was the woman Spain wanted there. He wouldn't show Stephanie any attention, even though on the farm he'd promised he would dedicate the first bull to her. Now the rules had been changed—again. He wouldn't publicly acknowledge her, and she struggled with the worse kind of misery she'd ever experienced.

I am going to be just like my mother. I'm going to let a man destroy me.

A guitarist struck a few dramatic chords, and Paloma pulled Miguel onto the dance floor. They danced the flamenco in beautiful sync to the bawdy cheers of the crowd. *Miguel is a dancer,* Stephanie thought, watching his velvet feet as he moved Paloma across the dance floor, up against him, around him, dropping her low for a light kiss.

Louder cheers brought Stephanie's attention to the club door.

Francosis had walked in with a retinue of men. The crowd parted from the door all the way to the dance floor, like in a biblical scene. The music came to an awkward finish.

Miguel, laughing, spun around, but the smile instantly vanished. Paloma gave a little cry, and put her hand to her mouth.

Francosis's eyes were narrowed, his fists clenched at his sides, when he took a step toward Miguel.

Later, Stephanie would not remember how it happened, but suddenly she had Francosis's arm. "Come!" She tried to pull him away, but the man was solid rock. *"Es urgente!"* she said in Spanish.

This was the one thing she could do for Miguel—

prevent a disastrous scene on the near-eve of *Las Ventas*. He could thank her later. But when Stephanie made eye contact with Miguel she knew there would never be thanks—pain and humiliation burned in his eyes. Domingo and Galleo, who grabbed hold of his arms and held him in check, halted his sharp step toward her.

Cameras snapped and flashes blinded everyone.

The night air came hot and punishing as they rushed out and gathered in a knot at the curb. A limo squealed up, offering refuge in its dark belly.

Stephanie slid in with Francosis and several other men, one a diminutive fellow smoking a long cigarette. "What do you want with the *matador, señorita?*"

Thank God, someone who could interpret for her! "Who are you?"

"His manager, Carlos Bottella." Carlos then said something to the driver and they sped away into the Madrid night. Stephanie turned in her seat and looked out the back window. A crowd had gathered, along with more TV crews and reporters, and Miguel—stood on the curb, watching her disappear with his challenger.

Think like a reporter! She spun around, fought off the confusion of seeing Miguel, and said, "What does Pacote have on Francosis?"

The limo came to a quick stop in front of Retro Park.

Francosis sat with his hands over his face.

"What does Pacote have on Francosis?" she asked again.

Carlos rolled down the window a little and tossed out his cigarette. His little eyes bore into her. He lit another one, blew out a long stream of smoke.

"Francosis is too shamed to tell you. Besides, you are a reporter."

"Francosis asked me to help him last night. Tell him I can, in exchange for what Pacote has on him."

Carlos explained this to Francosis. The *matador* took several drags of his cigarette; the tip glowed in the dark limo. *"Sí,"* he finally whispered.

His manager said something to the other men, opened the door, and let them out, then scooted up on the seat. "When Francosis was a small boy he worked on the ranch of Victor Manez on the weekends—a great *matador* who ranked up there with Juan Aguilar." Carlos smoked for a moment. "Pacote often came out to the ranch, you know, to watch Victor with the cape."

He opened a side panel and a light splashed into the limo. From this compartment he fished out a bottle of liquor and a few glasses. He poured three and handed one each to Stephanie and Francosis.

She ventured a sip. Gin.

"So one day Francosis is feeding the horses and he hears something. It is Victor come out to the stables. Francosis, he is just a boy, maybe ten, and he thinks that Victor is a god."

"Dios," Francosis whispered, and shot the glass of gin straight down without a flinch.

Stephanie looked at him, then back at Carlos. "What happened?"

"Victor was no god, *señorita*. He was a sick, sick man."

It took Stephanie a moment to realize where this was leading. *Oh, God, Francosis had been—*

"Pacote was on the ranch that day, and spied the whole thing—never tried to help the boy. When Francosis came up the ranks, Pacote at first was generous with his pen. But in the past year he has been unfair to my *matador,* and has convinced others to be unfair."

"But—" Stephanie looked at Francosis again. He looked miserable. "It wasn't his fault."

"Well, that depends. Who is going to believe that Victor was a beast? No one. Pacote promised to forget what he saw and write favorably of my *matador* if he challenged Miguel to this *mano a mano.*"

"Why?"

"Because Pacote hates *El Peligro* for the death of his brother, and wants to see him die in *Las Ventas.*"

"But Paloma—" Miguel *hadn't make the announcement—but I can't tell them the truth. What is the truth? Why would Pacote give Miguel an edge? What edge—this young* matador *was about to kill* Miguel. *Maybe if the bull didn't do its job, Francosis would do his—*

"Rafael knew my *matador* was in love with Paloma. He knew this announcement would tear Francosis's heart out of his chest."

But he didn't *make the announcement.*

She was almost afraid to ask the next question. "Does Miguel know Pacote blackmailed Francosis?"

"Señorita, I'm sure he knows Francosis had to make the challenge—maybe not why."

She'd been holding her breath, and hadn't known it until she heard it expel.

Francosis now sat with his hands covering his face, his shoulders caved in.

"Miguel isn't going to marry Paloma," she blurted. "Tell Francosis this is just a publicity stunt cooked up by Pacote to drive Francosis and Miguel further apart. Pacote is responsible for the announcement—not Miguel."

Carlos told Francosis the news, and the young

matador grabbed her and kissed her on the mouth, saying, "Gracias, gracias, *señorita*."

She wondered if Miguel would be as thankful.

The sun was streaming into the room when Stephanie woke up and focused on the profile of Miguel. He stood at the window looking out with the sunlight filtered around him, and he looked like an apparition, instead of a man.

Last night Francosis had brought her back to the villa, because she couldn't return to the club without making a scene. She'd waited for Miguel, but he never came back. She'd worried all night that he'd ended up with Jenna Starr, maybe out of spite. She'd dozed off at dawn, but not restfully.

She sat up, and he turned around. He wore the same clothes he'd worn the night before, had dark stubble on his face, and looked tired, wiped out—old. Taking a few steps, he tossed a rolled up newspaper on the bed.

"I waited up for you all night," she said, running fingers through her hair.

"*Señorita*, there is a car and driver waiting to take me to Domingo's. I need to sleep—I can't stay here today." He closed his eyes and pressed his palms to his stomach.

She scrambled out of the sheets. "What's wrong?"

He took a deep breath, and his eyes opened slowly, seemed unfocused. "I am always like this before a fight."

"I have to talk to you—about Pacote, what he's done. How he's used both you and Francosis."

"No talking!" he snapped in an angry tone.

She felt as if she'd taken a slap. "How can you

accept a challenge knowing Francosis was black-mailed into calling you out?"

"Because, *señorita,* it does not matter why he challenged me, or how the challenge came to be. It just must be dealt with. Just as it does not matter why I love you—I just do, and I must deal with you."

"*Deal* with me?" she said, a strange bitterness rising in the back of her throat. "What—"

He put up his hand and interrupted her. "I have lost myself in you for two weeks. I *donn* know where is Miguel Rafael. I *donn* listen to anyone—I put everyone out with worries, call my manager a liar—and hurt my sister by letting you stay here. And still, you break my foolish Spanish heart."

He turned and walked out. In her mind, Miguel Rafael had really been gone since yesterday morning.

Stephanie fought back a confusion of tears as she opened the paper. *Deal with her! Deal with her!* There on the front page was a picture of her and Francosis—in his arms—kissing her. Another one of her in Miguel's window, her breasts covered by a cheesy black strip.

Scrambling, she ran to Ray's room. She tore off his bedcovers. "Wake up. Read this. *Hurry!*"

"What the hell—" He grabbed the paper. "Shit."

"What does it say?"

Ray began to read: "Miguel not only killed our beloved Juan Aguilar by his reckless challenge, but he means to kill his very spirit by reprehensible behavior toward his daughter, the beautiful Paloma.

"Miguel has brought an American reporter to his villa who has been writing an exposé and will cover tomorrow's bullfight. The reporter works for an American paper, and she has never written anything about bullfighting, and does not even speak Spanish. She drinks and dances in the clubs of Madrid with other bullfighters, and her character is typical of loose women. She lives openly in Miguel's villa, and parades around the windows in the nude trying to get attention of the many reporters camped out.

"Miguel, trying to win the approval of bullfighting fans tomorrow—hoping they will forget his role in Juan's death—has announced his engagement to Paloma, Juan's beautiful daughter. Yet Miguel humiliated and broke the heart of this pure, innocent woman when she learned about his live-in lover last night at *Torero*.

"Miguel's conduct has let Spain down—Juan down—who on his deathbed asked him to care for his daughter. The fans at *Las Ventas* will show their disapproval during the most important bullfight of his career. They will back Francosis, a *matador* who shows promise, and respect to the profession.

"The American reporter has tried to corrupt Francosis—use him to make her *matador* jealous—and last night claimed her new lover in front of Miguel's family and friends. Those who witnessed it said it was nothing less than disgusting, and an obvious ploy to get even with Miguel for announcing his engagement."

Ray set down the paper.

Stephanie staggered a little, turned, and ran back to her room. She threw herself on the bed, but no tears came, just a sick kind of laughter. Ray followed her and sat on the edge of the bed.

"I don't know if this will make you feel any better, but Miguel knows better than anyone what a jerk Pacote is."

It didn't.

* * *

Stephanie and Ray arrived at *Las Ventas* the following afternoon. Remembering Miguel's story about the woman in the white hat—a lucky day for him—she decided to wear one as an offering of peace, and good luck. Yesterday she'd shopped in search of such an item, to avoid any downtime to think beyond the moment. She bought a bouquet of white roses, now opening up because of the heat, and a few white extra handkerchiefs to wave.

Miguel never called, and she didn't try to contact him, certain she'd run into one of his human roadblocks. Something told her Domingo or Galleo would be screening calls for the *matador.*

It was three o'clock and horribly hot and sticky when they stepped off the last red subway train that dropped them off in the plaza.

Through her personal pain, she tried to stay focused on what would be required today as a reporter. She had to give an unbiased report on this bullfight, and have it E-mailed within hours afterward to her offices in California.

La Plaza del Toros de Las Ventas was alive with the excitement. City double-decker buses lining the avenue carried huge posters of Miguel. TV news crews dragged their heavy cables around vendors selling all matter of bullfighting souvenirs—posters, *Your Name Here* coffee cups, toy swords and capes, T-shirts with Miguel's face silk-screened on them. Stephanie bought one of those to sleep in.

They fought their way into *Las Ventas* alongside the crowds. By the thousands, bullfighting fans streamed toward the beckoning Moorish arches of *Las Ventas.*

Rushing in groups from the two subway stops flanking the *Plaza del Toros,* the crowd came in buses, taxis, and cars, everyone impatient with each other as the emotional frenzy escalated. They struggled along the passageway that led upward until at last they emerged into the blazing Spanish sun and the noise of the impatient, gathering crowd.

Stephanie didn't realize at first that she herself was an attraction. She was recognized by the fans, who showed their disapproval with boos and jeers. Someone threw something at her, and it bounced off her white hat. She readjusted it to shield her eyes from the intense glare, and tried to see where the object had come from. Ray hollered something back in Spanish, which caused laughter.

"What did you say?" Stephanie asked, filled with alarm. It hadn't occurred to her that she might be in physical danger.

"I told them to save their rotten fruit and dead cats for Francosis Gaona!"

"Dead cats!"

"Let's go see Miguel before the fight," Ray said.

"Where is he?" This gave her pause. Maybe he didn't want to see her.

"In the bullfighters chapel. These press passes Miguel arranged for us should help us get around. I want to take some pictures of him in his suit of lights before he stains it with blood and sweat."

They threaded their way through a horde of reporters and photographers to the door of the bullfighters' chapel. Domingo blocked the door like a smoking wall, preventing anyone from descending upon his *matador* during his sacred moment of solitude.

"Domingo!" Stephanie cried over the throng,

squeezing between two bad-smelling men. "Is Miguel
in there?"

"Go away!" Domingo barked, and clamped his
stogie between his yellow teeth. Disapproving dark
eyes landed on her hat, and stayed there, and something else registered in the black depths.

"Let us by," she insisted.

Ray took over, and both fired off words in Spanish.
Finally, Domingo threw up his hands, frowned, took
a deep drag from his cigar and blew it straight into
Stephanie's face. *"¡Uno momento!"*

She coughed. "What did you say?" she asked Ray,
as they entered the foyer of the chapel.

"I just reminded him of what I'm sure he already
knew. Miguel called this morning and told me to
bring you here. You go in first. He's expecting
you."

"One minute, *señorita!"* Domingo cried before she
got all the way through the foyer. He grabbed her
hat off her head and crunched it in his hands. "I
will hold this for you!"

It was cool and dark in the chapel, and for a moment Stephanie's eyes refused to adjust. Then she
saw Miguel in the candle's glow. He was kneeling.
A wisp of incense swirled upward from a censer in
front of him. The light from the votary candles
danced off the sequins of his costume, spraying the
room with strange luminescence, reminding her of
that night at *La Libra* when he'd made love to her
on his magenta cape.

She watched him, mystified and at a loss as to why
she should be witnessing something so private. He
was praying, and because he looked so vulnerable
doing it she was suddenly terrified for him, didn't
want him to fight the bulls today. He looked over

one shoulder. "Ah, *querida.*" He rose, blessed himself with the sign of the cross.

"I—I didn't mean to disturb you." A tremor shook her. This was the first time she had ever seen him as full *matador de toros.*

El Peligro stood before her in all his glory.

The blue silk costume was heavily encrusted with gold embroidery down the legs of the pants, and down the sleeves of the bolero jacket. There were gold epaulets with tassels down the front, and under the vest a white shirt and black tie. Pink tights showed below his knees, and he wore ballet-style slippers on his feet. His hair had been cut, but a ponytail had been fastened to the back of his head.

At that moment she knew with certain clarity that she could not be a part of this life.

"Come here," he said in almost a whisper.

She obeyed and drifted into his arms. They stood holding each other for a few moments.

"Pray with me?" he asked.

She knelt with him before the altar, and tried to summon a prayer, but nothing would come but memories of the passions he'd stirred in her.

After some time he stood and helped her to stand. "Go to your seat, he said. "Go now."

"Ray said you'd wanted to see me, and I'm glad, because I'm leaving right after the fight—I'm sorry for all the troubles I've caused you. But I wanted to say thanks for—" A sob caught in her throat.

He gathered her up again. "Why are you always trying to run away? Where are you going to hide in this cosmos?" He took her chin between this thumb and forefinger and tilted her head up and looked into her eyes.

Tears slipped down her chin, and her breath

caught in her throat when she held down yet another sob.

His eyes were misted, too, filled with his own private pain. *"Querida,* you cause this *matador* a lot of troubles. But I love you always."

"I love you, too, but I don't belong here. No one wants me here but you, and after last night—"

"Wait for me, *señorita."* He kissed her on the mouth, pulled away a little. "Promise me you will wait. After the fight we will make things right between us." He kissed her again, then backed away.

She smiled through her tears, knowing she couldn't make any more promises, that there was nothing he could do to make things right except retire from the *corrida* and move to the States with her, and that wouldn't happen.

"Good luck, she said, and turned and left the chapel, her heart still with him in that cool, dark place. *Good-bye . . .*

Ray stayed behind to take pictures of Miguel.

Stephanie pushed and shoved her way down the aisle, tears forming and falling over her face, until she found her seat in the shade. Not Miguel's box, she realized. If she'd thought she could now take a breath and sort her thoughts, she was mistaken. Out of the crowd several reporters emerged, Pacote among them, all interrogating her. They asked horrible obscene questions, and she was trapped. There was no escaping them or their cameras. Ray was not there to protect her. It was only Paloma's sudden arrival that took the attention away.

Her hair had been brushed and coiled into a smooth, loose chignon and fastened with a pair of gilt-headed pins. Her pale yellow cotton frock drifted around her lithe body like a dream. Paloma glanced up from Miguel's box and waved at Stephanie. She smiled and waved back, thinking, *All must be forgiven.*

There was a handful of Miguel's relatives with Paloma. Stephanie had seen those faces at *La Libra.* Paloma received cheers and flowers from the crowd—unlike Stephanie, who was welcomed with rotten fruit.

I'm never going to fit in—Miguel's fans will see to what Domingo doesn't take care of—or that odious Pacote. Stephanie knew she had to leave—be the strong one. Once she was gone Miguel would forget about her, but she would never forget about him.

Ray finally showed up, carrying her hat.

The crowd roared and leapt to its feet, waving hats and handkerchiefs and chanting, *"¡Viva! ¡Viva! ¡Viva!"* as the *matadors* strode into the arena.

Ray, using a zoom lens, photographed Miguel undulating across the sand like a noble, his court in sync behind him. Stephanie thought he looked magnificent. Francosis cut a fine figure, too, in his yellow silk costume—it matched Paloma's dress!

Miguel's head was up, his body straight and proud as the crowd cheered. Women tossed him flowers, but Miguel looked detached as he came across the sand, while Francosis, on his left, smiled and greeted the crowd enthusiastically. Pacote's vile story had not hurt Miguel's rating with the crowd.

The two men continued single file with loose strides, one arm swinging, their chins up and their eyes on the president's box. They stopped, and both Miguel and Francosis bowed low.

Miguel stood now by the fence, but the crowd called for him. The entire plaza stood as one giant wave, everyone chanting his name. He took a few steps away from the fence and doffed his *montera*. Pandemonium forced him to remain, to take another step and pivot slowly, bowing his head. He then walked over to where Stephanie sat, tossed up a splendidly bejeweled blue cape. Ray caught it, and spread it out along the railing. This offering caused a few scattered boos.

Stephanie wanted to ask Ray why Miguel chanced turning the crowd, but he had run down behind the *burladero* to take pictures.

She could clearly see Miguel's face from where she sat. He looked unmoved by the crowd's unexpected approval. Domingo handed Miguel a big, folded, magenta fighting cape, and Miguel swirled it open with one hand and waved it back and forth across the sand. To the delight of the crowd, Francosis swung his own cape in several flashy moves.

"Francosis is such a show-off," Ray said when he returned. "Let's see him do that when the bull's charging!"

Miguel had since squeezed through the *burladero* opening, big enough for a man but too small for the bull, and he now rested his chin on his hand, his eyes fixed on the wooden gate that would soon release the first bull. His.

Ray leaned toward her. "The bull's name is *Amenaza.*"

Stephanie watched wide-eyed with anticipation as four men stood before the door of the *toril* where the beast waited. A lone trumpeter rose and sent out a clear high call that summoned the beginning of the bullfight. Silence pervaded the ring.

At first nothing appeared. Someone behind the gate swung a hot pink cape several times in front of the black hole. Then, like an explosion of chaos, *Amenaza* charged into the arena and skidded to a halt, startled by the bright light and crowd.

THIRTEEN

Stephanie felt her heart race, the same as she suspected the bull's heart must be pounding. A man suddenly ran across the bull's course trailing a cape, but the bull's sudden charge sent him in a nosedive back behind the barrier.

Ray snapped some pictures. "They test the bull to see if it has good vision, what horn it favors, and what kind of animal it is in general. Miguel is paying close attention right now."

Miguel still had his chin fixed on his hand, studying the animal from the edge of his *burladero*. After several more passes Miguel walked into the arena, passing the retreating caped man.

Amenaza trotted to the center of the ring and declared his new territory.

"Just so you know, Stephanie, this bull was raised for this moment—for brutality. His bloodline goes back to thousands who were maimed because they chose to challenge the horns. And that bull favors his left. Miguel's noted that, I'm sure. He'll watch the animal very closely to see if it has any quirks."

Stephanie scribbled Ray's words down on a small notepad for later use. She took a moment to straighten out her hat, crumpled from Domingo's brutal clutches and put it back on her head.

Miguel, his profile toward *Amenaza,* unfurled his cape and dug his *zapatillas* into the sand. The bull took the lure of the fabric as Miguel effortlessly swept its fold before the animals horns. Stephanie was fascinated with the way his feet played across the sand, as in a ballet dance. For a moment the cape seemed frozen around Miguel's hips, spread out in the air, suspended.

The crowd roared, *"¡Olé!"*

Stephanie held her breath and then exhaled sharply when the animal, bewildered, swiveled its body around and lunged for the cape. Miguel acquainted himself with the animal's reactions, and did a series of flat-footed movements, drawing *Amenaza* closer and closer.

Miguel finished by gathering the cape in against his body in a half *veronica* as the bull flew past and stopped short, stunned. He folded his cape over his arm, turned his back on the animal and strutted away.

"¡Olé!" deafened the air. Miguel returned the applause with a casual wave of his hand.

Stephanie leaned toward Ray. "I thought this crowd would be more hostile toward Miguel. Everything reported that led up to this fight made me think very differently than what I'm seeing."

"It's part of the hype, Stephanie. As long as Miguel takes chances, you'll only hear cheers and see handkerchiefs wave. Watch how close he'll bring that bull to his body. Very dangerous with a bull that hooks to the left. Francosis will have to match this— or do better with his bull."

Stephanie's attention turned to the entrance of

several horses, all of them blindfolded with patches over their eyes and their flanks hidden under rolls of quilted cotton canvas. The riders wore big felt hats, embroidered bolero jackets, and gold breeches. In their right fists the men clutched *picas,* eight-foot-long poles. These were the *picadors,* and among them Stephanie recognized Galleo, Miguel's brother.

Ray took Stephanie's hand. "This is going to be the most brutal, bloody task of the fight. You might want to look at your notes."

With the same perverse interest people had while driving past an auto accident, Stephanie was unable to look away.

The bull spotted the *picadors* with angry interest. The horned head dropped, and the bull charged forward and hurtled his black mass into Galleo's steed. Galleo, in turn, drove his lance into the animal's neck, and its bellow reverberated through the stands.

"Oh, God!" Stephanie cried. "That isn't fair."

"He's weakening that neck muscle. Otherwise Miguel could never get close enough for kill," Ray explained. "I thought you did some homework on the subject."

"I did, but to see it is another thing!"

In Stephanie's opinion the mattress didn't seem like much protection for the horses. Presently, the bull literally picked up Galleo's horse and toppled both animal and man. Miguel rushed to his beleaguered brother's side, waving his cape. He distracted the bull from the wobbling horse long enough for another man to help Galleo up. The crowd roared its approval for the horse's courage.

The oozing blood from the bull dripped onto the

sand, and seemed to sparkle in the sun. Stephanie didn't know how much more she could watch. After several more picks the task was finished, and the *picadors* rode out of the plaza.

She sighed in relief.

Miguel came out from behind the barrier carrying *banderillas,* a pair of decorated darts. The crowd went wild when they saw that Miguel was going to place his own. He snapped them in half over his knees to the cheers of the crowd, then ran with breath-catching elegance and drove them expertly into the bull's withers. His *banderillero* placed the next set, but not with the same grace and agility as Miguel.

Amenaza romped, tried to knock off the sticks.

Miguel lifted his *montera* from his head and gestured toward the box of the president, signaling he was ready for the final act of the bullfight and asking permission to kill his bull.

Ray dropped his camera and looked at Stephanie. "He's going to dedicate it to someone."

Miguel strode toward her and she felt her stomach quiver in strange little spasms when she realized the entire plaza watched where he headed. He stopped before her, his face and hair wet with perspiration under the brutal sun. Though he only paused there for a moment, to Stephanie it felt like a lifetime as his dark eyes pleaded with her not to go—to wait for him after the *corrida.*

A quick jerk of his hand, and his *montera* flew up, and she caught it in mid-air. The crowd strangely approved with an enormous roar, and several flowers showered down on her.

Miguel took his sword and carefully folded *muleta* from one of his men and took a quick drink from a water bottle—some of it trickled from his mouth.

Once again the crowd grew silent.

Miguel straightened up with a proud shake of his shoulders, walked out to the center of the ring, and planted his feet in the sand, a gesture that said this was where he would conduct his entire *faena*. The throng showed approval by waving handkerchiefs.

Miguel stretched out the *muleta* and swung it casually forward a few inches. Then, with a quick snap of his wrist, he jerked it to a stop and drew it back slowly.

He called to the bull. "*¡Toro! ¡Toro! Ha!*"

The bull made several beautiful, high passes, and with each one Miguel did an about-face with a series of quick, flat-footed steps that brought the animal past him, again and again, closer and closer until he actually leaned into the beast, staining his suit with blood.

Stephanie fought back the unease, thinking this was the most beautiful and the most horrific thing she'd ever watched. Someone behind them screamed in English, "*El Peligro! Kill him before he kills you!*"

It happened very fast, and Stephanie almost missed the moment of truth, when Miguel crossed his left hand, which held the cloth under his right, and sliced the sword into the animal's shoulder blades.

Amenaza staggered forward, looked around confused, took one step toward Miguel, and fell dead at his feet, a profusion of blood squirting from the mortal wound.

The crowd went wild. Miguel thanked them by sweeping an arm in the air, turning slowly on his black slippers until he had acknowledged the entire plaza. Then his eyes locked with Stephanie's. He bowed his head slightly, a faint smile on his lips.

Stephanie felt hypnotized, unable to keep her eyes off the crumpled, bleeding, black mass.

"That was an outstanding performance!" Ray cried, now on his feet, waving his own handkerchief. "The crowd is petitioning to the president to reward him."

There was a chorus of *¡Dos orejas y el rabo!"* around the ring. *Two ears and a tail.*

"I have to find a bathroom. I'll be right back." Stephanie fought her way through the crowds, more flowers showering her path, until she found herself running down a long cement hallway. Breathless, she leaned against a coarse, cool wall. Tears streamed down her face. The sound of *¡olé!* still reverberated in her distressed thoughts. She felt as if she'd taken the sword thrust herself.

She found her way to the restroom, splashed cold water on her face, stared at her pale reflection in the mirror, and knew she was going to be sick. She found an open stall and slipped to the stone floor, her hands in her face. How would she get the strength to go back out there and watch yet another animal be killed? She *had* to, had to complete this assignment, and wait for Miguel.

She did neither. She left *Las Ventas* immediately, much to the consternation of the cabdriver, who wanted to hang around outside the plaza and listen to the roar of the crowd on a day when he had the misfortune to be working.

Once in the villa, she hastily threw her bags together and wrote Miguel a note, which she left propped up against the woman statue in the room that smelled like incense.

Miguel,

Let me go—back home to my cats—to what makes sense to me. I'll always love you—that can't be taken away—but I don't fit in your world, and you don't fit in mine. You need a woman who understands the complexities, the traditions, who will appreciate and honor what you do, someone your family will honor. A woman who would be thrilled to have a bull's death dedicated to her. It isn't me . . . it never was.

Steph

She waited at the airport and caught the first available flight out of Madrid to New York.

Later she learned that Francosis took a horn from his second bull but was expected to make a complete recovery, with no serious complications. This news sent a shiver down her spine, and she wondered how Paloma had handled seeing her lover injured. The fates had turned away from Miguel and frowned instead down on Francosis.

Miguel had been victorious, and carried out of the arena on the shoulders of the crowd, awarded the two ears and a tail from his first bull, his fate forever changed at *Las Ventas.*

He doesn't need me anymore. His luck has changed.

In New York, she stayed for a few days—in a hotel bed, curled up into herself, trying to understand how she'd not only walked out away from an assignment, how she'd walked way from Miguel.

She wouldn't ever comprehend bullfighting. It had shocked and sickened her—and no matter how much she loved Miguel she didn't think she could watch him do that again—taunt, tease, and kill an animal. Writing about it had been an entirely different experience. She'd rather leave him than tell him the truth, hurt him that way, abandon her first chance at real happiness with a man. Besides, fans, Domingo, Miguel's family—everyone in his world—would interfere with that happiness until it was extinguished.

She tried to understand what had happened to her in two short weeks—a turbulent love affair, a disastrous career move.

She remembered with vivid clarity how her mother had sat curled up on the old chair, almost incapable of moving after their father left. For the first time in Stephanie's life she understood her mother's suffering, and why she hadn't been able to recover from her husband's betrayal. *She'd loved my father the way I love Miguel. Some soul thing you can't get over, that distorts your life.*

The difference between what Stephanie had felt for Steven and what she'd felt for Miguel was vast. She clearly saw now that she'd never loved Steven. Whatever she felt for him had never came close to the gut-wrenching need she'd felt for Miguel.

He was both disturbing and perplexing at the same time—fragile, yet the strongest man she'd ever known, and the bravest, to face a thousand pound raging bull with nothing more than a cape.

Over and over she saw him standing before her on the hot sand. This image came in dreams, haunted her, and she woke up in cold sweat wearing her *El Peligro* T-shirt. She would never forget what he looked like under the scorching Iberian sun, his suit of lights wet with sweat and bull's blood, twenty-three thousand set of eyes upon her as he'd tossed her his *montera* and she caught it.

While she struggled with facing reality, Richard and Adria were beside themselves with worry, and Ray had called and left messages everywhere trying to find her. When she finally caught a flight home, it took her a long time to clear her voice mailbox messages.

Nothing from Miguel. Leaving *Las Ventas* before the fight had ended was her ultimate insult after he'd dedicated the bull to her—a dangerous political move that could have turned the crowd against him.

One day Miguel would thank her for leaving, for coming to her senses. He would come to realize that he couldn't have stayed happy with her.

She found her house as she'd left it—not in neat order, the way one usually leaves before a trip. Instead, clothes were piled high, the coffee table littered, her bed askew, and dishes in the sink. Miguel had literally swept into her life and whisked her away.

Her home had an eerie atmosphere, as if someone who had left it in a hurry and met with some terrible demise. Now, all waited for her, including two impatient cats who wanted instant gratification and attention from the long awaited mistress of the house.

She picked up the phone and made the first of several dreaded calls.

"Good job, Stephanie," her boss Bob said, and it didn't sound condescending. In fact he sounded pretty happy.

"I know I screwed up." She sat down on the sofa, glanced into the fireplace. There, with curled up blackened edges, was the *People Magazine* Miguel had thrown into the flames. Leaning over, she fished out what was left, and peeled it open to Miguel's picture.

"I'd say everyone over at the *Variedades,* who said you couldn't do it, are opening their wallets and paying up painfully. I understand that Marc Garcia is going to offer you a job. Hope you don't take it. You know you're my favorite writer. One of the guys!"

She traced Miguel's face and left smudgy traces. "I am?"

"Hello? Are you in checkout land with Miguel? The picture of him throwing you his *montera* hit every newsstand in the world, so of course, *everyone* wanted to read *your* story. It was pretty damn fantastic, by the way—the in-depth research you did about his past, those personal quotes you got, that kid Renaldo, and how those kids follow *matadors.*"

Then it dawned on her how the story had been finished and submitted. Ray!

"Everyone's talking—and I mean everyone."

After she hung up from the half hour of unexpected accolades, she emptied her suitcases onto the festering pile of laundry, put on her souvenir T-shirt of Miguel, and lay back on the sofa with her charred *People Magazine* and her *montera.* She smelled the hat, put it on her head.

The phone rang, and she picked it up, still sitting on the sofa with the bullfighter's hat on. "Hello?"

"You okay?" Ray asked. "Everyone's been worried. Where you been?"

"Sorry."

"I'm still in Madrid, on my way to Cádiz."

"Ray, I don't know how to thank you, other than saying I told you all along that you should have written the story."

"*You* wrote it, and luckily you left your laptop behind when you bolted. I just finished the bullfight scenes."

"How's Francosis?"

"Healing. He and Paloma are officially engaged. Miguel gave a press conference right after the fight."

"I'm happy for them." She was.

"I sent you a package. Watch for it."

"Sure." *What about Miguel?*

"You hurt Miguel by leaving."

"I know."

"I'm the one who warned you about him, but I'm taking back all those warnings, Stephanie. He's really screwed up. Angry, I think."

He's really screwed up—angry.

After Stephanie hung up the phone she snuggled on the pillows in the same place Miguel had sat—in front of her phony fireplace—wondering if she would ever forget him. She crushed the blackened magazine to her breast. It didn't seem possible that she could ever face him again—with all the problems she'd caused, with all the interference from everyone, with his occupation. She needed a normal life—a boring, normal life with two cats.

Why do I need a normal life? she wondered.

Richard called her in the middle of the night to tell her Adria was in labor, and by ten the following morning a new Madison had been presented to the world. Justin Madison came in with a howl and a tuft of red hair.

The baby gave her new focus. After Adria came home from the hospital, Stephanie spent a good deal of time with the new family, helping out where she could, anything to keep her mind busy. Richard and Adria didn't say anything about Miguel, and she was thankful, especially when she knew it was killing Adria not to get the *details*.

The mystery package Ray sent was a beautiful photo album. It started with the rainy morning they'd left from LAX for Madrid, and ended with her standing in the first row of *Las Ventas*, Miguel in front of her, tossing her the *montera*.

Ray included all the newspaper clippings from Spain, and from the *Variedades*. The story was also featured in *6 Toros 6,* the glossy Spanish publication, and *Aplausos,* a weekly magazine devoted to bullfighting news.

El Peligro's lover walks out of his brilliant triumph at Las Ventas. *Read her story!*

Included in the package was a carefully folded poster advertising Miguel's fight at *Las Ventas*. She hung it over her bed with thumbtacks, and stared at it all night.

The photo album went to bed with her that night, and she cried for her dream lover, for the beautiful pictures she would have of him forever—not only in the photo album, but etched into her heart.

The following morning she had her period, and with it terrible cramps and a migraine headache. She wasn't going to have a baby that didn't look like her.

She'd been home three weeks when Ray called to say he'd read in the *Variedades* that Miguel had retired from bullfighting, without giving a reason.

Abracadabra. Poof! He's no longer a matador.

She waited for Miguel to call and complete the miracle, but he didn't. Why should he, after all her rejections? She wondered what he would do now, could imagine him out at *La Libra,* playing with Renaldo and the horn-board.

One week after learning of Miguel's retirement, Stephanie stood in front of the mirrored walls of Richard and Adria's house on Balboa Island, where it had all started. She suspected Richard was still handling the *matador's* business affairs here in the states, but he kindly never said anything.

This night Richard looked handsome in a dark blue suit, getting ready to take his wife out on the first night away from their baby. He handed Stephanie a glass of wine while he waited for his wife to finish feeding Justin upstairs. "Remember when you asked if I wondered about Dad?"

"Yes." *The night I took the flight into unreality.*

"Right." He scratched his nose. "Well, I more than wondered, Stephanie. I tried to find him."

"What?" She felt a wave of confusion come over her—happiness, no, anger. He'd abandoned them and their mother.

"He lives in Fresno—not with the woman he left Mom for—another woman he's been married to for about ten years."

Stephanie reeled with the news. "When did you find this out?"

"A week ago. I wanted to tell you, but with everything—" he didn't complete his thought. "Anyway, he wants to come down and see the baby. How do you feel about that? He wants to see you, too."

"Me? I don't want to see him," she snapped, and watched her brother's face fall.

"Stephanie, when did you get so stubborn? Did Steven do this to you? Did Mom? You've changed so much in the past two years that I can't recognize you anymore."

She blinked a few times to focus, as if to see Richard better. He'd never talked to her like this. "W— What do you mean?"

"I mean, you never used to be like this—this shutting everyone out—Miguel, for example."

For example?

"Frankly I don't think he deserves it. The man has called here every day—about you, not about business—but I've tried to stay out of it, tried to stay neutral. I can't anymore, not when I see you're this way with everyone and everything."

Miguel's called every day?

"What Dad did was wrong, and he's sorry for that—can't change what's under the bridge. I have to give him a chance—he deserves at least one. And so does Miguel."

Dad and Miguel? These two are not supposed to be in the same conversation.

"We'll talk about Dad later. Right now, let's finish this conversation about Miguel. Why didn't he call me?"

"I'm sure he's too *f'ing* proud, worried you'll reject him again."

Richard never said *f'ing*. Ray said *f'ing*, not Richard.

She felt she was spinning out of control again. She took a deep breath and a deep drink of wine, then said: "Richard, you just sprang this thing on me about Dad."

"Yeah, timing. I'm not good at it." Richard set his wineglass down and stood up as Adria came down the stairs looking spectacular. They were going to a business dinner.

"He should sleep," Adria said of the baby, "but if he wakes up and wants to eat, I pumped some milk for him. It's in the refrigerator."

"Don't worry." *Your baby-sitter just found out her father wants to see her after twenty years, and her Spanish bullfighting lover has been calling her brother every day. Everything is under control.* "Besides, I have your pager number."

Adria came over to her, and gave her a big hug. "Have a great night."

"Baby-sitting?" They both laughed. Stephanie thought she saw something in her best friend's eyes, then shook off the suspicion that Adria was up to something.

After good-byes were said Stephanie went upstairs to check on Justin. The smell of baby hit her hard, and it made her a little sad. How she'd wanted one of these—with a tuft of dark hair, not red.

She came back down the stairs, turned on the stereo to a Spanish station, and went out onto the balcony. It was a warm April night, and her blue jeans and tank top were just perfect for the weather. She used to think of Steven when she came out here. Now she'd remembered Miguel and the moonlit night that he'd boldly wanted sex in exchange for a story.

She smiled, and decided that when she got home tonight she was going to call him. She couldn't deny that she loved him—hell, the man was in her blood. *I don't want normal. I want the smell of laurel leaves and olives—green hills—and seed bulls in the distance. I want Miguel—in me, around me—everywhere.*

There were couples strolling on the sidewalk below, boats motored in on the glassy water, and the sun was almost set—an orange haze over the bay. Someone was smoking somewhere; she caught the smell on the breeze and closed her eyes, remembered when Miguel had given her a cigarette here on the balcony, and how she took up the habit in Spain.

While in Spain do as . . . she felt herself smiling as a new joy welled up in her—a sense of purpose. Then she felt a funny lightness go up her spine, and the doorbell rang.

FOURTEEN

Stephanie left the balcony and went to the front door and opened it. What registered first were Miguel's beautiful green eyes—framed in long, black lashes—as they looked her up and down, slowly.

"Buenos tardes, señorita," he said, showing perfect white teeth.

There it was—that physical response, a definite roll of her normally steady heart rate—only this time a wealth of emotions washed over her at the same time, the strongest one being love.

"¿Perdóneme?"

"No hablo español," she said, déjà vu coming over her, as well as a great happiness to see him again.

"Ah, I speak English. We are saved."

She smiled shyly and played along with this already written script. "If you're looking for Richard Madison, you've found the right place." She stepped back and let him pass. Miguel's sexy scent followed him, awakening her senses just as it always did.

He wore black linen pants and a white silk shirt rolled up at the sleeves, revealing his gold bracelet on one wrist and a watch on the other. His hair was longer, free of any gels, and touched his collar. He had a very healthy tan.

"Actually, I am looking for his sister," he said in his thick Castilian accent. Have you seen her, *señorita?*"

She tapped a finger on her chin, holding back the powerful urge to fling herself into his arms. "Can you describe her?"

"Ah." He leaned against the sofa back, and crossed one ankle over the other. "Let me think. *Sí.* She is very beautiful, but she does not think she is, which makes her even more beautiful. She has a dimple in one cheek when she smiles—which isn't often enough, in my opinion."

Stephanie took a few steps closer to him, relieved that he seemed in such good spirits after everything that they had gone through, this being the first time they were together.

"Anything else you can say about her?"

He slapped his hand on his chest. "She has broken the heart of *El Peligro,* when no one thought it could be broken."

Stephanie couldn't hold herself away from him, and took a few steps closer, reached her hand out, had to feel him, to know for certain this wasn't some twisted hallucination and she'd wake up and find herself alone.

As her hand moved up his chest she closed her eyes for a moment, relishing the experience, the feel of cool silk and the heat of his body rising to her touch. When she opened them she stared at the vein pulsing in his neck, felt his heart pounding fast against her hand. She lifted her gaze slowly until it locked with his. "Do I look anything like her?" she whispered, wetting her lips.

A Spanish song played in the background; a ferry's horn bellowed somewhere out on the water.

"Querida?" he said thickly, watching her mouth. "Everything like her. No—even more beautiful than I remember."

She moved all the way into his arms, and neither said anything for a long time—both drifted on some unspoken, deep need, in a reacquainting of souls, as if one could not live without the other for very long, and it would take a moment to fill each other back up.

He slipped his long, thin fingers through her hair, down her neck, around to her chin and tilted her face up, and kissed her gently, once, twice.

"Why don't you ever do as I tell you, eh? Running off like that in the middle of a *corrida* instead of waiting?"

His eyes were a shade of green she'd seen growing in the *Parque del Retiro* in Madrid. She brushed his hair back, since it had fallen loosely over his forehead, and he blinked. Then she touched his scar, ran a finger down it, to his lips, across his lower one, pulling it down a little. Their hips and legs were pressing each other, and she could feel him growing hard against her.

"The fight became too much—everything became too much. Oh, Miguel . . ." She laid her head against his chest, listened to his throbbing heart, and wanted this moment to last forever. She didn't want to talk about all their differences and what had thrown them apart.

He stroked her hair. "I knew you wouldn't see the *corrida* as a pageant—that you would see me as a killer of bulls. I worried so much, and in the end I was right to worry. But now, eh, I don't kill bulls. Now you can love me?"

She suddenly felt a little sad and unsure, and untangled herself from him, backed away a little. "I heard you retired. But Miguel, I loved you even as a *matador.*"

He raised a dark eyebrow. "Did you?"

Taking a deep breath, she walked across the room and turned the stereo down a little. She wasn't ready to take the conversation where he led it. Walking back over to him, she leaned against the sofa, letting her arm lightly graze his, feeling almost if she didn't keep a physical contact he might disappear.

"When you walked onto the sand, you looked like a king. I've never seen anything so beautiful as you in that suit of lights, and your colorful retinue behind you. I can't imagine you giving it up. Is retiring really what you want? Domingo must blame me."

The back of one of Miguel's hands trailed up her arm, and then he pushed himself off the sofa, stepped in front of her. He put both hands on her shoulders, ran them up her neck, and rested them on the sides of her face, made her look into his eyes. "Domingo does not blame you. Nor do I. It's what I want. I'm tired of that life. I want to enjoy my hard-earned millions."

She pulled out of his grasp, stood looking in the paneled mirrors of the dining room. She really saw herself now, wearing jeans, no makeup, while Miguel looked splendid in his linen and silk and smelled like heaven. She glanced up the stairs, thinking she needed a moment to collect her thoughts and make a few repairs, take a few deep breaths, and regain her equilibrium. Besides, she needed to look in on Justin.

"I'm going to check on the baby, and Adria has one of those infant speaker monitors around here.

I think I should bring it down so I can hear him if
he wakes up."

Miguel seemed reluctant to let her move around
him, and she felt him watching her leave the room.

Once upstairs, Stephanie sat on Adria's bed for a
moment and tried to collect her thoughts and her
emotions, hoping to sort through what was fact and
what was purely fantasy happening downstairs. Fact:
Miguel obviously cared about her, or he wouldn't
have called Richard every day, nor would he have
showed up tonight. Still, for all the things she loved
about Miguel, the *fact* remained that he had a gi-
gantic ego, and couldn't have really accepted her
leaving him in the middle of a bullfight.

She was afraid to get her hopes up too high with
all that lay between them—a country, cultures, re-
ligions, families. Maybe he just wanted to clear the
air a little so he could keep a decent working relationship with her brother.

Miguel looked as beautiful as she remembered
him, even more so, very relaxed now, years younger,
and when she'd opened the door earlier her entire
body had quickened in response to him. That hadn't
changed between them.

She couldn't, wouldn't, lose him again.

*Ladies and Gentlemen: This is your captain speaking.
It looks as if we've just reentered our atmosphere safely,
and we are headed for home. Please observe the No Smoking
and the seatbelt signs, and thank you for flying with our
airline.*

She rummaged around in her sister-in-law's closet
and found a sexy black dress and some matching
heels. Her hands trembled in anticipation as she
quickly fixed her makeup and hair, wondering

where tonight would lead, secretly hoping it would lead to making love with Miguel.

Adria had an array of perfumes lined up on her dresser, and Stephanie found her own scent and applied a light mist. *Hit him with everything,* she thought. Tonight he was going to be hers in every way—not at Adria's of course, but wherever he was calling home these days—The Newporter?

She stopped in the baby's room and checked on the sleeping bundle, grabbed the portable monitor. Justin was making little sucking movements, completely oblivious to what was going on in the house.

Miguel was outside on the balcony leaning against the balcony railing smoking a cigarette and drinking a glass of wine. He turned when her heels clicked on the wood.

"You look beautiful," he said, his gaze moving over her body. "But you looked beautiful in the jeans. You smell pretty good, too."

Setting the monitor down, she picked up the glass of merlot he must have poured for her and took a long drink. It was the first glass she'd had since she'd left Spain, and it tasted wonderful. Where had he found the wine and glasses? Obviously, Adria had something to do with this rendezvous.

"Thanks for the wine." She joined him at the railing, and looked out across the water at the lights on the Balboa peninsula. There was a ferry pulling away, and another waiting to dock. "This area gets busy in the summer months. The winter is the best time to live on the island."

They both watched until all cars were released and four more pulled on for the quick trip across to the island. A few boats motored in; their deck lights flickered on the water.

"I'm sorry for everything I put you through," she finally said, turning around to face him again, knowing he hadn't come to talk about the tourist trade on the island. A gentle breeze moved her hair, and a few strands caught on her lips, stuck there by her lip gloss. She reached up and freed it.

He swirled his wine around in the glass, then looked up at her, a faint smile on his lips. The breeze lifted his hair, too, moved it across his forehead. His cigarette smoke swirled around them both, and lifted away on the same current.

"Don't be sorry, *querida.*"

"Without me, your last fight wouldn't have been so controversial. You already had so much to worry about without added problems. I don't know why you brought me to Spain with you, or why I feel so responsible."

His gaze was contemplative as he seemed to study her face. "Without you *Amenaza* would have taken me down. He had the same *rosette*—insignia—that I'd seen in the dream. When I faced him at *Las Venas* to start my *faena,* I swear he winked at me, and when I turned to dedicate the bull and saw you with the biggest white hat I'd ever seen, I knew that my fate was changed and sealed forever."

He took a final drag from his cigarette and butted it against the railing. "*El Peligro* was always controversial. It's what made him so great." He deposited the butt in a trash can next to the covered barbecue.

"I didn't think I would ever hear from you again. I knew I'd injured your pride—and when you never called—"

"You didn't call me, either, *querida.*" His tone didn't sound accusing, more fact.

She turned back to the water, now looked out past

the leeway, toward the open ocean. "I thought I'd done the right thing by leaving, that someone had to take control of the madness between us. Before I met you, I had a pretty boring life—it's almost if I thought I *had* to have one, because it was something I could depend on. Someday I will tell you about my mother and father. Anyway, as the days passed and I looked through the pictures every night Ray had taken, I knew I didn't want boring, that I wanted you at any cost, for any length of time you would have me." She took a deep breath, struggled not to cry in front of him. "Tonight when I got home I was going to call you. I had to, at the very least, tell you I was sorry, and a big fool for running out. Then the doorbell rang."

"The fates seem to like you."

Even though he kept things light between them tonight, she could see real pain in his beautiful eyes. "I hurt you, didn't I?"

"*Querida,* my pride was very wounded." He fished out another cigarette, looked at it, and tucked it back into his pocket. "Everyone was talking about how you ran out on me. Playing it up—saying they were right about you. Your leaving hurt me—embarrassed me in front of my family and friends. I wish I could say I am not such a Spanish man with a big macho ego, but that would not be very true."

"But you're here now? Why?"

He smiled, his eyes shining. "You may think Domingo has no romantic heart, but he's the one who told me to shape up, to put away my tequila bottle and be a real man."

Stephanie looked at him with doubt.

"He said, and I quote, '*Matador,* I told you she was going to wreck you, but you *donn* listen. Now, you are wrecking yourself! You had better go find that woman and let her know who the man is before she is out of control and does you in for good.' "

Stephanie put her hand to her mouth and laughed. "Oh, bless his hard heart."

"But I didn't think I could take any more rejection from you, so I pestered your brother for information. I wanted to know if you were as miserable as I was." Miguel chuckled. "You must thank Domingo when you see him again, and thank Richard for letting me call him every day about his sister instead of business."

"I'll thank Domingo just to see his expression." Stephanie knew that it wasn't easy for Miguel to say these things, that in his culture men didn't come after women who scorned them, no matter how light he tried to make it all sound.

"Querida, I want you to understand a few things." He finished his wine, walked over to the table and poured more into his glass. "I don't want you thinking *El Peligro* is some kind of pig."

She shook her head. "You don't have to explain anything else."

"I want to clear it all up with you," he said, his voice smooth, but determined. "No more misunderstandings. I knew Pacote was behind the challenge, and that he had something on Francosis, but Pacote always has something on someone. I knew about Francosis and Paloma, because Madrid has eyes for *El Peligro,* but I never intended to use that information to hurt either of them. Domingo wanted to go forward with the announcement—it was too good a setup for a famous bullfighting manager to pass up. He finally agreed with his *matador* to shut up because *El Peligro* was going to cut off his paycheck."

Stephanie thought it was sweet the way he talked about himself in the third person. "I should have taken your calls, Miguel. I was just so confused, and had an ego of my own to deal with. I thought you'd end up with Paloma or that bitch Jenna Starr after the scene in the nightclub."

"That bitch?" He scratched his nose and smiled a little.

Stephanie felt her cheeks burn. "She was all over you, and you looked perfectly comfortable—oh, forget it." Remembering how his hand had slid down Jenna's body still hurt.

"If you had believed me when I told you that I loved you, that nothing would change that love, you would not have worried about Jenna Starr, or every pair of Victoria's Secret underwear that I receive in the ring or in the mail."

"If only I had understood all this before I got to Spain. Why did you keep so much from me?"

"Because I thought if you loved me, which was my aim, you would do what I wanted. Because that is how Spanish men think."

"I told you at my house—the night we sat before the fire—that I was a reporter. I needed that information for my story—for my sanity."

"And I told you that night to be a woman, and if you'd listened to me you could have come to Spain as my lover, nothing else—until you became my wife."

His eyes were full of longing, but caution.

"What am I now, Miguel? Someone who will do as you order?" She heard the petulant sound in her voice.

"No. I don't want that woman. I want you." He reached out and touched her cheek, ran a finger down her face, tilted her chin up. "My love. *Dios mío*, you are my love."

Stephanie leaned into him, lifted her lips to his, and let his mouth wet hers, warm hers. His arms came around her, pulled her against him. For a long time she stood in his embrace, returning his kisses, tasting him, filling up on what she'd lost all these weeks. She put her hands on his face, traced the scar, his eyebrows, and his eyelids, ran her fingers through his thick, coarse hair.

"Oh, Miguel. I thought I was doing you a favor by leaving, that one day you'd thank me for coming to my senses. I thought you'd go back to the plazas, and I didn't think I could live in hotels, or wait for you to return, or deal with the worry of every Sunday afternoon you being gored, or handle women throwing you more than roses."

He smiled, blinked a few times, tilted her head again and kissed her. "You must learn to trust me and stop running away, maybe learn to listen to your man once in a while."

"I trust you—it's myself I don't trust, or the many challenges. Where will we live? What about your religion? What about your family?"

"My religion?" He looked at her, a little confused, as if he'd figured everything out but this one thing.

"Anyone can see how important it is to you—it's what you'll want for your children—our children."

Miguel expression sobered some. "*Sí*. It is what I want for our children."

"Is it what you want for me? Could we even be married in your church?"

"You are old enough to make up your own mind about it, but for our children—perhaps we can agree to this one thing. And I will marry you anywhere, even in a courthouse."

She thought about what he said, and didn't have any immediate objections. "Where will we live?"

"You have so many worries. How do you sleep at night?" He waved a hand in the air. "I bought a house down the street, and we can live there for a while. Three bedrooms—an ocean view, very expensive. Your brother is spending my money like crazy."

He bought a house on the island. "I thought you were going to live at *La Libra* once you retired."

"I have houses all over." He scratched his head, his dark eyes on her as he leaned against the railing. "Domingo is going to live at *La Libra* and train his new *novillero*, a kid he picked up on the streets of Madrid—very talented but a little like Francosis— youth, and their changing ideas about the *corrida*. Domingo will be kept busy, and he will forget about *El Peligro*."

"No one will forget you."

Miguel winked at her in an agreement. "Renaldo is living at *La Libra*, too. He was an orphan—which I found out the day that I went to pick him up for the private *corrida*. I also found five boys waiting for their trip to *La Libra*, and not one with a decent home. I went to the local *padre* and gave him a bunch of money to set them up, and took Renaldo home."

Stephanie felt her heart swell. Miguel really was the most generous man she'd ever known. "What a wonderful thing you've done," she said, and smiled, remembering the little boy and his dirty feet.

Miguel shrugged. "My heart went out to them because I know that kind of hunger—to smell like fish. It makes a boy do things he wouldn't normally do.

You should see how puffed up with pride Renaldo is to be the new son of *El Peligro*. But he is too full of the bulls for his age. He needs to think about an education, and he's a smart boy, like his *padre*." Miguel winked again. "Would you want to be a *madre* so soon? He needs a mother."

"Yes—I mean, I want a baby right away. I tried—" she felt her face grow red at the unexpected confession.

"*Querido*, I know what you were up to." He drew her back into his arms. "You are such troubles for *El Peligro*, but troubles I do not mind." He smiled, and his gaze flicked over her face.

"Your family will never accept me."

He kissed a cheek, her nose. "They are already accepting you—if they want to keep living in my villas! I did not leave Spain until everyone understood that I would not return without a wife."

He kissed her, opened her lips with his tongue, and filled her with the taste of wine, smoke, Spain, and laurel leaves. "I told you on *La Libra* that I wanted to marry you. I always keep my promises—you, on the other hand, need to work on promises."

"Normally—" she tried to protest, but he cut her off.

"I told you I would always love you. Even when I have a proud ego, I still love you. Did you think running away could change that? Did you think you could find a place on this planet where I wouldn't find you? I told you we are in the same cosmos, and that I can't live without you. Still, you stomp on my heart."

He kissed her again, but she was dizzy, unable to really comprehend his words. "You need a Spanish woman—someone full of traditions, someone who understands bullfighting and can speak the language."

"*Querida,* it is your passions that make you Spanish, not your blood. And I know you are never going to understand the *corrida,* and I don't expect you to. Even though I'm retired, I will always be involved in bullfighting. Still, I don't think you'll mind very much, because at night I'm going to remind you why you fell in love with *El Peligro.*"

"But—"

Miguel silenced her with a kiss, then gently pulled back, his gaze flickering over her face. "Marry me right away, and take some Spanish lessons, if it's important to you. We'll live here for a while, then in Spain, maybe even in Paris, since I have a flat there, too. We'll have lots of children—if you want—at least two. If we have a son, we will take him to *La Libra* and Domingo can start making his big plans for him."

"Or if we only have girls, one of them can become a great *matador.* Times do change."

He laughed, and the sound was rich and full.

Suddenly, there was a noise. "Oh, *the baby!*" Stephanie remembered why she was there at her brother's in the first place.

"The baby is fine—that is just Richard and Adria."

Stephanie went into the house with Miguel, and sure enough, they had returned, with bottles of chilled champagne.

"What about your business dinner?"

Adria ran up to her and hugged her tight. "That was just a ruse to get you two together. Let's make a toast. Then you guys can get the heck out of here and head back to Miguel's new place. Steph, wait until you see it. We're going to have fun decorating!"

"I can see Richard is not the only one who is going to be spending my money!" Miguel whistled and laughed.

"How can I thank you for bringing us back together?" Stephanie asked Adria.

"Dear sister-in-law, I know what it's like to love someone the way you love Miguel." She walked over to Richard and put her arms around him. "I wouldn't be able to live without this guy, and you brought us together. Or have you forgotten?"

"But how did you know it would take Miguel less than an hour to win me back?"

Miguel drew Stephanie into his arms, kissed her forehead. "Stephanie is all the time worried about time. She must have a book someplace that tells her how long each event in her life should take."

Stephanie laughed and looked up at him, thinking she would never worry again—until her own son stood before the *toril* gates and waited for his mighty bull to blaze into the sun.

The *corrida* ran through Miguel's veins, and she knew that any son she had would have the same destiny. Her firstborn would grow up to become a great *matador*, just like his father. Though she didn't think she could ever really enjoy the spectacle, she'd nevertheless stand proudly in the plazas every Sunday waving her handkerchief, cheering her son on, wearing the biggest white hat she could find.